Advance praise for *Murder in Volume*

"A mystery lover's delight: clever, compelling, original, and chock full of detection lore. *Murder in Volume* is as much fun as finding a mint Christie hidden in your great-aunt's tea cosy."

—Carolyn Hart,
author of *Death on Demand*
and Henrie O Mysteries

"How ideal to play sleuth in the company of two such appealing and intriguing characters as Megan Clark and Ryan Stevens—especially when their "Dr. Watsons" include an eccentric hodge-podge of mystery fans. A great beginning for an exciting new series."

—Joan Lowery Nixon,
author of the Thumbprint Mysteries
and past president of Mystery Writers of America

"Wonderfully clever role reversals, a plethora of plot puzzles, an intriguing point of view technique, and an amazingly well-read author of mysteries old and new make this new series by veteran mystery author D. R. Meredith a delight for mystery lovers of all stripes."

—Marlys Millhiser,
author of *Nobody Dies in a Casino*

"Keeps the reader intrigued. More, more!"

—Charlaine Harris,
author of *A Fool and His Money*

And
Praise for D. R. Meredith's previous mysteries:

"D. R. Meredith's High Plains mysteries started great and got better." —Tony Hillerman

"The crime is imaginative, the characters memorable, the West Texas locale evocative, and the story hair-raising. Meredith has developed into a fresh, snappy voice of crime fiction." —*New York Newsday*

"The first mystery I've seen in which the truth is more frightening than fiction, the only mystery I have ever read in which I felt that I might be one of the ultimate victims." —Sharyn McCrumb

"A delight for the gourmet of mayhem: sparkling characters, a diabolically dovetailing plot, and some of the most brittle writing this side of McBain. Meredith is a bright new dawn on the tired horizon of the American mystery." —Loren D. Estleman

"Rivals even the best in the genre." —*Review of Texas Books*

MURDER IN
VOLUME

—⁓—

D. R. MEREDITH

BERKLEY PRIME CRIME, NEW YORK

MURDER IN VOLUME

A Berkley Prime Crime Book / published by arrangement with
the author

PRINTING HISTORY
Berkley Prime Crime edition / January 2000

The Penguin Putnam Inc. World Wide Web site address is
http://www.penguinputnam.com

ISBN: 0-425-17309-7

Berkley Prime Crime Books are published
by The Berkley Publishing Group,
a division of Penguin Putnam Inc.,
375 Hudson Street, New York, New York 10014.
The name BERKLEY PRIME CRIME and the BERKLEY PRIME CRIME
design are trademarks belonging to Penguin Putnam Inc.

PRINTED IN THE UNITED STATES OF AMERICA

10   9   8   7   6   5   4   3   2

To Mike, who cooked dinner every night
so I could write during the remains of the day,
and to Megan, my very own paleopathologist,
and to John, who rescued me from the scrap heap.

MURDER IN
VOLUME

PROLOGUE

Everyone enjoys a nice murder. But murder is not nice.

—ALFRED HITCHCOCK

Violet Winston plodded through the February dusk toward the bus stop, a bright red muffler wrapped twice around her neck, and a shapeless black knit cap pulled down over her ears. Neither muffler nor cap matched her iridescent yellow ski jacket, but she didn't care. Except for her nose, she was warm and that's what mattered, that and the fact that both muffler and jacket were free, hand-me-downs from one of the ladies she worked for. "Tote" they called it years ago. You worked for a family for fifty cents an hour and tote—which was clothes or food or geegaws the family didn't want anymore. Nowadays she worked for considerably more than fifty cents an hour, but she still liked her tote. There was nothing shameful about accepting other people's castoffs provided you needed them. It was nothing more than recycling.

Violet shifted the strap of her scuffed leather purse a little higher on her shoulder, and took a different grip on the white plastic bag stamped with the logo of a grandfather clock and the words "Time and Again Bookstore" underneath. Sometimes her fingers cramped when carrying a heavy bag. Arthritis, she guessed, but she couldn't complain of much else in the way of ailments.

Of course, her feet hurt, but then her feet always hurt these days. That's what age and cleaning other people's homes did to a person, gave her bunions and varicose veins and broken arches. No doubt about it, Violet Winston had lived a hard life. Forty-five years ago there wasn't much else a young widow with little schooling and a baby daughter to raise could do but what the politicians like to call "unskilled labor." Just goes to show that most politicians are men. Any woman could tell them a thing or two about what kind of skills it took to keep a house clean. She'd like to see a congressman try to figure out how to get a spot out of a carpet. Or the best way to clean a window till it sparkled. Or polish an antique sideboard till you could see your face in the shine. And do it all without using those fancy cleansers and waxes.

Not that she was likely to see a congressman except on TV, but if she ever did, she would straighten him out in a hurry. Nobody ever accused her of being a shrinking violet. Even her mother admitted she made a mistake naming her after a shy little flower you had to look for under the leaves in spring. Should have been called Dandelion, according to her mama, because she always sprang back up no matter how hard you stomped on her. Yes, indeed, she always spoke her mind when the occasion called for it. And sometimes when it didn't, just so everybody in the vicinity would know better than to try to take advantage of Violet Winston. A woman alone, especially one getting on in years, had to be a little stronger than she might be if she had a man to lean on.

That wasn't to say that she couldn't have caught another man for herself after her husband died, but somehow time got away from her, and when she finally stopped to look around, all the good men were claimed and what was left wasn't worth bothering with. She was lonely sometimes, living alone with just her beagle for company, and her daughter not much of a letter writer. Connecticut had post offices just like Texas, but Violet reckoned that telling Sharon that would just make the poor girl feel guiltier than she already did. If the truth were told—and sometimes Violet thought it ought to be—having a mother who was a "domestic" shamed her daughter. Not that Sharon ever admitted to being ashamed of her, but Violet knew just the same. That was why Sharon always visited her once a year, but never asked Violet to come stay in the big white farmhouse in Connecticut where Sharon lived with her husband and two fine boys. The fact was Violet fit Sharon's life in Connecticut like the glass slipper fit Cinderella's stepsisters. No reason for either party to be ashamed. Children ought to improve their lot over that of their parents, and parents ought to be glad of it. What kind of a mother wanted her only child to grow up to clean other people's houses?

Not Violet's kind.

She just wished her daughter would write a little more often than once a month.

Still, nobody who loved to read as much as she did ever died of loneliness. Violet figured she'd read the label on a can of peas if there was nothing better handy. But there always was. Agnes Caldwell down at the Time and Again Bookstore always saved her the best books that people traded, put them under the counter until Violet came in. Time and Again mostly sold used books with just a few new ones that Agnes knew she could sell without having any left over. Violet only bought new books when one came out by a local author, and since local authors were scarce on the ground in Amarillo, Texas, she figured she bought three new books a year at most. Otherwise, she traded in one sack of used books for another sack, paying a few pennies a title for the privilege. A transaction fee Agnes called it. In Violet's opinion Agnes could call it whatever she wished

so long as she stayed in business. And she probably
would. Started by Agnes's mother, the Time and Again
Bookstore had been in business on Sixth Street since the
days when it was still Route 66. Violet figured that a
family in business that long must have what it takes to
stay out of bankruptcy court.

Violet grunted as a pain shot through her foot. Good
thing her favorite bench was just up ahead, snuggled
against the faceted windows of an antiques store. She
just couldn't walk from the bookstore to her bus stop—
near one end of Sixth Street to the other—without resting a minute. Age catching up with her, she guessed as
she sank down on the old wooden park bench in front
of Time's Treasures, an antiques store housed in a building that dated from the 1920's. Violet hoisted the plastic
bag full of books onto the bench beside her, slid her
purse strap down her arm, leaned back on the park bench
and looked around. Lord, but Sixth Street had changed
in the last few years, ever since folks got all hot and
bothered thinking about old Route 66—America's National Highway, she'd heard one man call it. After they
re-routed 66 down Amarillo Boulevard in 1953, Sixth
Street suffered but survived. When I-40 opened up in
1968, traffic on Route 66, including Sixth Street, fell off
to nothing. Businesses started closing, and those that
didn't began to look shabby, like down-at-the-heels old
men in need of a bath and a shave. But as Agnes said,
who could afford a new coat of paint on their building's
trim when most business folks only made enough money
to put beans and cornbread on the table?

Those were the lean times.

Not like now with everybody suddenly nostalgic for
the past and Sixth Street getting the benefit. Instead of
cracked sidewalks, dim lights, and dingy buildings, there
were graceful black wrought-iron street lamps, fresh
paint and window glass, flower boxes and park benches,
and a brand new brick border along the curb side of

newly repaired sidewalks. Instead of palmists, tarot readers, and secondhand stores, there were quaint cafes and coffee shops, crafts shops, and antique stores that sold everything from Tiffany lamps to Route 66 memorabilia.

But not books.

Agnes cornered the market on books once folks who used to sell secondhand furniture found their calling as antique dealers. Since most used books are not antiques but just old, Agnes bought up every volume on Sixth Street for sometimes pennies on the dollar. Agnes said that for every ten titles fit for the garbage, she found one or two she could sell on the rare-book market. But her biggest find was just last week at an estate sale: old paperbacks, mysteries and Westerns mostly, some dating from the late thirties and out of print for decades. Agnes called them her retirement fund and was doling them out one at a time to her favored customers.

Violet stroked her bag of books. She had one of those old rare books, a mystery. Agnes gave it to her for being such a good customer all these years. She would start it tonight.

Anxious to get home to her beagle and her new-old book, she struggled to her feet and leaned over to pick up her purse and tote bag.

The glass store window behind her shattered, setting off a strident burglar alarm, and she jerked around to stare.

That's why the second bullet entered her back just under the left shoulder blade and pierced her heart—or so Lieutenant Jerry Carr of the Special Crimes Unit theorized.

1

You will remember, Watson, how the dreadful business of the Abernetty family was first brought to my notice by the depth to which the parsley had sunk into the butter upon a hot day.

—SHERLOCK HOLMES in Arthur Conan Doyle's
"The Adventure of the Six Napoleons,"
The Return of Sherlock Holmes, 1905

"Can fairies get sick like people can?"

The little boy was barely taller than the reference desk, and his straight blond hair looked as if he had combed it himself. The part zigzagged like a bolt of lightning from a cowlick at the crown of his head to just above his temple where an errant lock of hair kept falling over his eyes. Megan Clark, assistant reference librarian temporarily in charge during the noon hour, and at five foot two in her shoes, not much taller than the boy on the other side of the desk, knew the minute she looked into his worried blue eyes that she would not send him to the children's department. As good as it was, and Megan conceded that the Amarillo Public Library's Children's Department was one of the best in the state, it still was, well, a *children's department*, and this little boy's question, at least to him, needed a grownup's answer.

Slipping out of the hollow rectangle that was the reference desk, and resisting the urge to brush the youngster's hair out of his eyes, Megan cleared her throat, then spoke in the same brisk tone she used with adults. At least she tried to sound brisk, but Ryan Stevens told her she sounded sweet instead. Megan hated *sweet* nearly as much as she hated *cute*, having heard both adjectives applied to her since she was a toddler and her hair grew in very red and very curly. Her lack of height was an added curse. No one took seriously a short, cute, sweet woman under the age of one hundred. Probably not even then.

"I don't think anyone has ever asked me that question before, so I'll have to research it. Shall we begin with the encyclopedia? I always like to get sort of a general overview of the subject before consulting specific reference books. Don't you?"

The little boy shrugged his shoulders. "Guess so. Just as long as it tells about fairies and not witches. I know about witches. They're mean. I saw a witch one time. She hurted a lady."

"Is that so?" asked Megan, thinking the child had serious problems distinguishing reality from fantasy. He would probably grow up to be an award-winning novelist.

"She had a cape and everything. But she didn't have a pointed hat. Don't witches wear pointed hats?"

"I guess according to tradition they do, but it depends. I've studied cultures where a witch is called a shaman and wears no hat at all."

The boy looked dubious. "Ain't much of a witch, then. You sure you know about witches and stuff?"

Megan wondered if tall women had their credibility questioned by six-year-olds. Probably not. Even moronic statements sounded credible if uttered by a tall person instead of a short, cute redhead. Life was not fair. And the shorter you were, the less fair it was.

Megan lifted the F volume of the *Encyclopedia Britannica* and opened it to the pertinent article. "It says here that fairies are immortal. Do you know what immortal means?"

The boy wiped his nose on his coat sleeve. Megan couldn't help noticing that the sleeves were not only frayed, but too long for his skinny arms. "I heard the word on a scary movie about vampires . . ." His voice trailed off.

"At least popular culture increases vocabulary even if it doesn't instill an enlightened value system."

"Uh?" asked the boy, wrinkling his brow.

"Never mind," Megan said. "Being an anthropologist, I sometimes make statements on culture without thinking. It's an impulsive thing."

"Uh?" asked the boy again, the worried expression in his blue eyes increasing by the second.

Megan shook her head. "Immortal means that you live forever . . ."

"But Dracula always dies and he's immortal," protested the boy. "If he goes outside after the sun comes up, or if somebody sticks a stake in his heart while he's asleep. Can you kill fairies with a stake?"

"Thank God I turned down a position as a children's librarian," Megan mumbled under her breath before speaking aloud. "There's a difference between vampires and fairies. Vampires were people like you and me before they turned into vampires. Fairies are born fairies. So fairies are immortal, but vampires aren't really because they were once people, and if fairies are truly immortal, then they can't die and they can't get sick. So the answer to your question is no, a fairy can't get sick."

The youngster frowned, and Megan wondered if he believed her. Actually, she thought her argument was logical—for a discussion about imaginary creatures.

Suddenly the little boy smiled, revealing a gap where a front tooth should be. "I told my mama she was wrong when she said the tooth fairy was sick and it wouldn't do no good to put my tooth under the pillow, 'cause there won't be no money there when I wake up. I'm gonna go tell her right now." He turned and scampered toward the front door, leaving Megan with a premonition that she had just set a helpless kid up for the biggest disillusionment of his life.

"Wait!" she shouted, ignoring the uneasy stirring of patrons shocked by the sound of a raised voice.

Startled, the youngster whirled around like a dervish and streaked back toward her.

"I've got something for you. A fairy left it with me," she said, slipping back inside the reference desk. Kneeling down, she grabbed her purse and pawed through her wallet looking for the five-dollar bill she had been saving to spend at the Time and Again Bookstore. A little boy's illusions were more important than whether she bought five used mysteries or only one.

Stuffing the bill into an envelope, she stood up and looked sternly at the boy. "The tooth fairy left this with me last night when everyone had gone home. She told me a little boy with blue eyes and blond hair would ask about her, and that I was to give him this envelope."

"You sure she wasn't the witch?"

"She had long beautiful blond hair and wore silvery clothes," said Megan, wincing as she reinforced a sexist stereotype, but it was for a good cause.

"I got blue eyes," said the little boy, staring fixedly at the envelope.

Megan nodded her head. "I can see that, but how do I know you're the right little boy?"

"I asked about the tooth fairy."

"Tell me your name," ordered Megan.

"Jared Johnson!"

"That's the name the tooth fairy told me," said Megan, handing him the envelope. "So you must be the right little boy."

He dug in his pocket and stretched out his curled-up

fist. "Don't you want my tooth? The tooth fairy might be mad if I didn't leave my tooth."

"So did you accept his offering?" asked Ryan Stevens, leaning back in his chair and propping his feet on the corner of his desk where a dent in its surface just fit the right heel of his Tony Lama boots.

Certain men physically exemplified the culture into which they were born, Megan thought not for the first time, and Ryan Stevens was one such man. His family had ranched in the Texas Panhandle for more than a century, ever since General Ranald S. MacKenzie finally defeated the Comanches in the last battle of the Red River War, and Ryan Stevens looked born to wear the Levis, boots, and the silver belly Stetson of a Texas rancher, to ride and rope, brand and herd. He was six feet of broad-shouldered muscle, rugged features, wavy black hair going silver at the temples, and electric blue eyes with crinkly lines at the corners. He was the romantic loner, the wandering knight on horseback, the subject of late-night erotic fantasies indulged in by women of any age between puberty and menopause.

Which to Megan proved just how undependable appearances are.

In reality, Ryan Stevens was a forty-five year-old widower with four mostly grown children, curator of history at the Panhandle-Plains Museum, and allergic to horses. He was a disappointment to his family, who quietly passed the reins of ranch management to his younger brother. His aging father concluded there was a glitch in Ryan's DNA. It was the only respectable explanation for a rancher's son, a native-born Texan, who couldn't stand next to a horse without sneezing.

In Megan's opinion, she and Ryan Stevens were two of a kind, both masquerading in false colors. This masquerade created a bond between them more durable than sexual attraction, which in Megan's experience seldom survived morning breath or gastrointestinal emissions. She and Ryan were bosom companions and best friends, and she could not imagine it otherwise.

"Of course I accepted," said Megan, digging Jared's tooth out of her pocket. "It's a very fine example of the left deciduous incisor of a young *Homo sapiens*. See how the roots are completely dissolved, allowing it to fall or be gently pulled from the gum to make way for the erupting mature tooth. Also notice that it is quite small and more yellowish in color than an adult incisor."

"In other words, it's the front tooth of a little boy."

Megan frowned at him. For a reputable historian and museum curator, both very serious professions, Dr. Ryan Stevens was sometimes entirely too fond of levity. "That's what I said, although I didn't mention gender since one can't deduce male from female by examining deciduous incisors of young children. I can only assume it is from the jaw of a young male because Jared Johnson told me so. Scientifically I can't prove that, but circumstantial evidence—the gap where an incisor would ordinarily be—supports my conclusion that Jared Johnson was telling the truth, and that this incisor"—she held it between two fingers and waved it in front of Ryan's face—"is, or was, his."

Ryan sank farther into his chair in a boneless way that always reminded Megan of a cat seeking a comfortable position. "You don't need to be defensive with me. I accept your authority on the subject of bones. If you had told me it was the left front molar of an ape, I would have believed you."

"You shouldn't. To begin with, it's not nearly large enough for an ape. And I'm not being defensive. I'm being specific."

"You're always defensive when you're speaking professionally, Megan."

He was right, but she saw no need to concede the argument without defending her position. A short person learned to defend herself early and often. "You would be too, if you looked like me!"

"You mean?" Ryan asked, raising one eyebrow.

Megan nodded, wrinkling her forehead in a way her mother swore would make her look old before her time. "The C word."

Ryan lifted his feet off the desk and sat up, folding his hands and leaning forward. Megan braced herself for a professorial lecture. For as long as she had known Ryan Stevens, which was most of her life from the age of five until the age of seventeen, when she left for Austin and the University of Texas, he had always folded his hands before delivering a lecture aimed at correcting what he saw as inappropriate behavior, attitudes, or beliefs. Living next door and being best friends with Ryan's oldest daughter, Evin, Megan had observed these lectures firsthand. They always left her feeling grateful that her mother advocated the spare-the-rod-and-spoil-the-child school of discipline. A spanking cleared the air without any lingering confusion over the nature of cause and effect, right and wrong, good and evil. It was also quick. Ryan, on the other hand, practiced discipline as a cross between exorcism and positive thinking, a sort of Father Damian-meets-Norman Vincent Peale-approach in which evil is defeated by talking it to death.

Ryan cleared his throat. "Age has taught me one unpleasant fact about my fellow man—speaking generically, of course—and that is the low esteem in which the average person holds an educated woman. We, and I'm speaking generically again, since I find women as guilty as men, hold our stereotypes close to our hearts, and one of our favorite stereotypes is that beauty and brains are incompatible. I hope, Megan, that your being defensive in my presence doesn't mean that you think I'm guilty of believing that particular stereotype, because you are the last woman to whom I would apply it. You are one of the most intelligent and knowledgeable young women I know, and only a damn fool would doubt it, and I don't happen to be a damn fool."

Megan swallowed in an attempt to relieve the stinging in her throat. She doubted that she would ever receive such a compliment again. Too bad that Ryan missed the point in his lecture, a common failing according to his daughter Evin.

"If I fit that stereotype—if I was beautiful—then people would pay attention to what I said because I *was* beautiful. Beauty is always listened to; otherwise ad agencies would use ugly women to sell perfume. But I'm"—she swallowed again, then drew a deep breath to force the hated word out of her mouth—"I'm *cute*! Add to that the fact that I'm five feet, two inches tall only if I wear shoes with very thick soles, and my hair is not only red, it's *red and curly*. And I'm only twenty-six years old. If all that wasn't bad enough, I can't step outside in the sun without freckles popping out like mushrooms in a damp cellar."

"I don't think that's a good metaphor—" began Ryan.

"Oh, be quiet! I didn't interrupt your lecture, so don't you interrupt mine. Now where was I? Oh, yes, freckles. I have freckles."

"Actually, you don't," said Ryan. "Not many anyway, just a few across the nose."

"Ryan, do you remember when we went rock climbing in Palo Duro Canyon last month, the day you slipped and broke your wrist—do you remember how *speckled* I was after just a few minutes in the sun?"

"At the time I was more focused on my pain than your nose."

"Trust me. I was speckled. Don't you remember last summer, when we went water skiing at Lake Meredith and you fell and your ski flipped up and broke your nose—don't you remember freckles popping to the surface on my shoulders before I even had a chance to get my swimsuit wet?"

"My nose was bleeding at the time, Megan. I didn't pay much attention to your shoulders."

"You ought to be more observant, Ryan; then you would appreciate what I'm talking about. I can't count the number of older library patrons who address me as 'sweetie' or 'honey.' "

"I guess they never heard of sexual harassment suits."

"I can't sue an old man taped to an oxygen tank for harassment, Ryan. Or one who uses a walker, either. Besides, in the culture of their childhood, such endearments were not derogatory. But it just illustrates what I'm saying, that no one takes Dr. Megan Clark, Ph.D. in Forensic Anthropology, seriously. And if I dare mention my specialty, all I get are blank stares—disbelieving stares! No one is willing to admit a woman who looks like me is a paleopathologist—that is, if they know what one is, and most don't. You know what one of my regulars told me yesterday? That I should have majored in education so I could always find a job. If I had wanted to work with rug rats I would have taken the position as children's librarian when it was offered."

"Why didn't you?" asked Ryan. "The way you handled that little boy this afternoon was brilliant. You're a natural with kids."

"Why? Because I'm their size?" Megan waved her hands in the air. "Ryan, think about it! It's bad enough that I look like I do, but can you imagine what *National Geographic* would say if they read on my resumé that I was a kiddie librarian? Would they trust the autopsy of King Tut to somebody whose only job since graduating was as a kiddie librarian?"

"Are you planning to autopsy King Tut?"

"No! Even though I could do a more competent autopsy than the one done on Tut in the 1920s. But I'm just using that scenario as an example. You see my point, don't you? As an assistant reference librarian, I at least work with the genealogy society at their monthly meetings. Genealogy is human cultural past. Of a sort. Helping look up census records on ancestors may be far removed from digging up human remains, but it's closer to my profession than reading *Goodnight Moon* to preschoolers. It's the best I can do until I figure out a way of earning a living as a paleopathologist. The problem is that there aren't many mummies in Amarillo requiring autopsies."

Megan paced Ryan's study, stepping around or over books stacked at random on the floor. "The problem with me is that I'm bored. There's just so much rock climbing and water skiing and canoeing I can do."

Ryan cleared his throat. "About the canoe, Megan. I feel I ought to pay for the damage since I was the one who ran it into the dock. I never knew canoes were so fragile."

"And I ought to pay for your stitches since going canoeing was my idea. How long before your hair grows back? Did the doctor say?"

Ryan felt the back of his head. "I have a little fuzz already, so I think it'll grow in quickly."

"I have a new project for us, Ryan."

"If it's skydiving, I'll pass."

"Skydiving? Don't be ridiculous. That's dangerous unless you know what you're doing. No, I've signed us up for a readers' club, a mystery discussion group, Ryan! Isn't that terrific? I love mysteries!"

Megan stopped her pacing and leaned over his desk, apprehensive at his continued silence and the odd expression of cautious disbelief on his face. She was so used to his company that she hadn't considered that her new enthusiasm might not appeal to him. "You will come with me, won't you, Ryan? As much as we both love to read, I thought this would be a natural fit for us."

Ryan slid down in his chair and laced his fingers behind his neck. He tilted his head back and studied the authentic pressed-tin ceiling of his study. The ceiling was not original with his depression-era cottage, but salvage from an old hardware store in Chillicothe, Texas. As an archaeologist and anthropologist, Megan appreciated this remnant of America's architectural past, but failed to be mesmerized by it as Ryan seemed to be. Ask him a question and he studied that ceiling as though he found the answer there. When she was a little girl, Megan always wondered if there was invisible writing on the ceiling that only he could see.

Ryan lowered his head, sat up straight, and looked at her. "So we'll go to this bookstore and sit on chairs and just talk? No hanging suspended from a cliff a thousand feet in the air? No balancing on wooden skis behind a boat traveling at the speed of sound? No rowing a twenty-foot boat that's only eighteen inches wide? The most dangerous thing that might happen to us is a paper cut?"

"That's absolutely the only risk. I promise."

2

In my opinion, for what it's worth, our own little mystery began with the conception of Megan Clark, girl librarian and amateur sleuth.

—DR. RANDEL ANDERSON

My name is Ryan Stevens, curator of history at the Panhandle-Plains Museum on the campus of West Texas A&M University in Canyon, Texas, some twelve miles from Sixth Street, the setting of what those involved insist on calling "our mystery." I am a professor of American history as well, and teach two courses at the university: Manifest Destiny and Westward Expansion in the Nineteenth Century, and Frontier Life in the American West. I mention the latter because I want the reader to understand my motivations for serving as Watson to Megan's Sherlock Holmes. To be sure, that is not a good analogy, as many of you would point out, since Sherlock Holmes never confided to the public his own thoughts concerning any of his many adventures as the world's best known private detective, while Megan's thoughts, those she doesn't blurt out verbally, are as easily read as a large-print book. History will never know if Holmes feared the hound of the Baskervilles, or if his intellectual curiosity overrode such emotions as the ordinary man would experience. As your typical ordinary man, the ghostly hound would have scared the bejesus out of me.

But not Megan Clark. She might possibly show te-
merity face to face with a rattlesnake, but the supernatural wouldn't have a chance. Like Sherlock Holmes,
Megan would be too busy searching for the rational explanation to waste time being afraid of things that go
bump in the night.

But returning to why I'm Watson.

Because I'm not Sherlock Holmes.

I'm an historian, a tracer and recorder of human
events. I am a theorist who is at one remove from my
subject.

I'm not a problem solver.

Megan Clark is an anthropologist and archaeologist,
and in every other country but this one, that makes her
a scientist, a rational thinker who from an irregular bump
on a skull can deduce the probable disorder which killed
that particular individual. From the design on a pottery
shard she can deduce the time period and the likely culture of the potter. Give her a set of facts—the approxi-
mate time of death, the blood-smeared blunt instrument,
the body *in situ*—and she can trace the dead back to the
living. To Megan, artifacts tell a clear story of human
activities. Give me the same set of facts, and I pontificate
on the incivility of murder and its effect on human
events.

Activities and events.

Two different perspectives.

I can tell you what was, but Megan can tell you how
it came to be, in minute detail.

In a murder mystery the latter skill is the more valuable.

Some will say I'm downplaying the role of the professional historian, and perhaps I am, but this historian
is much better at recording events and indulging a secret
bent for storytelling than he is at looking at corpses *in
situ*. The tendency to faint at the sight of blood—mine
or anyone else's—is not a desirable character trait in the

lead member of a duo of amateur sleuths. I'm not good with blood, particularly when it is still in a fluid state and "seeping," but that doesn't make me a wimp; it makes me a Watson.

We took my truck to the reading group's first meeting because Megan's had an oil leak she hadn't been able to track down and fix before it was time to leave. For those unfamiliar with automotive terminology in the West, a truck is a pickup, one of those vehicles with a cab in front and an open bed in back, and they are common in Amarillo and other areas of Texas. Mine is a newish, white Ford Ranger, a small but comfortable truck with four-wheel drive. Megan's is an eight-year-old grizzled black behemoth GMC with an extended cab, manual shift, and 200,000 miles on its odometer the last time I looked. It growls when she turns the key in the ignition, and she swears she can drive it up the side of a mountain. Given my previous experience as Megan's companion, I could anticipate at least a broken collar-bone as the result of any such demonstration. Fortunately, we don't have any mountains in the Texas Panhandle, and not even Megan would attempt driving down the steep walls of Palo Duro Canyon, so I and my collarbone have been spared.

Megan claims she drives the truck because it is a practical vehicle for a woman in her profession—archaeological excavations not being commonly located in areas accessible to luxury sedans—and I suppose there is some merit in that assertion, but I'm convinced the real reason she owns such an outsized piece of automotive machinery is because she's compensating for her short stature. I've never shared that conviction with her. Certain subjects are best not broached with Megan Clark, principal among them her height.

An expectant look on her face, Megan bounded out her front door and across my front yard the moment I backed my truck out of the garage. She is a woman of fierce enthusiasms, and this latest one engaged her interest like no other project in my recent association with her, which dates back less than a year. I've known her longer than that, of course, ever since she was a little girl with scabbed knees and one extremity or the other in a cast every spring. Other than giving thanks that she never sustained her broken bones while on my property, I never paid any more attention to her than I would to any child who played with my children. Then she grew into adolescence and went off to school, and I hardly saw her for eight years. My first contact with the adult Megan Clark was a note I received from her when my wife died. I believe she was at the University of Tennessee at Knoxville at the time, doing research at that institute's body farm. I never inquired as to the nature of the research which, given what she later told me about the so-called body farm, is just as well.

I never actually saw Megan for another year, and by that time the numbness of grief had worn off and I was restless. Forty-five is too young to settle into a role as widower, but it is too old to make the singles scene without loss of dignity. Whether sitting on a barstool and ogling attractive women, or attending singles meetings in the church basement and sipping bitter coffee while ogling attractive women, one feels self-conscious and awkward. Or at least I did. There is something demeaning and hypocritical about pretending an interest in companionship and conversation when what one is really interested in is hot, sweaty, panting, musk-scented sex!

Perhaps that is why I became the best friend of a woman nearly two decades my junior: With Megan I felt neither self-conscious nor awkward, demeaned nor hypocritical. She was the boon companion of my eldest daughter, so my thoughts regarding her were as chaste as wind-driven snow.

Until lately.

Lately I'd caught myself watching her hair catch fire in the sunlight, and the muscles ripple in her thighs, but I'm not blind, and any man who failed to admire that vibrant hair and firm body was either blind, or a misogynist. There was nothing lustful in my admiration. I was old enough to be her father. She and I were comfortable together despite numerous personal injuries I sustained while accompanying her in many reckless pastimes. I never thought of myself as a clumsy man—I can walk across a room without bumping into the coffee table for instance—but I seemed to attract accidents when I was with Megan. It was a phenomenon I don't pretend to understand, but as long as she didn't mind driving me to the emergency room, I'd continue to be her companion, and in this case—pardon the pun—her Watson.

"It's the Time and Again Bookstore on Sixth Street," she announced, climbing into my truck and slamming the door.

"I've been there a time or two," I said, despite my throat tightening up until I thought I would choke the moment she disclosed our destination. Amarillo must have six or eight used bookstores and four chain stores without even taking into account the religious book businesses. Why the devil did this reading circle have to meet in this particular store? Furthermore, why hadn't I had the good sense to ask where the meeting place was that afternoon, while there was still time to decline Megan's invitation? Better yet, why didn't I just confess my taste in recreational literature and be done with it? I had nothing to be ashamed of, no reason to deny my love of the one literary form that is totally American.

Except . . .

In this time of revisionist historians, of emphasis on the roles of women and minorities in the settlement of the West, of debunking myth and legend and folk tale, to admit that you love traditional Westerns, shoot-'em-ups as my father calls them, is to be accused of racism, sexism, and probably some other "ism" which I can't remember at the moment. For a professor of American history, moreover, one who specializes in *western* American history, to proclaim an undying love for the Western is analogous to a Baptist minister proclaiming a belief in Christ at a convention of agnostics. We would create controversy but change no one's mind.

I'm as good with controversy as I am with blood.

No, I would have to trust in Agnes Caldwell's discretion.

3

In my lexicon, a girl is any female under twelve, and an amateur sleuth is Nancy Drew. I am not Nancy Drew.

—MEGAN CLARK'S JOURNAL

"That Sixth Street exists at all and is not a railroad bed of rotting timbers and rusting iron rails is one of those coincidences of historical fate."

"Hum," said Megan, tuning out Ryan's lecture on what she and Evin as children used to call Local History 101. Whether Ryan drove her and Evin to the pool for swimming lessons, the library for story time, or the park for softball, he told them the history of every city block between their homes and their destination. Not that Megan didn't enjoy his lectures on history then and now—Ryan was an eloquent and enthusiastic lecturer—but he was preaching to the converted. She probably knew as much about the past and present of Sixth Street as he did, since she had fallen in love with the district when she was a teenager, and any place she loved, she studied. To her, familiarity didn't breed contempt; it bred commitment.

"The discovery of gold in California ignited interest in building a railroad from St. Louis west along the 35th parallel, approximately along old Route 66 and Sixth Street," continued Ryan. "But the War Between the States intervened, and the South lost not only the war, but its chance at the country's first transcontinental railroad as well. Northern interests prevailed and the railroad was built along the 42nd parallel instead. Just imagine how different history would have been if the War had been averted."

"A lot less dysentery and gangrene," said Megan.

"What?" asked Ryan, glancing at her with a bewildered expression.

"Approximately eight percent of the male population, North and South, died in the War, but a majority died from dysentery and gangrene, not on the battlefield." Megan shrugged. "It's my profession, tracking diseases as cause of death. From my perspective, disease has altered history as much as any philosophy, and if not disease, then diet. We are what we eat, Ryan."

"Yeah," said Ryan, swallowing. "You know, Megan, you have a unique way of changing the subject."

"I'm sorry. What were you going to say about alternative history?"

He shook his head. "Nothing."

Megan felt a little guilty at the look of resignation on his face. It wouldn't hurt to keep quiet for once and listen to Ryan's professorial lectures. Her mother always told her she was too aggressive and scared men off, but what use was a man who was afraid of a woman's expressing her opinion? Not that she was interested in Ryan as other than a good friend, and not that he was afraid of her, but he was just too polite for his own good.

"Personally, I'm glad that Sixth Street exists, although I don't think any of the Okies who drove west on it to California would recognize it now," said Megan in an attempt to turn the conversation back to history, but her kind of history, that of individuals and families. She never had been fond of historic events with casts of thousands wielding spears or guns.

"I don't think Sixth Street had teashops and upscale little restaurants then. Or wrought-iron street lights and planters full of petunias either," she continued. "It was a business district with gas stations and mechanics and grocery stores and cleaners, and its restaurants probably served meat loaf and mashed potatoes, but if you use your imagination and squint, you can see the caravans of rusty old pickups and worn-out cars rattling down Sixth Street. What a contrast to the vacationing families just a decade and a half later! The Depression is over, the War is won! Life is possibility, and according to Mesdames Christie and Sayers, murder is domestic. Sixth Street has such atmosphere that I can't think of a better place for our reading group to meet. After all, the Golden Age of Sixth Street is contemporaneous with the first Golden Age of Mysteries."

"It's also contemporaneous with dust storms, Pearl Harbor, concentration camps, and the Bomb," said Ryan.

"Mysteries have the downside of human nature covered, Ryan. Have you forgotten Dashiell Hammett, Ross Macdonald, Raymond Chandler, and certainly James Cain? They all wrote about violence, corruption, and man's general inhumanity to man—so to speak."

Megan noted with satisfaction the look of confusion on Ryan's face. Obviously, he hadn't considered the whole spectrum of the mystery genre. "I hope you're not one of those men who, when they hear the word 'mystery,' think of murders in manor houses written by dead English ladies."

"N-no, I don't think so," said Ryan, stuttering a little in his denial.

"I'm glad. I'd hate to think I invited a male chauvinist mystery reader tonight."

"I'm not a male chauvinist!"

"I didn't think so, but so many men assume women only read 'gentle' mysteries. How ridiculous! Who do they think buys Sue Grafton and Marcia Muller and Sara Paretsky? I'll bet you haven't read a single title by any of those women!"

"I've been noticing their books in the grocery store, but no, I haven't read them," said Ryan.

"Well, you should! And while I'm on the subject, there isn't anything kind and gentle about the mysteries of Agatha Christie if one reads them objectively. What's kind about Dr. James Sheppard in *The Murder of Roger Ackroyd*? He set the standard for nasty, deceiving village doctors. What about *And Then There Were None*? Can you think of ten other characters in a modern novel you would be less likely to invite home for a drink?"

"Now that you mention it—" began Ryan.

"Of course, you don't!" finished Megan, smiling at her friend. "I'm glad we think so much alike, Ryan. We'll really enjoy this discussion group. And speaking of which, you just drove by the Time and Again Bookstore. You'll have to turn around and go back."

"Damn!" said Ryan, slamming on his brakes and swinging into a narrow alley. A car behind swerved around him, its driver making a digital remark about his driving. "Sorry, I guess I wasn't paying attention, but that doesn't excuse incivility from other drivers."

Megan smiled at his naiveté. If another driver slammed on his brakes in front of her, she would not only shoot him the finger, she would roll down her window and add verbal commentary. But not if Ryan was riding with her. Sometimes he was so sweet, he didn't seem to live in the same world she did, and she tried not to shock him any more than necessary.

The Time and Again Bookstore was a large, one story, L-shaped stucco building painted blinding white with a solid wood door stained ebony. A tiny parking lot with spaces for twelve cars nestled in front of the long wing of the L. Sometimes Megan liked to stand in the parking lot and study the mural painted on the side of the building. A collage of images from old Fords to road signs to extinct company logos such as the flying red horse of

Standard Oil evoked the era of America's Main Street: Route 66.

A huge picture of a grandfather clock, Time and Again's logo, was painted on the otherwise blank wall of the storefront. Wrought-iron bars covered its one window, behind which was displayed a colorful red, white, and black poster advertising the discussion group. "Join the Usual Suspects in the Murder by the Yard Reading Circle" it read. Surrounding the poster were mysteries: old Crime Club editions, glossy new original paperbacks, and hardbacks by both best-selling and would-be best-selling authors. From titles by authors whose names were household words to authors whose names were known only in their own houses, from Christie to Chandler, Babcock to Ball, Hillerman to Highsmith, Grafton to Gruber, McCrumb to MacDonald, the owner of Time and Again, Agnes Caldwell, had illustrated the incredible variety of the mystery genre from drawing room to mean streets, from urban cop shop to rural sheriff's office. Megan controlled her slobbering hunger to buy or steal every book in the display only with an effort of self-discipline that she considered second to that exercised by John the Baptist when faced by food other than honey and locust.

"Megan! I knew you couldn't resist joining my reading circle." Agnes Caldwell clasped Megan in a lilac-scented embrace the minute she stepped inside the bookstore. Agnes was a hugger and a toucher and an exuberant enthusiast of flowery perfumes, some distilled by her own hand. Rather than smelling of aging paper, as too many secondhand bookstores did, Time and Again smelled of flowers and spice and "everything nice," as Agnes was fond of saying. Tonight the store and its owner were fragrant with lilac. Megan immediately thought of her great-grandmother Christy, who always sprinkled lilac water in her underwear drawer. In fact, Agnes reminded Megan of Grandma Christy in other ways: Both resembled shriveled gnomes with silky brown hair twisted into a knot at the back of their heads, and faded blue eyes under hooded lids. Both wore support hose (brown), sensible shoes with crepe soles, and a sweater all year round. They differed in that Grandma Christy wore dresses that reached at least to mid-calf regardless of that year's fashion, while Agnes most often wore slacks. The other big difference was that Grandma Christy had been dead for years—since shortly after she divorced her fifth husband at eighty-seven. Agnes was alive and well and a spinster. "The best men my age are all taken, and the others are too young. Don't want to be accused of robbing from the cradle" was Agnes's way of explaining her marital state. Or lack of it.

Megan admired her as much as any woman she knew. Agnes was a very sharp lady with an almost encyclopedic knowledge of books of all kinds, but primarily of popular fiction. Unlike most owners of independent used-book stores, Agnes kept her inventory on computer and controlled her merchandise mix. "Otherwise, I'd have a store full of paperback romances and not much else," she once confided to Megan. "Not that I have anything against romances—Lord knows I sell enough of them—but there are more ways to commit murder than there are to have sex, and that makes murder more interesting."

It was an unique point of view, and Megan more than halfway agreed with it.

"Professor!" Agnes exclaimed, releasing Megan and hugging Ryan. "I didn't expect to see you here."

"I came along with Megan," said Ryan in a low voice, and Megan looked sharply at him. It wasn't like Ryan to mumble, and furthermore, he looked nervous and sweaty. She wondered if he was sick.

"Well, I'm glad she persuaded you to come," said Agnes, taking each by the hand and leading them farther inside the store.

To the right was the three-sided checkout counter, with a computer on one end. To the left was a small area with a couch, two easy chairs, and enough folding chairs to provide seating for twelve, all arranged loosely in a circle. Beyond the seating area and the checkout counter, row upon row of tall shelves filled the space to the walls. Subject headings printed on polished boards in the shape of grandfather clocks hung from the end of each row. A footstool with three broad steps stood in each aisle, in case a customer wished a volume from the highest shelf. Instead of dusty light bulbs, Agnes had installed track lighting down each aisle, imparting a feeling of light and space to the store. In an area just behind the counter were a series of slanted shelves holding Agnes's collection of rare books, each in a Ziplock plastic bag with a typed label showing author, title, publishing history, and current price. The rare books were also sorted by subject, the largest number of titles by far being mysteries and Westerns. In addition, Agnes had a separate section of old paperback mysteries and Westerns, not necessarily rare in terms of being worth a great deal of money, but rare in that each title was published in the late thirties, the forties, the early fifties, and their authors were obscure. That didn't mean Agnes sold these books cheap; after all, in the book market one never knew. What might be old and worthless today could be rare and expensive next week. These old mysteries were Megan's favorite. Finding a really good one was like discovering buried treasure. She liked to believe that the deceased authors—and almost all of them were deceased—knew from beyond the grave that she appreciated their work.

Megan smiled at the small group seated in the circle of chairs and squeezed Agnes's hand. "This is going to be so much fun. Isn't it, Ryan?"

4

Who studies human character as a whole? We leave it to the novelists and playwrights.

—DAVID FELTHAM, *Dear Daughter Dead,* 1965

Paretsky? Grafton? Ross Macdonald? James Cain? I had at least heard of Agatha Christie, but who the devil was Dr. James Sheppard and what did he have to do with Roger Ackroyd's murder? And what kind of a novel has ten main characters as apparently this *And Then There Were None* had? My knowledge of Christie was confined to seeing the movie of *Murder on the Orient Express,* and one called *Ten Little Indians.* And the only MacDonald I'm familiar with who wrote mysteries is John D. MacDonald, and the only title by him I've read is *The Girl, The Gold Watch, and Everything,* which isn't your classic mystery, but more of a thriller. I think. At least I would call it a thriller. As Agnes guided us toward the discussion circle I felt more and more like one of the witches of Salem being led before the magistrates to be judged.

I obviously needed expert advice to survive my travail.

"Agnes, if I might have a word with you?"

She patted my arm. Agnes is a contact type of person. "Certainly, Professor. What can I do for you? If it's about that first edition you want, I haven't found it yet, but I will. It's just that Louis—"

"No, Agnes," I said in a loud voice. Too loud, I realized when the small group of disparate individuals ceased their quiet discussions to stare at me. I felt sweat break out along my hairline. "If I could just speak to you about my bill?"

"I didn't think you carried anyone's credit, Agnes," said one of the individuals, a ruddy-faced man with a scraggly goatee. My heart sank to the vicinity of my knees as I recognized him as Dr. Randel Anderson, a professor of English at Amarillo College, and as big a pompous ass as I know.

"I don't," said Agnes in a tone of voice that ended the discussion of credit before anyone else could participate. She looked at me and smiled, a speculative look in her eyes, but one that was private between the two of us. "Did I make a mistake in addition again, Professor? I swear I have to get a new pair of glasses. These old eyes are having an awful time telling the difference between threes and eights."

I swallowed, so thankful that she was saving face for me that I could have hugged her again if I hadn't been allergic to lilacs. "Yes, but I think I owe you two dollars this time rather than the other way around."

I eased my way toward the counter and hopefully out of hearing range of the reading circle when Randel Anderson expressed his opinion. Randel's one dependable trait is that he always expresses an opinion whether the listener is interested or not. "I'll check my receipts when I get home tonight, Agnes. I seem to remember that the total of my last visit was a bit larger than I expected."

Randel is the only person I know who says *a bit larger* or *a bit smaller*, *a bit better* or *a bit worse*. He thinks it makes him seem more professorial in an English way.

Agnes didn't pay him any attention. To her mind the issue was settled. She slipped behind her counter and began riffling through receipts. "I keep copies of receipts from my steady customers, like you and Megan and Randel. I don't bother with the walk-in traffic unless they bring in books to trade. Some do and some don't. Now, Professor, what has you upset?"

I wiped my brow on my shirt sleeve. This was more embarrassing than I had anticipated and I felt ridiculous. "I would appreciate it, Agnes, if you didn't say anything about my reading tastes. Just keep a paper sack of my favorites under the counter and I'll buy them sight unseen at the end of each discussion group."

Agnes looked disapproving. "Professor, have you ever read a mystery in your life?"

"Yes! I've read Sherlock Holmes and I read Poe when I was at Nebraska as an undergraduate."

Agnes shook her head. "You're the only Texan I know who would admit to attending the University of Nebraska, Professor, but never mind, I won't mention it to anyone."

"I'm not ashamed of it! It's a fine school with a wonderful American history department."

Agnes added disbelief to her disapproval. I had forgotten she was such a loyal Texan that to her mind all other states are not only second best, but second-rate. "I won't mention your choice of recreational reading, Professor. It's no one else's business anyway, but I'll tell you right now that Poe and Arthur Conan Doyle alone won't be enough. You had better read a mystery or two, because I guarantee that this group will find out you're an imposter."

I felt myself flush and felt silly for being defensive. "I intend to be very quiet and just listen, Agnes. I know better than to try to bluff."

"Well, it's a good thing. Why did you come, anyway? Did Megan drag you along?"

"She asked me to join her, yes."

"And you do everything she asks? Never mind, don't answer that. I don't need to stoop to being nosy. I can see what's right in front of my face." She reached across the counter and patted my cheek. I don't think any woman had ever patted my cheek before, since I became an adult, that is. It made me feel young and foolish. "You go along and sit down, Professor. It's an interesting group here, and you might even enjoy yourself."

Feeling like a complete fraud, I smiled and nodded. It must have been a lackluster performance on my part, because Agnes just sighed and motioned me toward the circle.

Megan was seated in one of the folding chairs, the dark tan metal kind, and I made a note to myself to arrive early next week, so we could sit on either the couch or the arm chairs. Megan looks comfortable no matter where she sits, but those metal chairs leave me with numb buttocks.

Agnes clapped her hands, a gesture only someone of Agnes's authority and tact could carry off without offending. "I think everyone who's interested is here already. If not, then the best way to reproach the tardy is to start on time. I want to welcome you to the Time and Again Bookstore, where only the finest in used books are offered, along with a select few new titles ordered at the owner's discretion." She cleared her throat and patted the knot of hair at the back of her head. "I, of course, am the owner, Agnes Caldwell, to those who are visiting the store for the first time, and while I know most of you, you may not know each other. The first order of business therefore should be introductions. Everyone now knows my name and occupation, so let's start with my nominee for discussion leader, Megan Clark"

Megan blushed, as she generally does whenever she is the center of attention. It is a physical trait that distresses her, but which older observers find charming. I saw the two elderly ladies smile at her as though she were a favored grandchild. She rose and stood as straight as she could to maximize her height, a habit I've observed in short women, much as tall women tend to slouch.

"My name is Dr. Megan Clark," she began as she always does, and I saw the two elderly ladies nudge each other and *ooh* and *aah* that such an attractive young thing was a doctor. "And I'm a paleopathologist," Megan continued. "I autopsy mummies, but presently I'm an assistant reference librarian at the main branch."

The two elderly ladies appeared surprised at Megan's disclosure, but hardly as shocked as I expected.

"You mean mummies as in King Tut?" asked one of the ladies.

"Yes, but . . ."

"That's so wonderful!" exclaimed the other lady. "In my day young women didn't have the opportunity to enter such an exciting profession."

"You've forgotten Elizabeth Peters," said her companion. "She's an Egyptologist and she's nearly our contemporary. Close anyway."

"I've not forgotten her, but she's an exception," replied the first. "Do you read Elizabeth Peters, dear?"

"Yes, but . . ."

"I swear I feel like I'm walking in the deserts of Egypt whenever I read an Amelia Peabody mystery."

I thought this Elizabeth Peters would write under her own name rather than using a pseudonym like Amelia Peabody. But I didn't know much about mystery writers. Perhaps a name fit for a faded English spinster was a good marketing ploy. Certainly Max Brand was a better name for a Western novelist than Frederick Faust. The same could be true of Amelia Peabody.

"Dr. Barbara Mertz brings her professional knowledge to the mystery field," said a plain young woman in a soft, hesitant voice.

I wondered who Dr. Barbara Mertz was, and what she had to do with Elizabeth Peters-Amelia Peabody.

"We're getting off the subject, ladies," said Agnes. "Introductions first, then you can choose a book or author to discuss."

"Of course, you're right, Agnes," said one of the elderly ladies. "My name is Rosemary Pittman, and I am a fan of Agatha Christie. Well, really more than a fan, I'm a student of Christie. I've analyzed each of her crime novels in some detail. She is after all the Mother of the Murder Mystery."

"And I'm Lorene Getz, and I'm a student of Dorothy Sayers, and I can make a case that *she* was the Mother of the Murder Mystery. It's a friendly conflict between Rosemary and me that keeps us sharp." She looked at Rosemary, tilting her head to one side like an owl. "Shall we tell the Circle about our project?"

"Oh, certainly. And ask for suggestions of titles, Lorene."

Lorene, white hair long enough to touch her collar and somewhat frizzy, took a deep breath. "Rosemary and I are researching mysteries whose authors were influenced by Christie and Sayers. We plan to present a paper on the subject at the annual Conference on Popular Culture sponsored by Bowling Green University. Afterwards, we plan to submit it to *Mystery Scene Magazine*," she finished in a gush of words, then sat beaming at the others in the circle.

"But not the obvious authors and titles," said Rosemary. I noticed her hair was a mass of shining white curls. "We'll mention writers like Carolyn Hart, of course, but we're primarily interested in the early women writers who were more or less contemporaries of Christie and Sayers. We want to bring obscure writers to the attention of critics. There are many wonderful mysteries that are out of print and unavailable to the public. Agnes has been such a big help to us in our research. Each week she provides us with a sackful of old mysteries, mostly paperbacks, and we each read them and decide whether to include that writer in our paper."

"Depending on whether we decide the writer was influenced by Christie and Sayers," added Lorene. "Agnes has promised us some special titles of very old paperbacks that she's doling out to special customers. But she's not just a bookseller. Tell everybody about your own project, Agnes."

"Agnes is an encyclopedia on mysteries," Megan whispered to me. "What she knows about plots and characters of the major authors is astounding."

I nodded, I knew Agnes was a phenomenon as a bookseller. She'd even managed to locate a first edition of *The Girl, The Gold Watch, and Everything*. If she could just find a first edition of *Hondo* by Louis L'Amour, then as far as I'm concerned the woman deserved to sit on the right hand of God.

"I haven't actually started work on my project yet— I've been too busy preparing for this reading group— but if you and Rosemary think anyone might be interested, Lorene, I'll give a one-sentence synopsis."

"Of course, they'd be interested, Agnes." It was the other elderly white-haired lady, Rosemary, I think her name was. The two looked and talked so much alike, it was hard for me to keep track of which was which.

Agnes smiled, and pursed her lips in a coy manner, then spoke. "I plan to write a reference book on early paperback mysteries by obscure authors. I'm planning on using Rosemary and Lorene's bibliography as a starting point, so girls, you need to hurry along."

"Dr. Randel Anderson here, and speaking as an English professor," he said, preening a little. Actually preening a lot and looking ridiculous while doing it. Stroking a goatee went out of fashion about the time of Queen Victoria's funeral.

"I've had a bit of experience as a literary critic during my tenure at Amarillo College, and I would be pleased to look over your final selections. Sometimes obscure authors are obscure because they deserve to be."

Lorene and Rosemary looked at each other, then Rosemary smiled at Anderson. "We're flattered that you're interested in our research project, Professor, but Lorene and I feel that we should make the final selection of titles ourselves."

"We've spent so many years analyzing Christie and Sayers," added Lorene.

"But we would welcome your suggestions," said Rosemary. "We can't possibly know of or have read all the out-of-print mystery authors since 1929. Even at our ages that would be impossible. So if you would like to submit an annotated bibliography, Professor, we would be so grateful, wouldn't we, Lorene?

"Oh, yes, Rosemary, and we would like the help of all our fellow members."

They both beamed, and I wondered if Randel Anderson knew he had just been "handled" by a pair of experts.

"Aren't they sweet?" whispered Megan, smiling at the two white-haired mystery buffs.

"I'm not certain about that," I whispered back. "In my experience little old ladies are the most dangerous of *Homo sapiens*. Remember the two aunts in *Arsenic and Old Lace*?"

Megan gave me a disbelieving look, typical of the young who always underestimate the aging.

"Something else that Rosemary and Lorene are experts at is baking cookies," said Agnes, gesturing at a long table that held a coffeemaker, an ice chest of cold drinks, and platters of the most mouth-watering cookies I had ever seen. "They volunteered to provide refreshments each week for the Circle. If you would care to make a donation toward the cost of ingredients, I'm sure the girls would appreciate it."

"If we could finish the introductions before raiding

the refreshment table," said Megan in a firm voice as I started to get up, intent on being the first at the eats. "I believe you're next," she said to the plain young woman who had mentioned the author named Barbara Mertz.

The young woman blushed. "My name is Candi Hobbs," she said, looking down at her clasped hands, and pushing a pair of glasses in ugly black frames back up her rather long nose. "I'm a graduate student at West Texas A&M, and I'm doing my master's thesis on detective fiction."

"Bravo!" exclaimed Rosemary. "It's about time that colleges and universities recognized mysteries as literature."

Candi blushed such a bright red that it was a wonder there was any blood left in the rest of her body. "Thank you," she whispered.

"I guess I'm next," said a well-dressed man in a three-piece gray pinstripe suit. "I'm Herbert Jackson the Third, Herb to my friends, which I hope you all will be. I'm an attorney by profession, but my ambition is to write courtroom dramas. I joined this group for your expertise." He rose and began passing out folders. "I thought with Agnes's permission, and that of our discussion leader of course, I would pass out a chapter of my first novel at each meeting. It's strictly for your amusement, but if you have any suggestions to make, feel free to do so."

"Another would-be John Grisham," whispered Megan.

I nodded, recognizing the name from the grocery store book rack.

"You're next," said Megan, nodding at a youngish woman with shoulder-length blond hair, which owed its color to a bottle and its style to a fashionable salon.

"My name is Lisa Heredia, and I came out of curiosity," she said in a voice that was neither pleasant nor unpleasant, but soft enough to have us all leaning slightly toward her. She smiled what I can only describe as a half-smile, as if amused by the other members. Some women, like Candi Hobbs for example, spoke softly because they were shy. Certain others did so to control their listeners. I didn't think Lisa Heredia was shy.

We all waited, but Lisa Heredia had nothing else to say, and finally Megan cleared her throat. "Yes, well, I hope we can satisfy your curiosity. Ryan, you're next."

I stood up, introduced myself, and said I was looking forward to learning more about the mystery genre—which wasn't a lie, exactly.

"The next order of business would be to name our group," said Megan. "But Agnes anticipated us there."

"I didn't want to dictate to the members," Agnes said, "but I needed a name for publicity purposes, and I'm partial to calling our circle Murder by the Yard."

Rosemary and Lorene both clapped. "Marvelous idea, Agnes," said Rosemary. "I like the the play on words."

I must have looked bewildered because Megan nudged me and whispered, "Scotland Yard."

I still didn't get it, but everyone else seemed to think it a perfect name.

While everyone but me was making social conversation, I wondered if I could sneak over to the refreshment table and sample the cookies without drawing a dirty look from Megan. I hadn't eaten any homemade cookies since my wife died and I was salivating in anticipation. I wasn't the only one who was more interested in the refreshments than the conversation. So was a tall woman with thick shoulders and ankles, dressed in a bizarre outfit that I belatedly recognized as very similar to the clothing worn by Basil Rathbone as Sherlock Holmes: a long cape of some coarsely woven black material, and a deerstalker hat. She was stuffing cookies in her mouth and washing them down with Coke. It made my fillings hurt to watch her.

I leaned over and tapped Megan's shoulder. "I think we have another member who hasn't been introduced."

At that moment the woman turned around, cookie crumbs sticking to one corner of her small, thin-lipped mouth, and Megan sucked in her breath, then cried, "It's Annabel Edgars Crow!"

5

There are no hundred percent heroes.

—TRAVIS MCGEE, in John D. MacDonald's
Cinnamon Skin, 1982

Creative individuals, and Annabel Edgars Crow most certainly was in that category, are almost always eccentric, bizarre, frequently unlikable, and happier in imaginary relationships than real ones—strange, out-of-the ordinary weirdos who march to the sound of a different drummer.

In Megan's opinion, Annabel Edgars Crow's drummer should have his drum confiscated. Maybe then she could understand, if not like—she doubted she would ever really like—Amarillo's only published mystery writer. And she wanted to badly, but Annabel the private person kept getting between Megan and Annabel the mystery writer. Metaphorically speaking, no matter how much Megan wanted to worship at the feet of creative genius, the thought kept intruding that those feet probably stank.

Legs apart with feet pointing in opposite directions, Annabel sat on the edge of the couch between Rosemary and Lorene, stuffing cookies in her mouth and talking at the same time. To Megan, the writer's mouth resembled a garbage disposal with lips. "I don't intend to join your group," she said, spraying a cloud of cookie crumbs with her words. "I told Agnes that I would just sit in. Important to know what readers like in a mystery."

"Could you at least tell us where you get your ideas?" asked Candi, then turned red when the author looked at her.

"Do tell us, Ms. Crow," said Rosemary. "I'm particularly interested in *The Orange Pekoe and Pekoe Mystery*. How did you think to add the arsenic to the tea bag, so the longer the victim brewed his tea, the more poisonous it became? But I always wondered, wouldn't the tea taste bitter?"

Annabel's eyebrows nearly touched when she frowned. "That's why the victim put in three lumps of sugar—to disguise the taste."

"Actually, arsenic is virtually tasteless," said Megan. "That's why it's been the poison of choice for so many centuries. The French call it *poudre de succession*, "inheritance powder." And it looks harmless, so it can be mistaken for flour or sugar. Better yet, it can be dumped in *with* the flour or sugar and the murderer can slowly poison the victim because the effects of arsenic are cumulative . . ."

"And its symptoms resemble other illnesses," said Rosemary.

"Diarrhea and vomiting," added Lorene. "Like intestinal flu. I doubt the ordinary victim would even think to go to the doctor . . ."

"Until it was too late," finished Megan. "And speaking from a professional viewpoint, I doubt that the average doctor or pathologist today would think to check for arsenic poisoning. Of course, if either did check, then the murderer was dead meat—so to speak."

"Ms. Crow," said Randel Anderson, stroking his sparse goatee. Megan wondered if he had thought to use Minoxidil to encourage hair growth.

"I'm particularly interested in your novel *Breathless*," continued Randel. "That's the book in which you use crush asphyxia as your means of murder."

"What about it?" asked Annabel, belching a fine spray of cookie crumbs.

"I was a bit curious as to whether you considered the sexual connotations inherent in a large male murderer sitting on the chest of the victim? Might your use of both a female and a male victim be a subtle way of suggesting that the murderer is bisexual?"

"Love a duck!" exclaimed Lorene. "The only thing Ms. Crow was suggesting was that adultery is always a good motive for murder. The two victims were having an affair if you remember, Dr. Anderson."

"That does not eliminate sexual symbolism," insisted Randel.

"But I want to know where you got the idea for *Breathless*," said Megan, drowning out further comments by Randel. "You have to admit that crush asphyxia isn't an ordinary method of murder."

"Just thought of it one day," said Annabel. "Popped into my head."

"It must have *popped* in from somewhere," said Megan. "Were you thinking of Burke and Hare at the time? They sat on their victims' chests, deflating the lungs, then covered their nostrils and mouths simultaneously, interrupting the breathing mechanism. Of course, it helped that their victims were drunk at the time."

"Burke and Hare were body snatchers who sold cadavers to the medical school in Edinburgh, Scotland," said Agnes.

"Heavens to Betsy, we all know that," said Rosemary.

"There might be one or two who don't," answered Agnes. "Not all mystery readers also read true crime."

Megan couldn't imagine a fanatical lover of mysteries who didn't read true crime, but she supposed Agnes might know a few. She nudged Ryan. "Don't you have any questions to ask Ms. Crow?"

"No, I don't think so, not tonight. I'll have to think about it."

Megan thought his eyes looked glazed. Maybe he wasn't feeling well. "Do you want me to bring you a cup of coffee?"

"How can you think of food and drink after talking about arsenic poisoning?"

"I don't think Rosemary and Lorene have poisoned the cookies, Ryan."

"Probably not, but I don't feel up to taking any chances."

Megan counted out her last few cents for sales tax. She would have to brown bag it until payday, not that she cared much. She always went downstairs to the employee lounge to eat lunch and read, but she would miss not having a cold Dr. Pepper at afternoon break. Maybe she could borrow five dollars or so from her mother. No, she wouldn't either, not unless she wanted to hear a lecture on fiscal responsibility and making your money last. Her mother saw child rearing as crisis prevention, seizing every opportunity to teach some lesson necessary to prevent her child from living under a bridge in a packing case in her old age.

She'd borrow from Ryan instead.

She picked up her bag of used paperbacks and turned around.

"What did you buy?" The voice was fragrant with the smell of peanut butter cookies.

Megan swallowed an expletive that would have been out of place in Agnes's bookstore. Four-letter words did not go with the scent of lilac. "Ms. Crow! You scared the devil out of me!"

"I doubt that," she heard Ryan mutter.

"What did you buy?" repeated Annabel.

Megan gritted her teeth. Maybe Annabel didn't mean to be rude. Maybe she just had poor social skills. Writers were solitary people after all, and maybe Annabel was alone so much she forgot how to be polite.

And maybe Annabel was a jerk from infancy.

But she was the only mystery writer that Megan actually knew.

She would give Annabel the benefit of the doubt.

"I bought a Sue Grafton I didn't have, and a Lillian Jackson Braun, and one of Joan Hess's Maggody mysteries. And I bought a new copy of *Murder She Said*, although I like its original title better. *What Mrs. McGillcuddy Saw!* grabs the reader. But whatever we call it, I'm glad we chose that particular book to discuss next week. It's classic Christie. Are you coming again, Ms. Crow?"

"Probably. Will there be cookies?"

"Every week."

Annabel turned and stalked away, stopping to talk to Candi, who, Megan noticed, glowed bright red at being spoken to by the famous author.

"She's different, isn't she?" said Rosemary in a whisper. "Do you suppose all writers are that strange?"

"She certainly likes our cookies," said Lorene. "Look at her stuffing her pockets full. No wonder she's so heavyset."

"She's a little more than heavyset, Lorene, she's heavy, period," said Rosemary. "All that sitting in front of a computer must make weight control difficult. But I still think she's strange, poor thing. I guess she can't help it, though, given her circumstances. I feel sorry for her."

"In what way?" asked Megan.

"She's homely," whispered Rosemary. "I know a young lady with your looks doesn't understand what a burden it is to be homely. It's not something you grow out of—like asthma. I've always thought *The Ugly Duckling* misled children. In my experience the ugly duckling never turns into a swan."

"I'm glad she's such a successful writer," said Lorene. "It offsets her homeliness. It's not like she's a model or an actress. Nobody cares what a writer looks like as long as her books are good."

"Or smells like either," added Rosemary. "Thank goodness Agnes replenished her potpourri dishes for the occasion, although the lilac scent came in second best to *musty*!" She whispered the last word with a quick look around. The two elderly women looked at each other, nodded agreement, smiled at Megan and Ryan and walked out the door, their two white heads close together in shared confidences.

"I love the twins. They're so sweet and look so harmless that you'd never know they will be dissecting everyone here," said Megan

"What twins? Are you still talking about characters in books?" asked Ryan, looking bewildered. In fact, Megan thought, he had looked bewildered most of the evening.

"That's what I call Rosemary and Lorene. They're the same age, with the same white hair, and both are die-hard mystery fans. And they think alike. In fact, they came close to finishing one another's sentences. The only difference between them is that Rosemary has more money."

"How do you know that?"

"Elementary, my dear Ryan. Rosemary's hair is professionally cut and set and her clothes are expensive— I know, because I saw that outfit at the mall and it cost five hundred dollars. And the diamonds in her wedding ring probably cost more than my undergraduate degree. That all adds up to big bucks."

"I did notice the diamonds."

"They were hard to miss," agreed Megan. "Lorene, on the other hand, obviously does her own hair."

"Maybe she likes to."

"Women of her generation always go to the beauty shop if they can afford to. It's not only a sign of affluence, it's a cultural thing. Therefore, Lorene is not affluent and probably gets her hair done only for special occasions. Also, Lorene's clothes are off the rack. I know because my mother has a blouse just like Lorene's, and my mother's motto is 'I'll never wear my money on my back.' Another clue to Lorene's financial worth is the fact that she wears a plain gold band without even an engagement ring."

"Thank you, Ms. Holmes," said Ryan. "Now suppose you tell me how you know those two old ladies will—*dissect*, I believe is your word—everyone here. I thought you said they were sweet."

"Because they are just like my great-aunt Hazel and great-aunt Ruth except much nicer, discriminating instead of judgmental. My aunts deboned anyone who came close, but Rosemary and Lorene gently dissect a chosen individual to see what makes him work, then reassemble the body until you can hardly see the scars. They're probably discussing us right now."

"I'd rather be dissected by them than the Ice Princess."

"You must mean Lisa Heredia," said Megan. "She is strange, isn't she, watching us all evening and not saying a word? I kept waiting for her to pounce like a cat on a robin."

Before Ryan could answer, Candi Hobbs touched Megan's arm. "Excuse me, I just wanted to tell you what a wonderful discussion leader you are, and how I'm already looking forward to next week. I was a little scared because I'm not very good at explaining myself in discussion groups, but I'm so glad I came tonight! And Annabel Edgars Crow promised me an interview after the meeting! Isn't she the most terrific woman?"

Candi smiled, pushed her glasses back up her nose, and scurried off, a thin, plain girl whose shoulders were already too rounded for her age.

"I guess 'cute' is not so bad as I thought," said Megan.

"I like 'cute,' " said Ryan. "*Beautiful* intimidates, but *cute* is warm and fuzzy and comfortable."

"Ryan, here's your sack of books," said Agnes, interrupting before Megan could respond. Which was just as well because she wasn't sure what Ryan was implying. Was he comparing her to a puppy or a bedroom slipper?

"What did you buy?" asked Megan instead.

"You sound like Ms. Nosy Crow," said Ryan, tying the top of his sack in a knot. "And speaking of the same, she certainly is hooked on Poe, isn't she?"

"In what way?"

"Annabel from the poem *Annabel Lee*, Edgars from Edgar Allan Poe, and Crow is what most people call a raven. I'm not as knowledgeable about mysteries as you, but I know my Poe." He held open the front door.

Megan walked through, feeling like a fool. From Ms. Sherlock Holmes to a doofus in the space of five minutes. How could she have missed the Poe connection? It was so obvious when she thought about it—except. She stopped just outside the door. "Ryan, that's too obvious. No mystery writer as gifted as Annabel would choose such a transparent pseudonym. It must be her real name."

"Is she gifted?"

"Yes! Haven't you read any of her books?"

"Not a one. I could never get past the vision of her perched in a mesquite tree saying, 'Nevermore.'"

"Mesquite trees have long, sharp thorns, Ryan."

"I never said my vision was logical, just that I had one."

"I know she wasn't at her best tonight, but she's a brilliant writer," said Megan, trailing along behind Ryan with her own sack of books. "Maybe she writes more brilliantly than she talks. Many celebrities are inarticulate outside their particular creative environment. Maybe Annabel is one of those."

"Nevermore, quoth the Crow."

"Ryan!"

"I'm sorry, Megan, but Ms. Crow didn't strike me as

being more than middling smart, and middling smart is not gifted."

"But she is! Gifted, I mean. I have all of her books, and each one is so intricately plotted that she reminds me of Christie. Talk to her next week, Ryan. You'll see how wrong you are."

"As long as I don't have to watch her eat. Between listening to the arsenic discussion and watching her blow cookie crumbs, I lost my appetite. I didn't eat a single cookie."

"I'm not defending her social skills, just her writing," said Megan, following Ryan to the parking lot.

"What social skills?"

Megan clamped her teeth together. Most of the time Ryan was the most wonderful friend anyone could have, but there were times when he acted like any other guy: stubborn, unreasonable, and downright dumb. This was one of those times. Adding to her discomfort was the fact that she felt compelled to defend Annabel Edgars Crow when she didn't really want to. The woman was a slob, a publicity disaster for the mystery genre, and Megan did not like her.

But she was stuck with her. Maybe Annabel Edgars Crow grew on a person over time. Yeah, Megan thought, about like mildew.

She consigned thoughts of Annabel, her eating habits, and her personal hygiene or lack thereof to that part of her mind where she stored puzzles to be solved later, and listened to the throb of live music from the various clubs and restaurants, and the laughter of the young who came to Sixth Street to hang out, scope out the opposite sex, and maybe get lucky. Megan wondered at the abyss that separated her from those leaning against the old buildings or against the cars parked along the curb. Perhaps it was something so simple as living the moment instead of living in both past and present. Once you've touched a four-thousand-year-old mummy, time becomes infinite. She felt a closer connection to the ghosts of Depression-era Sixth Street than to her own generation, but that was the penalty she paid as a paleopathologist: She never felt connected to the present until it became the past.

"What are you doing in my truck, son?"

"Nothing."

Megan shook off her philosophical mood and hurried toward Ryan's white Ranger, where a small boy with blond hair, dressed in a too-big coat, was trying to wriggle out of Ryan's grip. "Jared?" she asked. "Jared Johnson, is that you?"

"Yeah."

"What are you doing out on the streets this late? And why were you in Dr. Stevens's pickup?"

"I was watching," said Jared, peering up at her while trying to twist his arm out of Ryan's grip.

"Let him go, Ryan. This is the little boy the tooth fairy told me about."

"The previous owner of that fine-looking tooth you showed me this afternoon?" asked Ryan, studying the boy without releasing him.

"The very one."

"You better answer the lady's questions, son. If she has an in with fairies, then you need to stay on her good side."

"What were you watching?" asked Megan.

"I was watching you. I was playing across the street and seen you and him go in the bookstore, so I hid in the back of his pickup. I figured to warn you if I saw the witch, and you could run and hide if you needed to. I don't know if the tooth fairy can protect you against a witch. Mostly I think they're just interested in teeth."

Megan rubbed her temples. This kid really needed professional help. "Jared, Dr. Stevens will protect me against witches."

"How?" asked Jared, sizing up Ryan and not appearing to like what he saw.

"I have a water pistol in my glove compartment," answered Ryan. "You know how water dissolves witches."

Jared hesitated a moment while he considered Ryan's statement, then nodded. "I guess you're smarter than you look."

"Thanks, son, I take that as a compliment."

"But it ain't no good in the glove box. You need to pack it, mister, in case you need it fast."

"You've got a point, Jared. Next week I'll be carrying. Now hop down and get in the cab, and we'll take you home," said Ryan.

Jared climbed out of the pickup bed. "Naw, my mom would whip my butt if I took a ride with a stranger. Besides, I just live right over there." He pointed across the street, and Megan and Ryan turned to look. When they turned back, Jared was gone.

"Are you sure he's a boy and not a sprite?"

"That's not funny, Ryan! He's a little boy and it's dark, and you never know who's lurking in alleys."

"Speaking as one who was once a little boy himself, I think Jared will be fine."

"But how do you know? It's different now than when you were growing up."

"Any boy willing to fight witches for the sake of a fair damsel is a boy who can take care of himself. The cowardly don't crouch in a pickup bed for three hours."

'Ryan, he's delusional!"

"He's a kid who knows evil and names it with a child's vocabulary. That's not delusional; that's acting with intelligence. Besides, there's a cop on every block of Sixth Street this time of year. He couldn't get into trouble if he tried."

"I forgot about the police," said Megan with relief.

"I didn't."

"Ryan, why a water gun?"

"Didn't you ever watch *The Wizard of Oz*? Water melts witches."

6

Never worry about what you say to a man. They're so conceited that they never believe you mean it if it's unflattering.

—CAROLINE SHEPPARD to Ursula Bourne
in Agatha Christie's
The Murder of Roger Ackroyd, 1926

I came prepared to the second meeting of the Murder by the Yard Reading Circle. I staked out a seat on the couch, opened my large-print edition of *Murder She Said* and laid it in my lap, folded my hands over my belt, rested my chin on my chest, and dozed through the meeting in the best college faculty style. I awakened whenever raised voices penetrated my subconscious. Generally, one of the voices belonged to Megan Clark.

"Dr. Anderson, Miss Marple's knitting needles are not phallic symbols! I'm not even sure they're symbols at all, but if they symbolize anything, it is the domestic nature of murder in Agatha Christie's England. Murder is a disruption of domestic tranquillity. Knitting needles in the hands of Miss Marple symbolically repair the torn domestic tranquillity, as her sharp mind solves the murder! Don't you see?"

Dr. Randel Anderson was in full-blown form. "My dear Miss Clark, I say the knitting needles are phallic symbols because of the masculine order at the time Christie wrote her mysteries. The police who must arrest the criminal are men; the courts, from judge to prosecutor to barrister, are men. Miss Marple, by holding the needles, is in fact holding the phallus of male dominated society."

"Ryan! What is your opinion?"

Judging by the way Megan was in high dudgeon, I thought I had better say something supporting her position. The fact that I hadn't read the book and therefore didn't know that Miss Marple knitted, was irrelevant. I am a college professor and can obfuscate with the best. "This is a very important issue, perhaps the pivotal one of our discussion to the extent that Christie's symbolism impacted upon her characterization. Randel makes an interesting point, but Megan's position is stronger in that it is supported by most literary critics, who agree that the domestic nature of Miss Christie's books is what might be the most significant feature of her style. I'm sure our Christie expert"—I smiled at each of the twins because I couldn't remember which was which—"will be able to supply the names of influential critics which have unfortunately slipped my mind."

Rosemary—it had to be Rosemary because her hair looked like she'd just stepped out of the beauty shop, which Megan insisted the well-to-do elderly must patronize—gave me a somber look, an indication that she took her expertise seriously. Or perhaps she was trying to decipher what if anything I had said. "I would be glad to share what little I know about critical opinion during Miss Christie's lifetime."

There was more to Rosemary's speech, but I, satisfied that no one would ask me to comment on any subject for at least the rest of the evening, dozed off again only to be awakened by the sound of a very frustrated Megan.

"The publication date of the novel is really immaterial to this discussion! It does not impact on the subject matter."

"I'm not disputing that in this case it may be, but I—I

just wanted to share what information I have about Christie. The original Dodd, Mead edition was published in the United States in November of 1957. And I think you were a year off in citing the American publication date of *The Pale Horse*. I believe it was September, 1962, rather than November of 1961."

"Thank you, Candi! I'm sure that Rosemary and Lorene are making notes of your expertise in case they need to consult you."

I noticed that Megan was grinding her teeth. Given the extent of her orthodontia as a youngster—braces from before puberty to high school graduation—I hated to see her endanger the results. I smiled in hopes of distracting her.

She ignored me in favor of Annabel, who was wearing her cape and deerstalker cap again, and lurking near the refreshment table. Periodically a chubby, thick-fingered hand darted out and seized an iced brownie. I hoped she got her fill soon, since I'd had my own eye on that plate of brownies from the time I walked through the door. At her present rate of consumption, I would go hungry.

"Annabel, which side are you on: knitting needles as phallic symbols or as representational of domestic tranquillity?" asked Megan.

Annabel stuffed the brownie in her mouth and displayed her masticating skills to the club members. "Most old ladies knit."

I thought it was a good answer. My grandmother always knitted, but if anyone had referred to her needles as phallic symbols, she would have rapped the presumptuous speaker on the head with those selfsame needles. At least Annabel pointed out the obvious, which neither Randel nor Megan seemed to have considered. Maybe the obvious was the last quality one sought in a mystery, I don't know. As I mentioned before, I don't read mysteries.

Annabel's answer seemed to have dumbfounded Megan and Randel, and it didn't help that Lisa Heredia giggled. Silent all evening and she chooses now to giggle. Both Megan and Randel sat speechless for a moment or two, until Megan rallied herself enough to comment. "You're saying that everything in Christie is nothing more than what its name implies, that Christie did not mean the reader to draw inferences? Is *that* what you're saying?"

Annabel stared at Megan, her mouth hanging open— which was unfortunate since it was partially full of masticated brownie—before finally replying. "All I'm saying is that knitting needles are knitting needles. I figure Christie thought the same."

Now it was Megan's turn to stare, only it was more of a glare—before finally shaking her head in either disbelief or speechlessness, I couldn't determine which.

Speechlessness didn't affect Herbert Jackson III— "Call Me Herb"—but then he was a lawyer, and I've never met a lawyer unprepared to talk at length despite having nothing important to say. "Megan, I've been listening to this debate, and being a writer myself, although as yet unpublished, I might be able to provide the group with insight on the issue of the knitting needles: Are They Phallic Symbols Or Not?"

I dozed off again to the drone of his lawyerly voice.

I woke up when Agnes Caldwell tromped on my foot as the Murder by the Yard Reading Circle adjourned to the bookshelves to fortify themselves with whodunits—I was picking up the vocabulary whether I intended to or not—and she leaned down and hissed in my ear, "Professor, you can wake up now. We're through for the evening, and it's a good thing, too, since you were starting to snore. If Megan and Annabel hadn't gotten into a knockdown-dragout fight over whether Lucy Eyelesbarrow was a modern feminist or a woman independent of stereotypes, everyone in the circle would have heard you."

I blinked myself awake and struggled off the couch. "I thought we were discussing Christie tonight."

Agnes gave me the same pitying look as she gave me last week. "I'm going to slip a reference book on mysteries in with the Westerns I've already bagged for you. If you're determined not to read the week's selection, then you need a cheat sheet of some kind. Think of the book as Cliff Notes."

"I'll make more of an effort next week, Agnes, but I have trouble suspending disbelief long enough to read more than a chapter or two about some amateur female sleuth sticking her nose into a murder case. Seems to me that the most logical thing to do is to call the police or your lawyer, depending on whether you're reporting a crime or have just committed one. Let the professionals do it; that's their job."

Agnes appeared pensive for a moment, then looked up at me. "What if the police can't do the job, Professor? What if there are no leads, no weapon, and most puzzling of all, no motive? Would you accept any help, even that of a amateur female sleuth, to solve the murder of a person you liked?"

I looked up at the ceiling. Megan tells me I do that a lot, but it's a mannerism I can't help. There's something about the blank expanse of ceiling tiles, a dusty light fixture with the shadow of a dead moth in its globe, the corner where two walls meet, that focuses my attention. I can't explain it, but I do some of my most philosophical thinking staring upward.

Presently I roused myself from contemplation and met Agnes's eyes. "If it were someone I love, one of my children for example . . ."

"Or Megan," she said.

"Or Megan," I agreed, content to let her think I classified Megan as one of my children. "I would call all my acquaintances with any political influence whatsoever to pressure the police to continue investigating. If necessary, I would hire a private investigator to look into the case."

Agnes interrupted me just as I was warming to the subject. "What if you were without political friends and had no money to hire anyone?"

"I don't know," I answered, exasperated at her intense questioning. "But I don't see myself calling on some amateur female sleuth to wave her magic knitting needle and solve the case!"

Agnes turned toward the checkout counter, where Call Me Herb was handing out the next chapter of his legal thriller to the members of the Circle. "I would call on whoever could help me," she said. "I wish I knew a Miss Marple. I wish one lived in Amarillo, and I would ask her to investigate why in the world anybody would want to murder a harmless cleaning lady!"

"Someone you knew," I said. It wasn't a question. Amarillo's population was around 160,000 on a busy day, with no more than two degrees of separation between any of us; maybe only one. A majority of the population knew a murder victim, if not personally, then second-hand. It is that kind of a town: close, gossipy, really a series of small towns within a city's boundaries.

Agnes nodded, her expression a blend of sadness and anger and frustration. "Violet Winston. She was a classmate of mine when Amarillo only had one high school, and she was one of my best customers for more than thirty years. She and I watched Sixth Street change from a home to palm readers and junk dealers, to an historical district when nostalgia became a national trend, and all of a sudden everybody was talking about preserving Route 66, and speculators bought up the old buildings. Violet had a lot to say about the changes. 'Artsy-fartsy' she called the tearooms and antique stores, but she liked them just the same. She and I had lunch together once a week at the restaurant down the street, where all the tables are antiques from different eras. She always said if Sixth Street could be 'prettied up, as old as it was,' then there was hope for two old women like us."

Agnes swallowed and drew a deep breath. Her eyes looked shiny and wet, as if the tears were only a blink away. I was mesmerized in spite of myself by her tale. "Violet never spent much money with me, didn't have it to spend most of her life, just traded one sack of paperbacks for another. Sometimes I'd ask her to review a new book for me, tell me who my customers would be for a particular title. That's the only way I could express my appreciation for her business, because she wouldn't take charity, not even a used paperback. She was a proud woman and a smart one, with lots of what my daddy used to call horse sense. All she had in this world was a daughter she saw once a year who was ashamed of her, and an old, fat beagle."

Agnes stopped, and a mystery was solved. "So that's where Megan got that beagle!" I said. "Damn thing barks at me every time I step inside her front door. Let him out, and he runs to my front yard to do his business." He also hiked his leg on my truck tires but I didn't think it appropriate to mention that to Agnes.

"I called Megan" she said, "when I first heard about the murder. I knew that the Humane Society would never be able to adopt that dog out. He was too old and set in his ways. He needed a tender-hearted girl to love him and put up with him, and Megan has as tender a heart toward animals as anyone I've ever known. When I contacted Lieutenant Carr of the Special Crimes Unit, he agreed with me. I think he must like dogs, too."

"That would be Jerry Carr?"

"Yes, do you know him?"

"He was a student of mine several years ago. I heard he was a cop."

"The youngest lieutenant in the police department."

"He must be thirty-five, thirty-six years old?"

"I believe he's thirty-one."

That was bad. Not only did Megan not tell me where she got the dog, but Jerry Carr, whom I remembered as looking like a young Harrison Ford, was fourteen years younger than I was. There wasn't a mirror around, but if I'd looked in one at that moment, my reflection would have been green. I don't know which was worse: that I was so jealous that my stomach hurt, or that Megan Clark kept a secret from me.

"So what happened to Violet?" I finally asked when I thought I could speak without saying something obscene about Jerry Carr.

"She was shot this past February. She stopped by and I gave her some books I wanted reviewed, and a couple of old paperbacks from my special stash that I called her salary, just to get her to accept a gift. She walked east to catch her bus, and stopped to sit on the bench in front of Time's Treasures, the antique store. And somebody shot her."

"And Jerry Carr never found out who?"

"No, but not for want of trying. Nobody could have done more, but there were no suspects, no weapon, and no motive. Why kill Violet Winston?"

I was out of my depth. I didn't enjoy fictional mysteries, and I didn't read about the real thing either. But it was interesting puzzle on an intellectual level. "A drive-by shooting?" I guessed.

"Special Crimes found a piece of a homemade silencer at the scene. Lieutenant Carr said that indicated that the shooting was premeditated. Drive-by shooters don't use silencers as a general rule, he said. The only thing he could figure was that the murderer shot the wrong person, because there was nothing in her life, no reason that someone should want to kill Violet Winston."

There was a pause in which I contemplated the ceiling, and she looked off in the distance, far beyond the walls of the Time and Again Bookstore. I looked down when I felt her touch my arm. "I'm sorry, Professor. I didn't mean to bend your ear with my story, but you do understand now why I wouldn't turn down an amateur sleuth if one appeared."

"Agnes?" Megan looked from one to the other of us, her expression as curious as the proverbial cat. "Agnes, I think everyone is ready to pay up, and Herb is waiting to give you this week's installment."

Agnes smiled, once more a pleasant woman whom one wouldn't guess had been describing a murder not five minutes before. Women are remarkable creatures.

"Goodness, I didn't realize that the professor and I had been visiting so long. Did you find everything you wanted?" Agnes lowered her voice. "Did you get your copy of Herb's chapter? I must admit that I've found his book very therapeutic. I read a little every night instead of taking a sleeping pill. Herb's fictional lawyer is as boring as Herb is, which may explain why no publisher will buy it. But I wouldn't hurt his feelings even if he doesn't spend enough each week to pay my utilities for the month. He's a nice man and he tries so hard to be one of the group. He can't help being stuffy. It's an occupational hazard." She smiled and patted my cheek, then Megan's.

After we paid for our books and said our goodbyes, Megan and I left the store. I could hardly wait to ask her about her beagle and Lieutenant Jerry Carr. As it turned out, I didn't have the chance.

"Phallic symbols! What kind of Freudian idiot believes that Miss Marple's knitting needles are phallic symbols? Randel Anderson's kind, that's who! Him and his moth-eaten goatee and his 'bit' of this and 'bit' of that. My God, the man makes me want to hurl. Not everything in literature is about sex and certainly not Agatha Christie."

"He does seem fixated," I said.

"Fixated? He's obsessed!"

"And then there's Candi Hobbs. She talks in footnotes, Ryan, so help me God! There has to be more to life than memorizing the original publication date of every mystery Agatha Christie ever wrote."

I refrained from mentioning that Candi's correction of two dates quoted by Megan might have contributed to her bad mood and her low opinion.

"And have you ever met anybody odder than that Lisa Heredia? She just sits there watching, watching, watching. I want to pinch her just to make sure she's not a mute."

"She did giggle tonight," I said.

"It's better than the smirk she always wears like a mask. Do you ever wonder what she's thinking, Ryan?"

"That smile reminds me of the Mona Lisa. Nobody ever figured out what she was thinking either."

"On the Mona Lisa it's a smile. On Lisa Heredia it's a smirk."

I wisely didn't argue the point. A man soon learns to pick his arguments with Megan, and Lisa Heredia was a sure loser. I glanced in the bed of my pickup instead, met Jared Johnson's bright little eyes, put my finger across my lips before he could say anything, and nodded my head in the presumed direction of his home. "She's on a tear," I whispered to him.

He nodded, grinned, and slithered out of the pickup bed and disappeared into the darkness.

"What did you say, Ryan? I don't know why you've suddenly started mumbling, but it irritates the devil out of me." Megan sounded very testy.

"I just said that you're on a tear tonight."

"I am not on a tear!" she insisted, then continued her tirade as though she had never interrupted herself. "And then there's Annabel Edgars Crow, Amarillo's only published mystery writer! She demonstrates more creativity in making excuses for her slovenly dress and personal habits than she does in making conversation."

Since Megan's favorite outfit is a worn Texas Crew T-shirt, khaki shorts, and hiking boots, I doubted she was in a position to judge fashion, but again, wisely, I kept my opinion to myself.

"Guess what she told me tonight? That she was allergic to antiperspirants! Like that was any excuse for B.O! I'm so disillusioned, Ryan. Annabel's books are much more clever than their creator. I was hoping for stimulating discussions and instead I get costumed performance art. If she wears that deerstalker cap and black cape to one more meeting, I swear I will not be responsible for my behavior!"

Suddenly I was looking forward to the next meeting. Megan on a self-confessed tear was a stimulating prospect which put tonight's performance in the shade. On the other hand, Megan on a tear was likely to lose all perspective, all tact, all sense of diplomacy; in other words, she was likely to become a force of nature, flailing right and left with a sharp tongue and regretting it afterward. For her own good I had to stop her.

"Megan, I think we should drop out of Murder by the Yard since it's upsetting you so much. It's obvious this reading circle is not what it was advertised to be. It's not a discussion group. It's a tag team boxing match."

She stared at me, her eyes shining in the soft light of the street lamps, hair wild and crackling with vibrant life. "Are you crazy? I *love* Murder by the Yard."

7

Real, deliberate, unprovoked rudeness can be quite as shocking as physical violence.

—In Michael Gilbert's *Fear To Tread*, 1953

Megan clutched her copy of *The Murder of Roger Ackroyd* in one hand and her notebook in the other. Of all the nights to be late Ryan had to pick this one, when the Circle was discussing Christie's most powerful novel, which if she had written nothing else, would have secured her a place in literary history. Megan didn't understand why he dithered around asking oblique questions about Rembrandt, her recently adopted beagle. You would think no one had ever adopted a dog before. He didn't shut up until she threatened to go to the meeting by herself. Then he argued about Murder by the Yard. His argument that the meetings upset her was such a weak one that she brushed it aside. The meetings didn't upset her, they stimulated her. She never felt so alive as she did when arguing with that jerk, Randel Anderson, or with Annabel Edgars Crow. Did Ryan think she had to agree with people to be happy? On the contrary, she and every other member of Murder by the Yard enjoyed disagreeing. Otherwise, there would be no need for a discussion group. You can't discuss a book if everyone's perspective is the same. What fun is there in that? No, a argument, as long as it didn't result in abuse or violence, was good for whatever ailed you. She just wished Ryan understood that.

Megan burst through the door of the Time and Again Bookstore, expecting to find everyone seated, their books open, and with Agnes leading the discussion until she arrived. Instead she found Agnes hugging the twins, both of whom were clutching wadded-up Kleenex. The three were huddled in front of the checkout counter, while the remaining members of the reading circle sat in the discussion area, almost motionless with only an occasional twitch or squirm to differentiate them from seated corpses. Not even the vanilla and cinnamon that Agnes had chosen for this evening's scents could reduce the funereal atmosphere. For a moment Megan felt as if she should tiptoe, as though she'd entered a mortuary.

"Rosemary! Lorene! What's wrong? Agnes, what's happened?"

Rosemary raised her head, her eyes red-rimmed and wet. Lorene, if anything, looked worse. Rosemary blotted her eyes and blew her nose before answering. "It's nothing but old age creeping up on us. Your skin gets thinner just like your bones, isn't that right, Lorene?"

Lorene nodded, looking years older than she had the previous week. "A month ago her nasty remarks would have gone in one ear and out the other. But it's different now. I'd been worried—Rosemary had, too—but one morning I woke up and found I'd forgotten to lock my door. I live in an old neighborhood, on Jackson Street close to downtown, and some of the houses have been turned into apartments—and well, some of the people are the here-today-gone-tomorrow kind. It's not as safe for an old lady as it was when my husband bought the house fifty years ago. How could I forget to lock my door, Megan? Can you answer me that?"

Megan blinked back tears. It hurt to see the old ladies so unhappy and scared, and they did look old tonight instead of only aging. "It's not as bad as you think, Lorene. Everyone, even me at my age, sometimes has a slippage in short-term memory. It's not enough to make you cry. Just tack a red bow on your door. Every time you see the red bow, you'll remember to lock it. When I was a kid I used to wear a safety pin on my collar, so I would remember to write my name on my paper in school. Safety pin, red bow, it's the same principle."

Lorene looked at her with unhappy eyes. "I've remembered to lock my doors for nearly fifty years. I don't believe I would suddenly begin forgetting unless something serious was wrong. And it's more than short-term memory loss—my mind is slipping away from me a piece at a time. I've misplaced everything lately. I even misplaced some of my notes for our paper."

Megan patted Lorene's shoulder. "Have you seen a doctor? I'll go with you if you don't want to go by yourself. Sometimes hormone therapy helps."

Lorene dabbed at her eyes. "You are the sweetest girl, Megan, but I don't think doctors have a pill to fix big holes in an old woman's memory. Even Miss Marple couldn't fix me with her knitting needles. And if my children hear I'm forgetting things, they'll start talking nursing homes again. Well, I'm not going to a nursing home! I'm not ready to start playing Forty-Two or canasta five afternoons a week. Or making little art projects. I never was very good at art, and the years haven't improved me."

Megan turned to Rosemary. "Can you say anything to Lorene to make her feel better?"

Rosemary's lip trembled. "How can I help her? I can't remember to lock my door either. And I can't remember where I put things even when I'm very sure I had them. I'm having the same problems Lorene is having. It's just age, Megan. A woman can't keep all her faculties forever. You'll see, it'll happen to you one day." Tears started rolling down her cheeks again.

"Stop crying, Rosemary, please, and you, too, Lorene. I'm not ready to consign you two to an old folks' lockup. Let's talk about your problem for a minute, and let's begin at the beginning. What is it you're missing? Rosemary, you go first."

"I bought a large bag of old, out-of-print paperbacks from Agnes, and so did Lorene." Lorene wiped her eyes and nodded. "It's not our imagination," continued Rosemary, once she had confirmation from Lorene. "Agnes looked up the sale on her computer. I thought I set the bag down on a little display cabinet in my hall. I was tired and had a book I was finishing up, *The Christie Caper* by Carolyn Hart, so I didn't take the bag into my bedroom because I knew I wouldn't be reading any of those books. The next morning I looked in the bag to do a bibliography card on the titles we intended to cite in our paper, and all those old books were gone!"

"Maybe you put them in your office. Do you have an office?" asked Megan.

Rosemary nodded. "Of course, I do, and it's the first place I searched. Those books aren't anywhere in my house that I can tell, and I looked in drawers and closets that haven't been opened in years. What on earth could I have done with them?"

"The same thing happened to me," said Lorene. "Except I lost my books and my book bag, too. All those old paperbacks! Gone! Disappeared! Vanished! The only thing I can think is that Rosemary and I took those books out of the bags to talk about them when we stopped at the pancake house for a late-night supper."

"We enjoy having breakfast late at night," added Rosemary.

"And we left the books in the booth—just walked off and left them," said Lorene.

"Have you called the pancake house?" asked Megan.

"They hadn't found any books," sobbed Rosemary. "I imagine they thought it was trash and threw them out, but I even drove back over there and looked in their dumpster. No books."

Beginning to feel a sense of helplessness, Megan

glanced back and saw Ryan listening to the twins. "Can you think of any place Rosemary and Lorene might look, Ryan?"

"No, but my grandmother was forgetful sometimes, and she said if she just stopped looking, whatever she lost would show up sooner or later. Why don't you ladies come over to the circle, talk about the Christie we all read, and when you both get home tonight, I'll bet you remember what you did with the books. The important thing is not to panic."

"I don't think I care to go back to the circle," said Rosemary, blowing her nose and tossing her Kleenex into a wastebasket.

"I don't either," echoed Lorene. "I want to go have a stack of blueberry pancakes and two eggs over easy."

"But we need your expertise tonight. This isn't just any Christie, it's *The Murder of Roger Ackroyd.* It's her masterpiece!" said Megan, looking at each twin in turn. "Agnes, tell them how much they will be missed."

"I can't, Megan, because if I had been humiliated like Rosemary and Lorene, I wouldn't go back to the circle if you paid me. In fact, I don't know that I would ever again set foot in this bookstore if I were them."

"Oh, we would never take it out on you, Agnes," said Lorene, hugging the bookseller.

"Certainly not," agreed Rosemary. "It is not your fault that certain people are rude and ill-bred. But I think it would be best if Lorene and I left."

"But you haven't looked for books yet," said Agnes. "I have a stack of old paperbacks that I put under the counter for you. There are several that I think you might want to include in your bibliography."

Rosemary smiled, a poor effort, but one Megan was glad to see, and she joined Agnes in cajoling the twins. "That's right! You two go home early and work on your paper."

Rosemary and Lorene exchanged glances; then Rosemary took the lead, as Megan noticed she often did. "Lorene and I will not be writing a paper for the Conference on Popular Culture. If we can't even remember to lock our doors and keep track of the necessary books, we certainly can't do a paper."

Megan wiped her own eyes on the sleeve of her Texas Crew T-shirt. "Please don't decide now. Ryan's right about panic making you more forgetful. You become the thing you fear the most. I think Shakespeare said that or somebody else famous, but anyway it's true."

Rosemary stepped close to Megan and lowered her voice. "Lorene and I make jokes about being forgetful old ladies, Megan, but this time it's no joke. It scares a woman my age when she can't remember important things like books, and locking her door. The next thing I know some policeman will find me wandering downtown in my robe and house slippers, and no idea under heaven where I live or even who I am. You're too young to understand. You don't know how frightening it is to forget something that you *know* you could call to mind a week ago. Being absent-minded is not funny. What could possibly be humorous about being absent of mind? What are we but mind? When that is gone, one might as well be dead."

Megan stood stunned as the ladies exited, holding one another as though they were both feeble old women. And they weren't. "My God, Agnes, what happened here? Two weeks ago those two could have kept up with me on a cross-country hike. They were sharp, quick-witted, funny. I don't believe their minds have suddenly deteriorated."

"They were quieter than normal last week, Megan," replied Agnes, wringing her hands. "But after that witch made fun of them, they just fell apart."

Megan felt icy inside her belly while her face turned suddenly hot. Somewhere inside her head she told herself not to completely lose control. No violence except verbally.

"What witch, Agnes?"

"Lisa Heredia."

"But she hasn't said five words altogether in two weeks," said Ryan.

Agnes looked up at him. There were dark circles under her sunken eyes, and the only color in her face came from two splotches of rouge. "Well, she's said enough already tonight to last me a year."

Megan whirled and marched toward the discussion circle, her hiking boots making clicking sounds on the tile floor. She stopped in front of Lisa Heredia, who sat with that same half-smile Megan hated. "What did you say to Rosemary and Lorene that upset them?"

Lisa glanced up. "Oh, it's Megan. And the professor. I think it's nice that a father and daughter can enjoy doing things together." She giggled and batted her eyelashes.

"I beg your pardon," said Ryan in a voice so cold that Megan wondered why the temperature in the room didn't drop to freezing. She wished it would. Then she would break off Lisa's bleached blond hair exactly one-half inch from her skull.

Megan touched his arm. "Just a minute, Ryan. I asked Lisa a question and I'm waiting for an answer. What did you say to Rosemary and Lorene?"

Lisa frowned just enough to form a tiny line between her hooded eyes. Hooded like a snake's in Megan's opinion. Apparently she expected a reaction from Ryan and was disappointed. Too bad, thought Megan.

Lisa licked her lips, then pursed them into that half-smile. "I don't know why they got so upset. I did disagree with their opinions of Christie and Sayers. I have a more modern perspective on those two authors, which I shared with Rosemary and Lorene. I *am* entitled to my opinions." She twitched in her chair and crossed her legs, exposing them to the middle of her thigh in the process.

"Why don't you tell me what your perspective is," said Megan.

Lisa sighed as if she were put upon, and Megan barely held back from slapping her. "I told them that Miss Marple and Hercule Poirot are yesterday's icons. Don't you think today's readers would laugh at Poirot's wearing a hair net on his mustache? And Lord Peter Wimsey is such a geek. Nobody cares anymore about those characters. Really."

Megan counted to ten under her breath and clenched her hands to hide their shaking. "Of course you're entitled to your opinion, Lisa, but you're not entitled to deliberately humiliate two elderly women by making fun of their opinions."

Satisfied that she had said as much as her temper allowed without resorting to four-letter words, Megan sat down and drew a shaky breath. "Let's begin by discussing the ways Christie used Dr. Sheppard to narrate events while at the same time confessing his responsibility. How did Christie achieve this narrative device? Randel, have you any ideas to share with us?"

"Doesn't he always?" asked Lisa, wagging her finger at Randel. "Now, Dr. Anderson, let's be careful about sexual symbolism in this novel, or do you believe that Poirot is gay?"

Randel flushed an unbecoming shade of puce. It was the first time Megan had ever seen anyone turn that particular color. "I certainly do not! And I don't appreciate being sneered at."

Lisa opened her eyes as wide as physically possible. "I wouldn't do that, Professor Anderson. I was just anticipating your comments. I mean, you can't argue that Poirot's hair net is not a feminine symbol. And I always wondered what his relationship with Hastings really was."

Randel stood up, knocking over his metal folding chair in the process. It hit the tile floor with a metallic clang that caused Megan to start. There was nothing metallic about Randel's response. Megan expected to see the words erupt from his mouth wreathed in fire and smoke.

"You, Miss Heredia, are the kind of woman that drives a man to celibacy! Megan, I refuse to continue in this reading circle if Miss Heredia is a member. She doesn't appreciate the civility that such a group requires."

Straightening his jacket and smoothing his hair, Randel exited in grand fashion, squared shoulders and head high on a rigid neck.

"You had no right to talk to Randel—Professor Anderson—like that. You're an ugly person!" With that final comment Candi Hobbs burst into tears and ran out the door after Randel.

"Do you suppose the little thing is in love with Randel Anderson?" asked Lisa, tapping her long nails against her cheek in what Megan thought was a very stagy gesture.

Suddenly Herbert Jackson stood up. "I'll be leaving the group, too, Megan."

"Herb, what's wrong? What did Lisa say to you?"

"Oh, I didn't say anything," Lisa protested. "And I don't know why he's so angry. He asked us to make comments on his work in progress, didn't he?"

"Herb, what did she say?" repeated Megan, rising to grab his arm.

With a glance at Lisa that was filled with as much rage and hurt as any Megan had ever seen, Herb slapped one of his folders in Megan's hands. "I have defended murderers who were kinder than her."

Megan opened Herb's folder, knowing what she would find. Inside was Chapter two of his courtroom drama, bleeding red ink from a savage line-edit. Lisa had changed words and phrases, rearranged sentences, and scribbled editorial comments in all the margins. "Stilted dialogue!" "Really, this is such a silly description! Can't you be more realistic?" "This character isn't even two-dimensional! If you can't do decent characterization, you should at least have a strong plot! I don't see any kind of a story line!" "Don't give up your day job! I hope your closing arguments are better than this unfocused tripe!"

Megan closed the folder and gave it to Ryan. "Murder by the Yard is not a writing critique group, and even if it were, this is not a helpful critique, Lisa. I don't think I've ever read anything so cruel."

"No one told me not to critique his novel. He did ask for comments." Lisa pouted as if the reading circle was responsible for her conduct.

"You know, if you ever had a kind thought, the shock of it would probably kill you," said Megan, feeling hot all over. She noticed her hands were shaking again.

"If you could replay my words from tonight's meeting, you would see that I haven't said anything as tacky as the insults you and Randel Anderson exchange each week. It's not my fault that my words are taken the wrong way." Again that innocent half-smile appeared on Lisa's lips.

Megan started to retort, but hesitated, thinking over Lisa's comments that night. Much as she hated to admit it, Lisa was right. Taken one way, her words were no worse than many remarks Megan herself had made. Taken another way, Lisa Heredia could have taught the serpent in the Garden of Eden a few things. There was something so familiar about Lisa's technique, something that reminded Megan of someone else. If she weren't so angry, she might remember who.

"Megan, could you please lock up for me?" asked Agnes, distracting Megan from Lisa. "I have such a migraine, I don't know if I'll even be able to open in the morning."

Turning toward Agnes, Megan was shocked at the woman's pallor. "Ryan and I will take care of the store, Agnes. Do you want me to help you to your apartment?"

Agnes lived in a comfortable two-bedroom apartment in the wing of the store facing the parking lot. Not many people were aware of it, and most of the time Agnes walked outside to a door in the back of her building, so as to "pretend I don't live in the bookstore." Apparently she would be using her outside door tonight as she staggered toward the store's front entrance.

"Thank you," said Agnes. "You're a lifesaver, Megan." Grabbing the brass door handles to steady herself, she turned back to face Lisa. "I don't want you in my store again, and you are not welcome back to the reading circle."

"Legally, I don't believe you can prevent me from coming to the reading circle," said Lisa, her half-smile replaced by what Megan believed was a sneer.

"Try me, young lady. Just try me." Agnes jerked the front door open and let it slam behind her.

"Why are you doing this?" Megan said to Lisa. "Your total contribution for two weeks has been your name and a giggle. Now—now suddenly you're the bitch from hell. Why the sudden about-face? What's in it for you, Lisa? I'm really curious as to what you think you will gain from acting like this."

Lisa rose from her chair, stretching like a cat. "Now you're talking like this is a class in self-analysis. You are all so full of yourselves, talking about symbolism and presenting papers and writing drivel, that I just had my fill of it tonight. There is only one person in the Circle who's interesting, and that's Annabel Edgars Crow. Are you hiding among the bookshelves, Annabel?"

Megan looked over her shoulder to see Annabel

emerge from the last aisle, still wearing her deerstalker hat and black cape. "I'm here, but I didn't see any need to sit with the rest of you and be a target."

"Didn't you hear me, Annabel? I'm fascinated by your writing. Each book is so unique and different from the next."

Annabel lumbered over to the refreshment table. "Where are the cookies? Didn't anybody bring cookies?"

"Did you hear what I said?" demanded Lisa, her hands on her hips in a very thirties theatrical pose.

"I heard you. We'll talk. Have to check my calendar first." With a lingering look at the empty refreshment table, Annabel walked out without ever acknowledging Megan or Ryan.

"Get out of here, Lisa," said Megan. "And don't try to come back to the reading circle. As badly as you wounded Herb, I'm sure he would look until he found a reason for a restraining order against you."

"I don't think so," said Lisa. "I haven't threatened anyone, and you can't find anything in my language to prove differently. I don't think you can get a restraining order because you don't like someone."

Megan couldn't remember hating anyone more than she hated Lisa Heredia at that moment. "I don't know why you are the way you are. I don't care if you were abused as a child or abandoned or feel the world has cheated you, I just don't care. You're hateful because you choose to be. From now on, be hateful on Tuesday nights somewhere else besides the Time and Again Bookstore."

Lisa picked up her purse and ambled toward the exit, her very posture radiating disrespect. She opened the door, then looked over her shoulder at Megan. She smiled and licked her lips. "Did anybody ever tell you that freckles are ugly?"

With a scream like the sound of fingernails on a blackboard Megan ran for the door, intent upon tearing Lisa Heredia's bleached hair out by the black roots. She took two running steps before Ryan grabbed her around the waist, whirled her about, and tossed her on the couch. Before she could roll off, Ryan had her pinned beneath his body.

"Megan! Listen to me, damn it!"

Shocked at Ryan's use of even mild profanity, Megan stopped fighting. "What are you going to say?—and it had better be good."

"You can't beat up Lisa Heredia!"

"I wasn't going to beat her up; I was going to tear her hair out. There's a subtle difference between the two acts," said Megan with as much dignity as she could muster while pinned to the couch.

"And she would have filed charges against you, and then where would you be? Maybe a felony conviction, no job, no prospects of ever digging around inside a mummy. If you hit her, she wins, Megan. That's the way she plays the game."

"But why, Ryan? I don't really understand."

Ryan sat up, grabbed Megan's hand and pulled her up beside him. "I don't understand her either, Megan. Maybe she's so unhappy with herself that she can't stand for anybody else to be happy."

"No, that's too obvious an explanation, and Lisa is anything but obvious. She was taunting us, Ryan, like she was playing some secret game or telling a joke, then laughing at us because we didn't get the punch line. And she reminds me of someone else, but I can't remember who."

"It doesn't matter," said Ryan. "Lisa did a one-woman show that she can't repeat next week, because everybody will be ready for her."

"But everyone quit but us, Ryan. And maybe Annabel."

"Trust me, Megan. Everyone will be back next week

just to see if she will. And she won't. She doesn't want
to argue one on one; she wants to win. So she ambushed
us tonight and won. I don't think she'll risk her victory."

Megan leaned against his shoulder. "Are you mad that
I didn't challenge her about calling us father and daughter?"

"Well, I couldn't hit a woman, so I depended on you
to put her in her place. Why didn't you?"

"It's like asking a man if he's still beating his wife.
There's no good answer. If we deny being father and
daughter, then you're robbing the cradle. If we say nothing, then you're committing incest. It doesn't matter that
everyone else knows better. That soft little voice and
innocent look will take them in for just a moment and
they will all wonder. As my mother would say, least
said, soonest mended."

Ryan slipped his arm around Megan and hugged her.
"For a short, cute, *young* redhead, you're pretty smart.
And I like your freckles."

Megan smiled and kissed his cheek. "And for a tall,
cute, older man, you're my best friend."

Ryan hugged her again, to hide his wince, then looked
up at the ceiling. "Is that how you see me, Megan, as
an older man?"

Megan thought about laughing, but realized that
Lisa's comments had hurt Ryan more than they'd hurt
her. "I'm a paleopathologist, Ryan. There's no such
thing as too old."

8

Don't tell me that women have not ten times as much intuition as the blundering and sterner sex; my firm belief is that we shouldn't have half so many undetected crimes if some of the so-called mysteries were put to the test of feminine investigation.

—MARY GRANARD of the Female Department
in Baroness Emma Orczy's
"The Ninescore Mystery,"
Lady Molly of Scotland Yard, 1910

I guess to Megan I was an older man. At least she didn't say I was a father figure. I never tried to act like one toward her despite the twenty-year difference in our ages, and she never indicated to me that she viewed me as the father she lost in childhood. In fact, she bristled with indignation if I offered any advice that might be construed as parental. I suppose any young woman who owns a well-stocked and well-used toolbox is not in need of a surrogate father unless he has a working knowledge of the internal combustion engine.

Not that I wanted her to substitute me for her father. I didn't. I didn't want to be her best friend either. And that was a growing dilemma that I had to solve before I made some ill-advised romantic gesture that would horrify Megan, and incite her to physically retaliate in some unspeakable, but potentially painful, manner.

Was I suffering a midlife crisis? Was the past year's celibacy warping my brain? And when did I embrace celibacy? When Megan came home and first knocked on my front door. Damn Lisa Heredia for letting the fox in the hen house. If she hadn't made that father-daughter remark, I wouldn't have been analyzing my relationship with Megan, and discovering feelings that should have been buried so far in the back of my mind that I would never act on them.

As an historian, I knew that disrupting the status quo leads to reprisals. Revolutions have started from less.

Once more I was looking at the broad spectrum of human events. Megan, as usual, focused on mundane human activities, so she was not as stunned as I at our discovery. She told me later she was only surprised that Lisa Heredia lived as long as she did.

I locked the front door of Time and Again Bookstore behind me, joined Megan, and we walked down the sidewalk toward the parking lot. There was a wrought-iron street lamp at each end of the short block that Agnes's bookstore occupied, and a dim light shone from the store's one window. Still, the sidewalk was more dark than not. In front of the store, on either side of the entrance, were two six-foot-long planters filled with petunias, already blooming as it was late April and warmer than normal. A round planter with a frail tree just leafing out stood on the sidewalk's brick border at the corner of the short front wing of the store. Beyond was the parking lot in front of the long back wing where Agnes had her apartment, and storage areas into which she planned to expand if, as she said, "business stays good and I live long enough." Farther down Sixth Street were the clubs and restaurants with their live music and crowds, although the crowds were small on a week night.

As I said, the sidewalk was mostly dark, and anyone could have crouched behind the planters and not been seen. Or waited out of sight against the side of the book-store, which is the scenario Megan likes best, because the streetlight didn't penetrate that far.

It was Lisa Heredia's misfortune that the night was cloudy and there was no moon to cast a killer's shadow.

If Megan and I had not been walking side by side with my arm resting on her shoulder—in a companion-able way, of course—she would not have stumbled over Lisa's foot, and the body would have been discovered by someone else. I like to think that if Megan hadn't been the one to find the body, she would not have plunged headlong into the investigation.

And if wishes were horses, beggars would ride.

On reflection, I know that keeping her out of the investigation would have taxed the ingenuity of an Einstein, and Lieutenant Jerry Carr, although I suppose intelligent enough, was no Einstein.

"How long between the time the victim left the store and you and Megan Clark locked up?" asked Jerry Carr, tall and lean and sure of himself. And young. How could anybody thirty-one years old look so young?

I was sitting on the couch inside the bookstore clutch-ing a vial of what I supposed was smelling salts or its modern equivalent. A large knot on the back of my head throbbed in 2-4 time. I wiped my forehead with a damp cloth someone had given me—the paramedics, Agnes, Megan—I didn't remember who. As a matter of fact, I couldn't remember how I got back in the store. The last thing I *do* remember was hearing Megan cry out "Don't step in the blood!" At that thought, I grew nauseous, and sweaty and cold at the same time.

"Where's Megan?"

"She's already talked to us and so did Agnes while we waited for the paramedics to finish."

"Then Lisa Heredia is alive. With all the blood, I thought she had to be dead."

"She is dead. The paramedics worked on you. According to Megan Clark, you slipped on the blood and fell backward into the planter full of petunias, knocking yourself out."

I took a quick whiff of the vial at the mention of blood. Leave it to Megan to cover for me. "I don't remember."

"I don't imagine you do—at least about finding the body. Now, could you answer my question? How long between Lisa Heredia leaving the store and yours and Megan's departure?"

"I can't be sure. We had to count the money and turn off the lights except for the one over the counter, and lock the door. Maybe thirty minutes?" I didn't mention that Megan and I had sat on the couch talking about Lisa Heredia for a good fifteen or twenty minutes. I included it in the thirty-minute estimate instead.

"How long before that did Ms. Annabel Edgars Crow leave?"

"Five minutes? Ten minutes? I can't be sure. I wasn't watching the clock."

"And Candi Hobbs?"

"I'm just guessing here. Don't take my word as gospel. Candi ran out maybe fifteen minutes before Annabel."

"Why did she run out?"

"Did I say run?"

"Yes, you did. Can you tell me why?"

I swallowed. I hated to say anything to Candi's detriment. If Jerry Carr made me nervous, and he was a former student *and* I was innocent, I could imagine how poor, shy Candi would react. "I said run because Candi ran after Dr. Randel Anderson. I guess she had something she wanted to say to him. And if you're thinking Candi had anything to do with killing Lisa, well, that dog won't hunt. I doubt if she would step on a cockroach."

"How did you know Lisa Heredia had been killed, Dr. Stevens? How did you know it wasn't an accidental death? You've been out cold over forty minutes."

I felt my mouth drop open. How *did* I know Lisa was killed? "There was all that blood, Jerry. You don't bleed like that from a skinned knee."

He nodded, wrote something in a small spiral notebook, and looked at me again. I've read the expression. His eyes pinned me like a butterfly, but I'd never been on the receiving end of such a look until then. I didn't remember his being so forceful when he was a student. It was probably the reversal of roles. He was in charge and I wasn't.

"Dr. Stevens, did you have some other reason to suspect that Lisa Heredia was a murder victim?"

I took another whiff of the vial and swallowed. Funny how dry my mouth was and I still needed to swallow. "Lisa was not well liked."

Jerry nodded again, his eyes never leaving my face. "Megan called her the bitch from hell. Is that a fair description of her personality, Dr. Stevens?"

Megan needed to learn not to volunteer information. I guess since she knew she was innocent, she didn't realize how bad her words sounded to someone else. "I don't know that I would put it quite so strongly as that. Megan is a stereotypical redhead in some respects. She tends to exaggerate when she's irritated."

Jerry Carr smiled, his eyes just the least unfocused. "I know Megan, Dr. Stevens. She is a firecracker."

I didn't like his smile, his eyes, or his choice of words. Just what the devil did he mean exactly when he called Megan a firecracker?

"Go on, Dr. Stevens. You were talking about Lisa Heredia," he reminded me.

I cleared my throat and tried to corral my stampeding thoughts. "Uh, yes, Lisa rubbed people the wrong way, but just tonight. The first two meetings she gave her name and giggled. Otherwise, she sat and listened."

"Like Madam DeFarge?"

Wouldn't you know he was just what Megan liked: a well-read man. "Madam DeFarge is a character from a *Tale of Two Cities*, which is not a mystery, and she knitted. Lisa didn't knit. That was Miss What's-her-name in Christie's mysteries."

"Marple."

"What?"

"Miss Marple is a character in Christie's crime novels who knits," said the lieutenant.

"That's right. Slipped my mind for a second. Must be the bump on my head."

"Must be," agreed the lieutenant. "Leaving out literary allusions, isn't it odd that Lisa Heredia suddenly changed personalities? Which one is the real Lisa Heredia: the silent, Ms. butter-won't-melt-in-my-mouth, or the nasty bitch? What's your guess, Doc?"

"I don't know. Megan and I talked about it after Lisa left, and we couldn't come up with any reasonable explanation."

"So how long did you talk, Doc, or didn't you pay any attention?"

Tricked fair and square! Jerry Carr rose in my estimation. I confessed to neglecting to divide our talking and our closing up into separate segments. He seemed satisfied with my explanation, but I couldn't be sure. He was an expert at suppressing facial expressions.

"So let's go through the order of departure again, just to make sure you have it right. You and Megan left last, is that right?"

I nodded. I wished he would stop calling her Megan. To him, she was Dr. Clark.

"Before you, Annabel Edgars Crow left."

I nodded again.

"Wasn't Agnes the next to leave?"

"I forgot about Agnes. Yes, she left before Annabel."

"She lives in an apartment in this building, is that right?"

"Yes, that's right. She had a migraine and asked Megan and me to lock up."

"And before her?"

I thought a minute. "Herb Jackson."

"I understand Lisa Heredia didn't like his novel."

"To be honest, Lieutenant—Jerry—none of us like his novel. It's pretty bad."

Jerry showed me the folder with Herb's chapter. "Is this the folder she gave Herb Jackson? Is this her writing in the margins—and all over the pages?"

I nodded.

"Pretty ugly critique. I imagine Mr. Jackson's ego was bruised black and blue."

"He wasn't happy," I said, which was as close as I intended to get to the truth. Herb Jackson had been royally pissed.

"Who left before Jackson?"

"Candi Hobbs. She ran after Randel Anderson as I told you before."

"And before Anderson?"

"Rosemary Pittman and Lorene—I don't remember Lorene's last name. They're both very old ladies, very forgetful, very fragile. They had to help each other out the door."

"So everyone left the store before Lisa Heredia did—except you and Megan?"

"That's right. And her name is Dr. Clark."

Jerry Carr smiled. "Fond of her, are you, Doc?"

I hate being called Doc. And my feelings toward Megan were none of his business. They had no bearing on who killed Lisa Heredia. "I've known her since she was a little girl. She's my daughter's best friend."

"Is that how come you forgot to mention that Megan Clark left the store first by a good five minutes and waited for you outside?"

I debated whether or not to fake unconsciousness, but decided I wasn't a good enough actor to fool Jerry Carr. I remembered him as a sharp student, and I doubted he'd lost his edge in the intervening years. "It slipped my mind, and it doesn't have anything to do with this business anyway. Lisa had been gone a good twenty-five or thirty minutes before Megan went outside."

"So you think Lisa Heredia was killed immediately after leaving the store?"

"Of course, don't you?"

"That blood was still wet when we got here, Doc, not even a hint of congealing, and it would have been fresher still when you allegedly stepped in it."

"Why would Lisa Heredia hang around on a dark street for twenty-five or thirty minutes? That doesn't make sense."

"Maybe she was waiting for someone," he suggested.

"It wasn't Megan! I was there all the time and they never arranged to hang out together on a street corner!" I was trembling and took another whiff of whatever was in the vial. I hoped it would clear my wits if not my head.

"I never said they discussed a meeting. I said that Lisa Heredia was evidently waiting for someone because she was a fresh kill, Doc."

"Megan didn't kill Lisa Heredia, damn it! Nobody in the reading circle would kill Lisa Heredia! Yes, she was a bitch, but that's not a good enough reason to kill her!"

"Is that why you're lying, Doc, because you don't believe anybody in your reading group would bludgeon a woman, then slit her throat from ear to ear and prop her up against the side of the bookstore because she insulted him or her?"

I leaned over and put my head between my knees to keep from passing out. The very image of Lisa with blood spurting from a sliced jugular vein made me light-headed. Finally I got control of myself. "I didn't lie about Megan or Lisa or anybody, Jerry—Lieutenant. I didn't tell the story word for word, but that's because I didn't want a bunch of old ladies and harmless eccentrics suspected of murder!"

Jerry Carr swung a chair around and straddled it, resting his folded arms on its back. "Let me tell you something, Doc. I've locked up a man who beat an eighty-five-year-old woman to death for thirty-five cents and a portable TV that wasn't even a color set. His neighbors said he was a good man, just a little different. I guess different would be the average person's word for eccentric, wouldn't it? I locked up another guy, the sole support of his blind mother, but you see, he liked to put on a ski mask and rape five-year-old girls. His neighbors were surprised, too, when I arrested him. I could go on with even more graphic examples, but you understand what I'm saying. You can't tell a murderer by looking, Doc, so how about you tell me everything that was said and who said it."

Feeling as if I were picking my way through a minefield, I recited as exactly as possible the dialogue as I remembered it. By speaking in a monotone I managed to take the sting out of much of what Lisa said. You had to actually be there to understand the viciousness of her remarks, because it wasn't so much what she said, as it was the way in which she said it. Much worse were the responses to Lisa's words. I kept remembering the promise in Agnes's voice when she told Lisa, "Try me." And the rage I saw expressed in Herb Jackson's eyes. And shy, homely Candi Hobbs. Did she have a crush on Randel Anderson? Hard to imagine any woman seeing Randel as a romantic figure, but maybe Candi took her glasses off when she looked at him. Would Candi feel protective enough toward Randel to wait for Lisa, argue with her, hit her over the head, and lean down to cut her throat?

Or did Randel do it? He was vindictive enough from

what I knew of him, but I couldn't see him splashing blood around. He might get some on his wool tweed jacket with the leather patches.

Last of all were the twins. Impossible to imagine two little old ladies bludgeoning a woman half their age. On the other hand, I wished they didn't remind me so much of the aunties in *Arsenic and Old Lace*.

"Can you think of anything else you want to tell me, Doc?" said Jerry, those laser-sharp gray eyes of his watching me.

"Doc, did you hear me?"

"I am Dr. Stevens, or Ryan to my friends. I am not 'Doc.'"

"I apologize, Dr. Stevens. I was trying to get under your skin, so I could weigh your reaction. The paramedics vouched for you, but I wanted to see for myself. There was a small, very small, possibility that you killed her and Megan is lying for you, but that explanation felt wrong to me. You're free to go, Doctor. Of all the members in this reading group of yours, you are the only one who is not, and probably never will be, a suspect. I'm reserving judgment on the others."

"Why am I not a suspect?"

He stood up and laughed, flashing straight white teeth suited to a matinee idol. "I examined the scene, Doctor, and there were no footprints in the blood. No skid marks, so you didn't slip. It wasn't a bad story Megan made up on the spur of the moment, but it wasn't true. More likely you fainted and hit your head on the petunia planter. The paramedics told me they have never seen anyone with such an aversion to blood. Every time they revived you, your eyes would fly open with an expression wilder than a March hare's, and you'd scream, 'My God, the blood,' and pass out again. They said you ought to be written up in the medical literature. One of them suggested therapy, too."

"I'm sure I'll furnish a good story over coffee break

for the next ten years, unless paramedics are subject to confidentiality like doctors," I said, getting off the couch and testing my legs. A little weak, but they would hold me up.

"I don't know, but I'll have a word with them. Ask them to at least call you John Doe." He was grinning when he made the offer, so I was less than appreciative.

"Thank you," I said, trying not to choke over the words. "Where's Megan? I'm sure she's ready to go home. This has been a hard evening for her."

"Megan? A hard evening? Yeah, well, you might want to slip out the back way and go on home. The body's still out front, and Megan is jawing with the Justice of the Peace for this precinct, pointing out injuries and generally charming the old man out of his boots. She's trying to talk him into letting her assist in the autopsy on the basis of her being a forensic specialist, but I don't think it's going happen, no matter how cute he thinks she is."

Why couldn't Jerry Carr call Megan cute in her presence? His comment would surely make me look more favorable by comparison. "Why can't she assist at the autopsy? She's probably more qualified than whoever does them."

"There's probably a law somewhere about a *suspect* doing an autopsy."

My mouth gaped open in shock, and it was several seconds before I could speak. "What are you talking about?"

"There's a lot of blood on Megan's clothes for somebody who only discovered a body."

9

There are some blokes what was borned to be a husband of a nagging wife. There is other blokes what was borned to have sixteen kids. And there are some other blokes which are borned to be murdered. Kendall was borned to be murdered. The surprising thing is that he was murdered so late in life.

—SAM THE BLACKMAILER in Arthur W. Upfield's
Death of a Swagman, 1945

"Jerry, this was not a premeditated murder. It was decided upon no more than five to ten minutes before the killer met with Lisa Heredia. It was a spur-of-the-moment kill. The fact that blood was still seeping from the throat when Ryan and I stumbled over the body indicates that although she was dead, she had not been dead long enough to have completed bleeding in those areas subject to gravity. In other words, I missed witnessing a murder by five minutes at most, and probably closer to three."

"It was darker than Hades at this particular spot, Megan, so how did you know the blood was still seeping?" asked Lieutenant Carr.

Megan swallowed. She supposed that Ryan would hear that she left him unconscious, lying spread-eagled beside the planter while she gave the body a cursory examination in what light the tiny flashlight on her key ring afforded. But examining a corpse *in situ* and immediately upon discovery was so important. Ryan would understand.

She hoped.

She explained to Jerry, waving her hands about in their surgical gloves, which she had begged from the Justice of the Peace after Special Crimes refused her. It was a case of locking the barn door after the horse was stolen, since her hands had been bloodied when she examined the body before the JP and Special Crimes arrived. But she didn't have a choice. You can't assume a body is lifeless. You have to find out for sure, and you're going to get bloody if the corpse is seeping. She would have to remember to soak her T-shirt and hiking shorts before tossing them in the washer, since both articles were bloodstained. She just hoped Lisa Heredia didn't have any infectious diseases.

The JP ruled the victim dead and ordered an autopsy, then left after telling the lieutenant how wonderful she was. Megan sensed that Jerry didn't think she was nearly as wonderful as the JP did.

"A flashlight on your key ring?"

"Yes, but it was enough light for me to see that her throat was still bleeding, but very slowly, so that I knew gravity had nearly done its job. If the murderer had been more proficient and propped the body up with its head tilted back at an angle, there would have been little more bleeding than the initial glut when her throat was first cut—which happened just around the corner. From the laceration on the temporal fossa, near the squamous suture and close to the mastoid—the side of the head above and slightly behind the ear, to the layman—I theorize that the murderer struck her from behind, knocking her to the ground either unconscious or nearly so, then lifted her head by her hair or collar—I'm not sure which—and slit her throat from left to right while standing above and behind her. The Jack the Ripper scenario, to put it in historical context, because Jack probably stood behind his victims, and one at least, Elizabeth Stride, was lying on the ground when he cut her throat."

"You're amazing," said the lieutenant.

"I hope you don't mean I'm amazing for a woman," said Megan.

"No, you would be just as amazing as a man. Anything else you'd like to tell me?"

"Well, I can tell you a good deal after I do an autopsy. Not that I enjoy performing one on a fresh body. There's not a lot of challenge to it. Now a mummy, that's a challenge! If this body were three thousand years old, I would have no clues left except his injuries and whatever was left in his tomb, if anything."

Jerry Carr was shaking his head. "Pretty damn amazing. You're probably the only woman like you in the entire Panhandle."

"I know I am. There are only about fifty paleopathologists in the country and I know them all and none of them live around here."

"You said this body wasn't a challenge—so tell me more."

"Well, after the murderer cut the victim's throat and waited for the initial bleed-out, he dragged her to this spot and propped her against the wall. And Jerry, if you search the gutters and alleys and dumpsters around Sixth Street, you have a chance of finding a redwood plank from the planter that holds the tree. I notice one is missing, and from the looks of the break area, it was broken off recently. I theorize the murderer broke off the plank, so he could whop the victim up beside the head, so to speak. But he didn't do it immediately, or else the body wouldn't have still been bleeding out, so he and the victim must have talked for a few minutes before he . . ."

". . . whopped her up beside the head," finished Jerry.

"Exactly."

"So you're calling this is a spur-of-the moment murder?"

"That's the way I see it," agreed Megan.

"How about the knife, Megan? Why do you suppose he was carrying a knife, or do you think he found a sharp instrument lying around handy?" asked Jerry.

"If you don't find a bloodstained sharp instrument along with the redwood plank, then I would guess the murderer took it along, and I would further guess he had to because in some way or another that object is associated with him, and he dare not discard it."

"That would be my guess, too," said Jerry. "So which of the three men murdered her?"

"I didn't say she was murdered by a man. I used the pronoun he as a generic term because it's easier than saying 'he slash she.' A woman could have done it, Jerry. I don't see any of the steps I've described requiring an extraordinary amount of strength. Even breaking the plank would not have been difficult because you'll notice the planter has two mental bands—one around the bottom and one two-thirds of the way up. I think anyone could take hold of a plank and bend it back against that top mental band, so you have leverage against which to push. Snap and you're done. Which is exactly how the missing plank was broken."

Megan peeled off the surgical gloves so each was inside out, thus keeping the blood from touching her skin. One of the five evidence techs from Special Crimes who had been watching and listening to Megan, hurried to take the gloves and dispose of them in a hazardous waste container inside the Special Crimes van. She flexed her hands and nodded her thanks to the man. Jerry, she noticed, was frowning.

"Something wrong? Did I miss something?" she asked.

"I just wondered how you managed to get my five evidence technicians and the Justice of the Peace dancing to your tune in less than an hour."

"I guess they just recognize expertise when they see

it," said Megan in an offhand manner while surreptitiously watching Jerry for his reaction. What was his problem, anyway? She was practically dating him—if you called a couple of lunches and dinner and a show dating.

"Megan, I don't want you to take this the wrong way, but you can't perform the autopsy. You can't assist either."

Megan bristled at the firm command. "Why not? I'm perfectly qualified with a degree in forensic anthropology with a specialty in pathology. Just because I do most of my work on mummies doesn't disqualify me to perform an autopsy on a fresh body."

"You discovered the body—you and Dr. Stevens—and it's a rule of thumb that until the individual who discovered a murder victim is investigated . . ."

"Are you telling me that I'm a suspect?" demanded Megan, a cold spot beginning to form inside her chest.

"No, or I would have read you your rights, but I can't let you near the body again, Megan, until you are cleared of even the least suspicion . . ."

"You *know* I didn't murder Lisa Heredia, Jerry, you know it!"

"I have procedures I have to follow, Megan, and I can't bend those procedures just because we have a—relationship. You are a civilian and I can't let you mess around with the evidence. I'm sorry." He did have the decency to look as if he regretted his words, but Megan didn't think simple regret was enough.

She looked at the pool of blood drying on the parking lot asphalt, at the smaller pool of drying blood in front of the store, at the place where the plank was missing from the planter. "So you're refusing the help of the most qualified person in the entire Panhandle? That's what you're telling me?"

Jerry shrugged his shoulders. "That's what I'm telling you."

"And I suppose that the rest of the members of the reading circle are also suspects?"

"Not yet, but I have to investigate them. It may be that one might become a suspect."

"Well, Jerry, I'll just have to see to it that doesn't happen. If you're done with the third degree, I'll leave.

"I'm done for now, but I want you and the professor at Special Crimes tomorrow morning to give me a statement."

"We'll be there with bells on, as the expression goes," said Megan, wondering how a man could kiss you until your toes curl one week, and act like an official jerk the next. She turned toward the bookstore.

"Megan, I think the professor is in his truck. I sent him out the back door. Can't tie up the paramedics all night reviving him."

Megan twirled around and walked toward the parking lot. "Your last statement was unnecessary," she said as she walked around Carr.

"I'm sorry, Megan, you're right. That was a smart-ass remark that I intended to be humorous. It wasn't, and I apologize. I let my personal feelings get in the way for a second."

"What personal feelings?"

"Jealousy."

"Of Ryan? You're jealous of Ryan? If there weren't a body lying five feet away I'd laugh. Why are you jealous of Ryan? He's my best friend."

"Stupid, isn't it? Just forget it, Megan. Take the professor home, and the two of you come to my office about ten in the morning."

"Okay," said Megan, hurrying toward Ryan's truck. She glanced in the bed, but no little tow-headed boy grinned at her. The cold spot in the middle of her chest grew larger until she shivered. Please, she prayed, don't let Jared have seen the murder.

"Megan?" Jerry walked across the parking until he

was a few feet away. "Megan, keep your nose out of this. Will you promise me that?"

She put her hands behind her back and crossed her fingers. "I will not stick my nose into your investigation."

"Thanks, Megan, I feel better." He leaned toward her, but caught himself before he kissed her. "I better go back and give orders to the troops. See you tomorrow."

"Tomorrow," echoed Megan, uncrossing her fingers. She hadn't promised not to do her own investigation.

10

*As long as we're going insane we may as well go
the whole way. A mere shred of sanity is of no value.*

—PHILO VANCE in S. S. Van Dine's
The Bishop Murder Case, 1929

I sat in the passenger seat while Megan drove, my eyes
closed until I judged we were several blocks away
from Time and Again and Lisa Heredia's body. Then I
jumped on Megan.

"You lied to me."

"What! What are you talking about, Ryan? I haven't
lied to you," she said, glancing at him in surprise.

"You promised me the most that could happen if we
joined Murder by the Yard was a paper cut! You never
mentioned cut throats and dead bodies."

Megan pulled over to the curb on Georgia Street, put
her forehead against the steering wheel and started
laughing. I reached over and hugged her as best I could
while sitting in a truck with bucket seats. "It's all right,
honey. Just let it all out. It's the delayed reaction from
finding the body."

She laughed harder. "Ryan, you're so funny sometimes. Expecting a paper cut and getting a dead body
instead."

"I didn't mean to be funny, Megan. I just meant that—
oh, I don't know what I meant, except this is worse than

breaking my wrist or my nose or any of the injuries I've accumulated in our adventures together. This is a dead body of someone we knew! And somebody we know probably killed her. Jesus, Joseph, and Mary, but this is one damnable mess!"

I let go of Megan and settled back in my seat. Not only did she seem not to need my comforting, but there was the faintest scent of copper hanging about her, a sweetish smell that I knew was blood. The smell of blood doesn't ordinarily bother me like the sight of it does, but I was in a fragile state. I also felt like a wimp. I was sure Jerry Carr didn't faint at the sight of blood.

"I don't think you know how much of a mess it is," said Megan. "We're all suspects—the Circle that is. Not that Jerry admitted we were suspects, because then he would have to give us our Miranda warning and we could hire lawyers and the whole nine yards. But he as much as said we were all under suspicion. All but you, that is. He said anybody as sensitive to the sight of blood as you couldn't possibly bludgeon anyone to death. So you are without blemish in the eyes of Lieutenant Jerry Carr, and that's why we're having the meeting at your house. The police won't be visiting you, and I can't say the same for any of the rest of us."

I sat up straight, all my alarms ringing. "What meeting, and what difference does it make if the police should visit?"

"A meeting of Murder by the Yard at your house," explained Megan in her let-me-explain-this-simply-to-a-simpleton tone of voice. "We are all under suspicion and I refuse to believe that any one of us committed murder. Particularly that murder. It really was grisly, Ryan."

"Would you stop talking about it, please? I keep remembering your screaming at me to watch the blood and shining your flashlight at that wide red ribbon around Lisa's neck, only it wasn't a ribbon . . ." I stopped and swallowed, wishing I had kept the little vial of whatever it was. I needed a hit now to keep me from being sick all over the front seat of my pickup.

Megan pulled over and pushed my head down between my knees. "Breathe deeply and think of yellow roses in spring. Think how sweet they smell. Think of us walking in your rose garden picking roses until all the vases in your house are filled."

I closed my eyes and thought hard of one perfect yellow rose—and how beautiful it would look against Megan's red hair. I sat up. Thinking of Megan that way was madness, because I certainly wasn't thinking of her as a friend or a child. What was wrong with me? Did finding bodies make me amorous? If that was true, the paramedics were right: I needed therapy.

"I'm okay, Megan, I'll be fine, don't worry about me. Let's go back to this proposed meeting. I say *proposed*, because I have no intention of hosting a secret meeting of suspects behind Jerry Carr's back. And what did you plan to do at the meeting, anyway?"

Megan drove back onto the road. "I'm going to assist the police in solving this crime. Not only am I uniquely qualified, but I know all the suspects and circumstances."

"I know what made me ill a few minutes ago and it wasn't blood. It was the smell of conspiracy. What you're contemplating is illegal, Megan. You're not some female sleuth. You're an assistant reference librarian. You're not Miss Marbarry . . ."

". . . Marple. It's Miss Marple, Ryan."

"Marple. You're not Miss Marple! You're Megan Clark! This is real life, Megan. A do-it-yourself murder investigation is fantasy. If you don't get this idea out of your mind, I'll only be seeing you on visiting day at the women's prison."

Megan drove up in my driveway, turned off the ignition, and turned to face me. Not that I could see more of her than the left side of her body where my outside light shined into the cab. "Ryan, you're being ridiculous. I know I'm not Miss Marple. I don't go looking for murder cases to solve, but I'm already involved in this one, so I'll just ask a few questions to assist Lieutenant Carr."

She put her hand on my cheek and looked up at me. Her hair was the color of darkest burgundy in the faint light, and I could barely see the gleam of her eyes. "Now that I've explained what I'm doing, may I use your house, Ryan?"

I sighed—and capitulated. "Yes."

They parked their cars blocks away and darted from shadow to shadow down Ong Street, lurking momentarily behind tree trunks and creeping from shrub to shrub, then slithering along the side of my house and knocking three times on the back door, behind which Megan and I waited in the light of three candles set out on my kitchen counter. I'd argued for leaving the light on over the sink, but Megan said the cops might see it. To demonstrate how paranoid I was becoming, I agreed with her. I felt as if I were caught in a James Bond movie— and I wasn't James Bond. I was his best friend—you know, the junior agent who always dies in the first few minutes of the film.

"Quit squirming," Megan hissed at me.

"I'm not squirming. I'm practicing walking with chains around my ankles. When I'm convicted and sent to prison do you think the warden will let me work in the library?"

"Will you hush! You're not going to be convicted for anything; you're not even going to be arrested for anything, so shut up!"

Just then someone knocked three times. My heart sped up until I felt it was going to jump right out of my chest. Why did I let Megan talk me into these adventures?

Lord, I promised, if I live through this without going to jail and sharing a cell with Guido the three-hundred-pound biker, I will break off all association with Megan Clark except for church on Sunday.

"Who's there?" demanded Megan.

"Why are you asking that?" I demanded. "You know it's someone in the group."

"I wanted to be sure, so I told everyone to pick a favorite mystery as a password."

"Oh, my God, this sounds like a sorority initiation."

"Hush, Ryan! This is a means to bond the group together."

"I'm sure bonding is very important in a conspiracy." She dug her elbow into my ribs and I concentrated on getting my breath back.

"Who's there?" Megan asked again.

"*The Pale Horse*," said a falsetto voice.

"And *The Nine Tailors*," said another voice, as bass as the first one was falsetto.

Megan opened the door and Rosemary and Lorene slipped in, each in identical black sweat suits.

Rosemary pulled off a close-fitting knit hat. "That was fun. I feel thirty years younger. Well, fifteen anyway."

Lorene unwrapped a long black scarf from around her head. "Rosemary wanted to wear ski masks, but I was afraid somebody would call the police. Or shoot us."

Megan hugged each one of them. "I'm glad you came. Ryan thinks I'm crazy, or that we'll all go to jail."

Rosemary—or was it Lorene—patted my check. "Ryan, you're much too young to stop taking a chance on life."

"Life! This doesn't have anything to do with life—unless we're talking life without parole."

"Hush, Ryan. I think I heard someone curse. I think he walked into your pyracantha bush."

"It's not called the fire thorn for nothing," I said, hoping that it was Randel Anderson with his butt full of thorns.

The three knocks came. "Identify yourself," ordered Megan. I heard the twins giggling.

"*And Then There Were None*," said a hoarse voice.

"Wonder why he chose that title?" asked Megan. "Unless he sees the whole book as Christie's statement on necrophilia."

The twins smothered their giggles, but I was appalled. I didn't want to believe that Megan even knew what the word meant.

Megan opened the door and Randel Anderson fell through onto the floor. "Pull them out," he moaned, pointing a tiny flashlight at several long thorns in his left buttock.

The twins and Megan looked at me. Unfortunately, I had no one to pass the buck to, so I crouched down by Randel. "This is going to hurt you a lot more than me. Rosemary, hold the flashlight. Megan, get him something to bite on."

"Just a minute," he gasped, then squealed as I pulled out the first thorn. I must give the pompous little jerk credit. He had the widest range of squeaks, squeals, squalls, and screams I've ever heard. If there had been police outside, they would have already rushed the door.

I pulled out the last one as another of our conspirators knocked. "Who goes there?" I demanded in my deepest voice, then winced when Megan made her best effort to bury her elbow in my side again.

"*A Is for Alibi*," a soft voice answered.

"What a marvelous choice!" said Rosemary, clapping her hands.

"Such imagination!" said Lorene. Or maybe it was vice versa. I still had trouble telling the twins apart, especially in the dark.

"She knows something besides the publication dates

for Christie's seventy titles," said Megan, opening the door. "Enter Kinsey Millhone."

Candi Hobbs swaggered—there's no other word for it—into my kitchen in a tan trench coat, a fedora, and a cigar clamped between her teeth. "I parked the VW down the street and around the corner. Put mud on both license plates."

Everyone but me burst into leg-slapping laughter. I couldn't figure out what she said that was so funny. And I didn't get the significance of Kinsey Millhone either. Who was Kinsey Millhone?

Call Me Herb and Agnes arrived together. Call Me Herb chose *The Rainmaker,* which I remembered seeing next to the checkout counter in the grocery store, and Agnes picked *Death on Demand,* a choice which had the troops applauding her "appropriate choice for a bookseller." I hoped it wasn't an omen of our fate.

Megan led the way into my living room which was dimly lit by two table lamps. She had confiscated all my blankets which she taped *over* the drapes. No ray of light need attempt to escape the room. London wasn't so well prepared during the Blitz. There was much conversation among the members, all boiling down to How Clever of Megan. I sat in my recliner and watched a girl barely older than my oldest child take over my house as she had taken over my life. Would I have had it any other way? I didn't answer that question. I was afraid to.

Megan chaired the meeting and designated Candi as the recording secretary, a good choice as Candi was an obsessive note taker. Most graduate students are. They live in mortal fear of not taking down the right remark from their professor, so they take down all his remarks, a wasted effort as only about half of what a professor says is worth remembering. I know; I'm a professor.

"The first topic is to discuss our relationships with the victim," said Megan. "We each need to detail everything we know about Lisa Heredia, and every time we met her. Randel, we'll start with you."

"I didn't have a relationship with her," said Randel, stroking his goatee. "I had never seen the woman before the first meeting of Murder by the Yard. Not to speak ill of the dead, but she was not the type of woman I enjoy getting to know. In my opinion, for what it's worth, she was a cold, controlling woman."

Megan had a pensive expression on her face, but I couldn't guess what was troubling her. "Thank you, Randel. Agnes, what about you?"

Agnes was silent for a moment while she gathered her thoughts. "She came in the bookstore three times before the first meeting. She didn't say much the first two times, just asked if I would take a check. I remember she lived on the south side of town in one of the apartment complexes on Bell Street. The third time she asked about Annabel—did I know her, did she ever come in, would she mind if a fan called? Then she saw the flyer about Murder by the Yard, and asked if Annabel was likely to attend. Of course, I didn't know. Who knows what Annabel will do next? But I told her I thought Annabel might drop by once or twice. The other times I saw her were at the meetings, and you were all there. And I agree with Randel, she was a cold woman."

"What about Annabel?" I asked. "Isn't she coming?"

"I left a message on her answering machine, but she hasn't called back. I'll try her again now."

I tossed Megan my cordless phone and watched while she dialed Annabel's number from Murder by the Yard's membership list. I didn't know there was a membership list. I certainly didn't remember signing it.

"Annabel, this is Megan Clark. Are you alone? Can you talk? You can't talk? The police are there? Oh, well, I won't bother you, then. I just wanted to tell you about Lisa Heredia. The police just told you? I guess they would, wouldn't they. Annabel? Annabel? Hello, Annabel? Oh, hello, Jerry." I couldn't hear the other end of the conversation, but I didn't need to. I watched Megan's face instead.

"I am not interfering with your investigation, Jerry! I was calling Annabel to tell her about Lisa, and to ask if she wanted to go in with the rest of the group for flowers. If you think that constitutes interference, then you'll just have to arrest me. Goodbye!" She clicked off the cordless phone, and looked at each of us. "You heard. The lieutenant wouldn't approve of our meeting like this. If you feel you should go, that's fine. I don't want anyone to get into trouble with the police. I mean, more trouble than we're already in. So, what do you want to do?"

"I think I'm next," said Candi. She had taken off her trench coat to reveal a rather nice figure in a red T-shirt and tight jeans. Randel Anderson certainly thought so. His beady little eyes were about to fall out of his head.

"I never saw Lisa Heredia in my life until the first meeting," continued Candi. "And I can't say that I missed making a good friend. Lisa struck me as the type who didn't have any friends, or if she did, she didn't trust them." She blushed when she realized everyone was looking at her. "That's just my opinion, of course. It might not be true at all, but it feels true. If you know what I mean."

Everyone nodded, including me. However badly she expressed herself, Candi had pegged Lisa Heredia instinctively. A cold, distrustful, hurtful woman would have friends exactly like herself. No other kind of woman would come near her more than once.

"Herb, what about you?" asked Megan.

Call Me Herb had removed his jacket and, informally dressed in his vest, shirt, trousers, and wingtips, sat relaxed on my couch with a cup of coffee close at hand. It was the closest to human I'd seen him. "I have thought about Lisa Heredia since walking out of the meeting. To the best of my knowledge, I had never seen her before the first meeting. She isn't an old client of mine or I would remember her. Besides, my practice is primarily criminal work. I might add that I prefer the company of my thieves and murderers to that of Lisa Heredia. If she were still alive, that is."

"Rosemary, Lorene, did either of you know Lisa outside of Murder by the Yard?" asked Megan.

The women looked at one another; then as usual, Rosemary answered for both of them. "We never met her before, Megan, which is odd in a way. As long as Lorene and I have lived in Amarillo, and given the fact that it's not a huge city, I'm surprised that we haven't seen her at least once in our lives. But we haven't."

"So there is no prior connection between any of us and Lisa Heredia. The only common link is Murder by the Yard. I don't know about the rest of you, but I don't believe that a love of mystery fiction and a nasty mouth are sufficient motives for murder. Somebody benefits from Lisa's death, and I want to know who that someone is. I intend to find out."

Agnes cleared her throat and waved her hand for attention. "Megan, it occurs to me that within this group we have eight people, who, if you add all their years of reading together, have several hundred years experience solving crimes. I know that real crime is different from the fictional kind, but the principles are the same: motive, means, and opportunity."

"Bravo, Agnes! That is just what I was telling Ryan before the meeting. I plan to do a little investigating on my own. Personally, I am offended to be suspected of murder, but we all had the opportunity according to Lieutenant Carr."

"When did he say that?" I demanded. "I don't remember his saying that." I was on the verge of an anxiety attack listening to Megan and her familiars planning to interfere with a police investigation.

Megan gave me a look that would have stripped the hide off an elephant. "Ryan, Jerry is a very clever cop. I explained to you why he didn't come out and say we were suspects, but we are, whether he said so specifically or not. It's the same with opportunity. We all had it. Any one of us could have waited for Lisa to leave the store."

"What about it? Did anyone trip over anybody else on their way to the parking lot? No? There you have it, Megan. Nobody hiding in the parking lot or in the petunias waiting to bash Miss Heredia over the head. We alibi each other and the case is closed." I spread my arms and bowed to the assembly. "I don't know about anyone else, but I want to toast my deductive reasoning with something stronger than coffee or tea. I'll even bring out my best stock. Anybody else want a little Jack Daniels?"

"Do you want to tell him or shall I?" said Agnes, giving me that pitying look again.

"Ryan, if everyone alibis everybody else, who alibis me? I was the last one out of the store a good five minutes before you. That was ample time for me to bludgeon Lisa and slit her throat. And don't forget, I know my way around the human body. I would know exactly how to do it."

11

If you convey to a woman that something ought to be done, there is always a dreadful danger that she will suddenly do it.

—FATHER BROWN in C. K. Chesterton's
"The Song of the Flying Fish,"
The Secret of Father Brown, 1927

Megan knew more about the Special Crimes Unit of Potter, Randall, and Armstrong Counties than the average citizen, thanks to a degree of curiosity that Ryan claimed approached nosiness. Actually, personal curiosity accounted for only part of her knowledge. The other part came straight from the horse's mouth, Lieutenant Jerry Carr being the horse in question. One of her mother's most valuable hints on how to trap a man into thinking you are the most wonderful woman in the world is to ask him questions, then listen with total concentration to his answers. Of course, her mother's advice was directed at enabling her daughter to catch a husband, a quest upon which Megan had no intention of embarking at this time. There were archaeological sites to dig, mummies to discover, ancient organs to examine, a whole world to explore, and Megan intended to do it all before settling down to two o'clock feedings and PTA meetings. In the meantime, she utilized her mother's advice to learn more about Special Crimes than Jerry Carr realized he was teaching. She knew for instance that

Special Crimes was organized to investigate any suspicious deaths in the three-county area, and that in Texas, any death was deemed suspicious until the Justice of the Peace of that particular precinct or county ruled it to be suicide, homicide, accidental, or by natural causes. Despite the anti-gun lobby's publicity to the contrary, the majority of deaths in Texas were from natural causes, followed by accidental death and suicide. Homicide is the least frequent cause of death. But when it is the cause, Megan would advise a murderer leave the country rather than have Special Crimes under Lieutenant Jerry Carr target him for investigation.

Megan knew Special Crimes' solve rate was one of the highest in the country, knew its evidence technicians were some of the most meticulous gatherers of bits and pieces from a crime scene, knew it called upon experts in ballistics, serology, questionable documents, and fingerprints. She also knew that Jerry Carr and Special Crimes enjoyed a friendly working relationship with the FBI. Unlike many local police forces, Special Crimes didn't see the feds as their natural enemies.

When Megan thought about what she knew of Special Crimes—and the intelligence of Jerry Carr—she wondered at her own audacity and that of Murder by the Yard. Special Crimes and Jerry Carr definitely held the home field advantage in any competition between them and the Megan Clark-led troops. There was an outside possibility that Ryan was right: She was crazy.

She and Ryan entered the building on SE Third, and waited on the first floor until somebody from Special Crimes came downstairs to escort them. Butterflies fluttered madly in her stomach, and her palms were wet. She noticed that Ryan, leaning against the wall next to the elevator, looked so relaxed he might as well have been sitting behind the desk in his study.

"Aren't you nervous?" she whispered with a smile to mislead the gimlet-eyed cop at the so-called front desk, which was really a window open to the foyer.

Ryan raised one eyebrow, a mannerism he used when he wanted to irritate her, because however much she tried, she could never duplicate it. "Nervous? Why should I be nervous? I resigned myself last night to spending the rest of my natural life in prison. Once you accept your fate, stoicism sets in and you relax."

"Would you please quit exaggerating, Ryan? What would you rather do? Wait for officialdom to take its bureaucratic time investigating a murder in which I have a legitimate interest?"

"What interest? Are you an undercover cop and just failed to tell me? Are you wearing a badge on your underwear? If not, then your interest is about as legitimate as William the First."

"William the Conqueror was illegitimate!"

"My point exactly. So is your investigation."

The elevator opened to reveal Jerry Carr, with a smile on his face that Megan noticed stopped short of his eyes when he looked at Ryan. Maybe he hadn't been teasing her last night. Maybe he really was jealous of Ryan. She had never seen it fail. Show a man a little attention, and he went into his macho mode and made a fool of himself.

"Megan, Dr. Stevens, get in, please." A somber expression replaced his smile. "I'll escort you to individual interview rooms upstairs. We'll tape the interview, type it up, and you can read it over and sign it."

"How long will it take? I have a class at one o'clock in Canyon," said Ryan.

"You should be done long before noon, Doctor," said Jerry. "In your case it will just be a matter of going over what you told me last night for the record. Unless you thought of something else you want to tell me—something you might have forgotten." Jerry raised his eyebrow, and Megan wondered if all men could lift one eyebrow at a time. Maybe it had something to do with male chromosomes.

"I can't think of anything," said Ryan, still so calm Megan wanted to pinch him.

The elevator door opened onto a hall, and Jerry led them around the corner and down another long hall to a reception area where a secretary sat behind a large desk. To the left was an enormous tank where equally enormous fish swam languidly through the water. Megan watched the fish open and shut their mouths, turning their bodies this way and that to study her. She'd never thought of it before, but there were disadvantages to having an eye on each side of your head and no neck. After this murder case was over she might read up on how a fish saw the world. Did they combine the two separate images, one from each eye, or was each image processed individually?

"Do you suppose those are piranhas?" Ryan whispered. "Do you suppose they feed them recalcitrant suspects who refuse to talk?"

Megan looked around, but Jerry was talking to the receptionist in a low voice.

"They are not piranhas, and I wish you would take this seriously," she hissed.

"I am. You're the one who thinks this is Amateur Sleuth Hour."

"Megan, if you'll come with me, we'll go in my office," said Jerry, taking her arm. "Dr. Stevens, the sergeant will take your statement."

"I'll wait for you downstairs, Megan," said Ryan, no longer looking so collected.

"I wouldn't wait if I were you," said Jerry Carr. "Megan's statement may take a while longer than yours. I'll see she gets home."

"I'll wait," said Ryan, an obstinate expression on his face.

"I drove my truck," said Megan. "I'll get myself

home. But thank you for the offer, Jerry." She smiled at him and watched his eyes crinkle as he returned the smile.

Megan sat down in a typical government issue, thinly padded chair in front of Jerry's typical government issue metal desk. His office was small and cramped, with barely enough room to walk between door and desk, chair and filing cabinets. She wondered if government employees, whether local, state, or federal, got free therapy for claustrophobia. Perhaps government offices were designed specifically to narrow minds enough to fit in the standard bureaucratic mold. It was, she decided, a different slant on the nature versus nurture argument.

Jerry sat down behind his desk and turned on a cassette recorder. He recorded the date, his name and area of responsibility in Special Crimes, the case number, and finally Megan's full name and address. Megan wasn't intimidated as she thought the ordinary citizen suspect would be. As an anthropologist slash archaeologist, she recorded information using much the same format as Jerry. She didn't assign case numbers to her bodies exactly as he did, but the result was the same.

"Megan, if you would tell me again the sequence of events of last night, and the dialogue spoken in your presence as nearly as you remember it," Jerry said, pushing the recorder closer to her.

If you were innocent, the best way not to get caught in a lie was to tell the truth. If you were guilty, the best way not to get caught in a lie was to call a lawyer and say nothing at all. Megan was innocent, and other than that unwitnessed five minutes she spent in front of the store listening to music from down the street, nothing she did or said could be construed in any way but the actions and words of an innocent woman. However, since she spent that five minutes not more than ten feet from a bloody—no, make that bleeding—corpse, Jerry had no choice but to put her on his "A" list of suspects.

She understood that. What infuriated her was his insistence on being objective about it. He ought to know she didn't murder anybody, and he ought to be out working to prove it. What was the point in having friends in high places if they weren't on your side?

"Did you see anybody walking away from the store while you were waiting for Dr. Stevens, and Lisa Heredia was dead or dying a few feet away?" asked Jerry.

"Just you wait a minute, Jerry Carr! Lisa was past *dying* at *that* point. When her throat was cut practically to her spinal column, the massive blood loss killed her within minutes—I would say three at the most, but there is room for disagreement among pathologists on the time factor. You're making it sound as if I'd been paying attention, I would have seen her and administered first aid to save her life. One, I didn't see her, and two, a dream team of surgeons couldn't have reattached her head and saved her life! She was nearly decapitated!"

"You didn't see another person walking away while you were by yourself in front of the store?" repeated Jerry as if he had not heard her outburst.

"No! I would have told you last night if I had!"

"Where do you think the murderer went after killing Lisa Heredia?"

"There were no cars in the parking lot except Ryan's and Agnes's, so I assume that the members of the reading circle had already left. We can eliminate them. If the murderer had a car, and I would suppose that he did, then he parked it elsewhere. Since I didn't notice a car pulling away from the curb within a block or two of the store, I would guess he parked in the alley that borders the parking lot. After murdering Lisa and arranging her body for me to fall over, he ran across the parking lot, up the alley, and drove off. Speaking of the alley, that reminds me, Jerry, there might be a witness . . ."

"A witness, and you're just now telling me!"

"A little boy named Jared Johnson, and he might not be a witness at all, but—"

Jerry slid forward on his chair and grabbed a pen and notebook. "Why do you think he might have seen something?"

"He's been hiding in the bed of Ryan's truck during the meetings. I saw him there the first time, but pretended I didn't the second time. He's been protecting me, or watching out that a witch doesn't get me."

Jerry sat back and tapped his pen on the desktop. "A witch. The kid thinks a witch is after you?"

"He's six years old, Jerry! Cut him some slack! Kids that age believe in the tooth fairy and Santa Claus and witches. Anyway, I thought about him last night, but he wasn't in the pickup, and I couldn't imagine his not watching all the commotion, so I figured he skipped last night's meeting . . ." She stopped and tried to swallow the lump in her throat. "We've got to find out if he's all right, Jerry, please."

The lieutenant picked up his phone and punched a few buttons. "Damn it, Megan, if you had told me last night . . . Yo, Lester, you got any missing kid cases, called in late last night or this morning?"

He noticed Megan watching him and swung his chair around so that his back was to her, and spoke quietly into the receiver. Megan tried to listen, but her heart was pounding in her ears too loudly for her to hear more than an occasional word.

Finally Jerry hung up the phone and turned back to face her. "According to the Juvenile Officer, your little friend Jared Johnson is the number one curfew violator in the entire city. Claims he can't tell time, so he doesn't know when it's past curfew. Lester is always picking him up and taking him home. But he didn't pick him up last night, and his mama hasn't called this morning. So far as Lester knows, Jared is safe at home. I'll go out there this morning with one of the women officers and talk to the kid."

"Let me go with you, Jerry. He knows me, he'll talk to me. I'm the one he was protecting after all."

"Megan, I'm going to say this once more. You are a civilian. You discovered a body. You have not been cleared yet, and even if you were, you're not a cop. And by the way, we tried to question the rest of your discussion group and didn't catch any of them at home until nearly three-thirty this morning. Guess what? Nobody would tell me where they had been other than visiting friends who wouldn't want to be involved with the police. If three of them hadn't been my grandmother's age, I would have arrested them as material witnesses. You wouldn't happen to be the friend in question, would you?"

"Jerry, I'm already involved with the police. There would no point in the group protecting my identity."

"Somehow I don't take a lot of comfort from that answer. Megan, I'm warning you. Stay out of this case! If you obstruct justice by sticking your nose in my investigation, I'll arrest you so help me God."

"Do you have high blood pressure?" asked Megan.

"No!"

"Your face is red, so I wondered."

"Stop changing the subject, damn it!"

"Watch your language, Jerry! And you ought to be happy that someone besides your mother is concerned about your health."

"You know my mother?"

"She's a member of the genealogy club. She visits with me for a few minutes every Saturday."

"Oh, my God."

"Just imagine the harm to the Special Crimes' public image if you arrested a CUTE librarian on some trumped-up charge of interfering with an investigation. In my twenty-six years of being cursed by lack of stature and CUTENESS, I've learned that my looks prevent ninety-nine percent of the population from taking me seriously. Nobody would believe I'm guilty of anything except, maybe, speeding. And imagine what your mother would think of your picking on 'that sweet little librarian.' You'd be lucky if she ever invited you to Thanksgiving dinner again." Megan nodded her head once when she finished, satisfied that she had demolished any idea Jerry Carr had of sticking her in some jail cell.

"You don't have to draw me a picture, Megan. I know when I've lost an argument." He buried his head in his hands, and Megan took the opportunity to sneak a look at the notebook where he wrote Jared's address. "My own mother would betray me." Jerry moaned.

Megan sat back down a split second before Jerry raised his head. She didn't assume an innocent look. She didn't have to. Nature had endowed her with an innocent look that a Hollywood makeup artist couldn't improve on.

"Get out of here, Megan."

"Don't I need to sign my statement?"

"Go sit out in the lobby and watch the fish. The secretary will bring it to you after she types it."

Megan rose and tugged her blazer straight. "Thank you, Jerry. And Jerry?"

"What?"

"I'm not interfering with a police investigation. It's not my fault that I stumbled over a corpse. I never intended to discover a dead body—not a fresh one anyway, since I prefer the mummified kind, but once I did, it was my civic duty to offer my special insight into human psychology and criminal motivation, gained from degrees in anthropology, archaeology, library science, and my recent study of true crime. Think of it this way, Jerry. I'm not interfering, I'm assisting."

12

God preserve me from idiots and men in love, which is the same thing.

—In M. N. HEBERDEN'S
The Lobster Pick Murder, 1941

I was leaning against my car waiting for her and conjuring a series of images that gave me heartburn: Jerry Carr putting the moves on her; Megan succumbing to his charms; Megan looking soulfully into those gray eyes. Many more such scenes and I would storm Special Crimes ramparts and punch Jerry Carr's lights out. When Megan came hurrying out of the building like the devil himself was after her, I was certain he was.

There's no one more pathetic than a man infatuated with a woman half his age, and if I didn't get my libido under better control, I would find myself in that category with no idea when or how it happened.

"Get in my truck, Ryan. We've got to beat Jerry Carr," said Megan, unlocking the door of her behemoth black vehicle and climbing behind the wheel. Since the seat is approximately at the height of her breastbone, climbing is the right verb.

"What are we beating him at?" I asked, sliding into the passenger side and turning sideways before buckling my seat belt. Anybody more than five feet two cannot ride comfortably in the front seat of any vehicle driven by Megan Clark without his chin resting on his knees.

Even with the bench seat pushed toward the dash as far as it would go, and adjusted as high as it would go, Megan still peered through the spokes of the steering wheel. Watching her shift gears in a truck with a standard transmission gave new meaning to the phrase "scared spitless." I always found religion riding with Megan.

"We're not beating him *at,* we're beating him *to.* We're going to go ask Jared Johnson some questions."

"Oh, no, we're not. That's interfering with a police investigation in anybody's book. You may be determined to go to prison for the rest of your natural life, but I'm not. Take me back to Special Crimes so I can pick up my car, drive to Canyon, and teach college sophomores all about the Oregon Trail and westward expansion in five easy lessons. Besides, this is a school day. Jared will be in school, and there's no way you can persuade some elementary school principal to let you talk to him."

"I've got to try," said Megan, then sniffed.

I was stunned to see tears rolling down her cheeks. Most men are horrified and helpless when faced by a woman in tears. I'm more horrified and helpless than most. "Stop that crying, Megan. I'll go with you. I won't let you break the law by yourself. Maybe I can make friends with Guido, the three-hundred-pound biker I'll be sharing a cell with."

"Don't make jokes! This is not funny!" She sobbed and let the truck drift toward oncoming traffic.

"Watch out!" I yelled as I lunged for the wheel.

"Oh, my God!" she exclaimed as she yanked the wheel to correct the truck's drift.

A man in a brand new BMW veered to his right. I glanced out the rear window in time to see his car climb the curb and take out a street sign. The driver rolled out of the car and gave us a digital salute accompanied by the most imaginative profanity shouted at the top of his lungs.

Megan glanced in the rearview mirror. "Some drivers are so careless. That BMW we passed just jumped the curb and hit a stop sign."

"I thought it was a street sign."

"That was after the stop sign."

"At least you're not crying anymore," I observed. It was the wrong thing to say.

The tears flowed again, this time with commentary. "I forgot about little Jared, and now Jerry Carr thinks I'm awful because I didn't tell him Jared might have seen the murder until this morning. Even though the Juvenile Officer said no one called in a missing kid report on Jared, that doesn't mean the murderer didn't follow him home last night and kill him and his whole family. I might have been the cause of a mass murder because I was so selfish and only thought about outdoing Jerry, and look what happened." She ended in a sob.

"Nothing's happened, Megan," I said, unbuckling my seat belt and sliding over to put my arm around her shoulders, and keeping the other hand free to grab the wheel. "You're getting hysterical for no good reason. Don't waste a good crying jag over what you imagine happened. Wait until you know it happened."

Those aren't the most comforting words I've ever spoken to a woman, but I was still reacting to her claim that Jerry Carr thought she was awful. Crying over a potential mass murder is one thing; crying over what Jerry Carr thinks of her is another.

Megan wiped her eyes on the sleeve of her blazer. "I'm sorry I upset you, but I'm so scared. How could I have forgotten a little boy?"

"Stumbling over a dead body might have something to do with it, Megan. You may think bodies don't bother you, but you're not personally acquainted with your mummies during their lifetime. Seeing the corpse of someone you know is different."

"That's why I never called her by name when I examined the body and talked to Jerry last night. I always called her 'the victim.' I never do that with my mummies. I always give them names."

I patted her shoulder. "Jared's fine. Trust me."

Jared lived in the San Jacinto district of Amarillo just a couple of blocks south of Sixth Street. Since the national craze of nostalgia over Route 66 has revitalized this area, the old homes are being snapped up and remodeled and San Jacinto is once more a good place to live. However, Jared's block appeared to have missed out on the general refurbishing.

Megan and I pulled up in front of a frame duplex that dated back to the early twenties, and hadn't been painted since. We climbed out of the truck and were assailed by the sour smell of poverty. If you've never smelled that particular blend of stale urine, stopped-up plumbing, too many unwashed bodies in too small a house, a thousand meals of brown beans and hamburger, cheap wine spilled on threadbare carpets and worn furniture, then I envy you, for once you've smelled poverty you never forget it.

Expressions of horror and pity fought for supremacy on Megan's face, and both lost to the kind of fierce determination most often associated with Mother Teresa. Nobody stopped her from helping the poor, and I don't see anybody stopping Megan.

We knocked on Jared's door without speaking. There probably aren't half a hundred families in the entire Panhandle who lived in Jared's kind of poverty. I was ashamed there was even one.

The door opened to reveal a young woman carrying a toddler. I say young because of the toddler and the fact there was no gray in the woman's hair. In all the ways that counted she was younger than I.

"If you're after the rent, I got it now. My husband got paid yesterday and I kept out the rent money. Just a minute and I'll run and get it." She spoke in a monotone, often the sign of clinical depression.

"No, we're not here to collect the rent. I'm Megan Clark, the lady who gave Jared money from the tooth fairy, and this is Dr. Stevens. Is Jared at home?" Only if you knew Megan well would you hear the tremor in her voice.

The woman smiled as if she had forgotten how. "The tooth fairy lady. Jared still talks about you all the time. That was a nice thing you done, Miz Clark. My husband took him out to that toy store by the mall and Jared bought a toy. Wasn't much, just a little plastic truck, but he's mighty proud of it."

I heard Megan catch her breath, and hoped she didn't cry in front of this woman. Mrs. Johnson didn't have much she could claim as her own but pride, and I didn't want to see that hurt.

"Could we talk to Jared if he's home, Mrs. Johnson? We need to ask him if he was on Sixth Street last night."

"He wasn't. He broke out with a hard case of the chicken pox and been laid up for three days. Been so sick he ain't even left the house. First time since last February I ain't had to go looking for him at bedtime."

I saw Megan close her eyes in relief. If she'd been Catholic, she would have made the sign of the cross. "Dr. Stevens and I have both had the chicken pox, so if we could just come in for a moment and say hello to Jared, we would appreciate it."

Mrs. Johnson opened the screen door. "You're welcome to come inside if you'll pardon the mess. I been trying to fold clothes while my husband reads to Jared."

We stepped inside the duplex, and Mrs. Johnson led us down a hall off which all the rooms opened. On the other side of the wall separating the duplex units would be an identical hall. It was a common blueprint for such dwellings built in the late teens and twenties. What shocked both of us was not the threadbare carpet, peeling paint on the walls, or the old, barely held together furniture, but the cleanliness of every surface. Mrs. Johnson apparently believed that cleanliness is next to godliness, and did her best by her beliefs.

"Jared's in this last room, Miz Clark. He's not feeling so good right now, but I figure he'll start feeling better when the pox start drying up."

We stepped inside Jared's room and a very tall, gaunt man rose from his seat on the bed and turned to face us. Both Megan and I tried to keep our faces expressionless. Jared's father wore a patch over his right eye, and his left sleeve was pinned up as far as his shoulder.

"Motorcycle accident," said Jared's father in a matter-of-fact voice. I admired his way of accounting for his deformities and getting the subject out of the way.

"This is my husband, Leon," said Mrs. Johnson, shifting the toddler from one hip to the other. "This is the tooth fairy lady, Leon. She's come to see Jared."

"That was a nice thing for you to do, ma'am," said Leon as he leaned over to nudge Jared. "Hey, Jared, wake up, boy. You got visitors."

When Leon stepped back so we could move closer to the bed, we saw the extent of Jared's "hard case" of chickenpox. Not a square inch of the skin we could see had escaped without at least one pox. I knew one thing for certain: there was no way Jared Johnson had been on Sixth Street last night.

"I'm awful sorry I ain't been able to watch out for the witch lately."

"Don't worry about Miss Clark, Jared," I said. "I've been packing my water gun wherever I go, and I haven't seen a single witch. But if I do, I'll draw my pistol and soak her down and watch her smoke."

He didn't smile as I expected him to. "She's there, mister."

I had underestimated how seriously Jared took his witches. "I know she is, Jared, but she's been behaving, so I haven't had to soak her."

He nodded. "So long as she don't trick you."

"You don't have to worry, Jared," said Megan, brushing the hair out of his eyes. "Dr. Stevens is a premier witch killer."

He nodded and closed his eyes. "She hurted a lady once."

We waited but he said no more. We thanked the Johnsons and left just as Jerry Carr pulled up with a female police officer.

"We're caught with our pants down, Megan. We've got no excuse and no alibi."

"Damn it, Megan," said Jerry Carr in a loud voice, climbing out of his car and slamming the door. "I warned you about interfering in this case. You're going to force me to arrest you."

Megan walked up to him, grabbed his tie, and jerked his head down to her eye level. "You shut up about arrest, Jerry Carr, and listen to me. I'm having a bad day. Jared Johnson is having a bad day. In fact, he's having a bad life. Jared Johnson has the worst case of chickenpox I've ever seen, so he saw nothing last night. But I want you to go in there and interview him, tell him you need his help, and ask him about witches. It will take his mind off his chickenpox, and it will let you meet the family and see the inside of that duplex. Then I want you to go back downtown and call the Department of Human Resources and the social security office and get these people some help. At the least, they should be eligible for rent subsidy, food stamps, Medicaid, and the father ought to be receiving Social Security disability. Every deadbeat in this country rips off the welfare system, and it's time we spent some money on a family who needs it and has earned it by being as decent and as self-reliant as their means allow. And I don't want to hear excuses. I want action!"

Jerry Carr pulled his tie out of Megan's grasp, and nodded his head. "I hear you, Megan. And I'll take care of it."

"You better, or I'll tell your mother you're a loser."

"You would, too," he said as he leaned down and kissed her.

A giant fist closed around my heart.

13

I cannot agree with those who rank modesty among the virtues.

—SHERLOCK HOLMES to Watson
in Arthur Conan Doyle's
"The Greek Interpreter,"
The Memoirs of Sherlock Holmes, 1894

Murder by the Yard met on its usual night the following week, but Megan substituted true crime for fiction. "Does anyone have anything to report on the Lisa Heredia case? Yes, Rosemary, you've learned something about our elusive victim?"

"Lorene and I divided the ladies' clubs—between us we belong to almost all of them—and called the individual membership chairwomen. Lisa Heredia belonged to no ladies' clubs in Amarillo. I even called one of my Hispanic friends—Heredia is a Spanish surname—but Maria had never heard of her. And believe me, Maria would know. Finally, Lorene and I called all the Heredias listed in the phone books for the entire Panhandle. Thank goodness the library has copies of each community's phone book, but it took all week, and left poor Lorene hoarse. We found no one who claimed her as a relation."

"If she was no more pleasant to her family than she was to us, I wouldn't claim her either," said Randel.

"Oh, Randel, you're so bad," said Candi, elbowing him in the ribs.

Watching them, Megan decided that being in love or lust or infatuation or however the two defined their relationship, encouraged childish behavior. When she elbowed someone, she meant it.

"Other than your evaluation of Lisa Heredia's probable family relationships, do you have any information to offer us, Randel?" asked Megan.

Randel stroked his goatee, which was nicely trimmed for a change. Probably Candi's influence. "She never attended Amarillo College, at least under that name. She seems to have sprung full grown from the head of Zeus."

"I spent my time checking the census records," said Megan. "The genealogy club helped me after I told them we wanted to send a card to her family, but we didn't know where they lived. We didn't have her in the census, at least not in Texas. If she had been there, my ladies would have found her. There's not a woman in that club who can't trace a fourth cousin back ten generations and tell you when he was married and buried. Finally, in desperation the ladies turned to Salt Lake City . . ."

"The Mormon Church," said Agnes. "They have the finest genealogy records in the world. It has something to do with their religion, I believe. Did they find her, Megan?"

"Yes, she was from New York . . ."

"Literary agent," said Annabel in her deep voice. Startled, the women in reading circle emitted squeals; mild expletives came from the men.

"We would appreciate it, Annabel, if you would make some kind of announcement of your presence," said Agnes, holding her hand over her heart and breathing deeply. "After the murder we're all a little jumpy. I don't know about Rosemary and Lorene, but I'm too old to have a scare like that."

"Thought you knew I was here," said Annabel. "I

came early to find something to read. Mailed off my manuscript today."

The reading circle clapped—Agnes, the twins, and Candi enthusiastically—the rest more restrained. "Bravo!" cried Candi.

Megan noticed that Randel seemed to be bringing Candi out of her shell—along with whatever else he was persuading her out of.

"You said that Lisa was a literary agent. What was she doing in Amarillo?" asked Megan. "This is not exactly the center of the creative writing world, and it's a little far to commute for a business lunch."

"Pestering me," replied Annabel, reaching for one of the twins' tollhouse cookies and stuffing it in her mouth. She continued talking as she chewed, spraying crumbs. "Called me a couple of weeks ago. Wanted to represent me, but I said no. Got an agent I'm happy with."

"She came all the way to Amarillo to court you, Annabel?" said Rosemary. "How flattered you must be."

Annabel shrugged, and Megan realized the writer had finally shed her cloak and deerstalker hat. Without them she was still thick through the shoulders, waist, and ankles. "She wanted to make money off me. Wanted to take twenty percent. I wasn't interested."

"But she acted as if she had never talked to you before the last meeting," said Megan.

"All an act," said Annabel. "Nasty piece of work, would steal the coins off her dead mother's eyes. Twenty percent! Nobody charges that kind of fee."

"From what I know of the book business, that does sound pretty high. Why on earth did she think you would change agents?" asked Agnes.

Annabel shrugged and crammed another cookie, this one oatmeal, in her mouth.

"For her to invest money coming out here and renting an apartment, she must have expected to make some big bucks from you, Annabel," said Randel. "The mystery writing business pays better than I thought."

"I make a living," said Annabel.

"To think that Jerry Carr had all this information and never told me," said Megan.

"He doesn't have to share information with you, Megan," said Ryan. "Remember, you're a civilian."

"He doesn't know everything," said Annabel. "Told him she tried to sign me up and I told her no. Figured that's all he needed to know. More likely she'd cut my throat than the other way around. I didn't like her. Not the kind to turn your back on."

It was the most animated Megan had ever seen the writer. Lisa must have really irritated Annabel for her to be so loquacious. Her expressiveness was always confined to the written word. In person she spoke like a case of arrested language development.

"But she must have had another reason to come to Amarillo besides trying to talk Annabel into paying an exorbitant fee for the privilege of having Lisa represent her," said Megan. "Do you suppose that she approached other local writers with offers to represent them? But that doesn't make sense either. How would anyone know that Lisa was in the reading group, and how would he or she know to wait for Lisa on that particular night? And even though she insulted all of us and tried to con Annabel, I still don't see that any of us had a strong enough motive to slit Lisa's throat."

"Thank you, Madam Leader, for that vote of confidence," said Randel. "I feel so much better knowing you don't suspect me."

"I think the biggest puzzle of all is why no one killed you, Randel," said Rosemary. "You can get under a person's skin like a sand flea."

"Well, excuse me for living!" said Randel, glaring at Rosemary.

"Please don't take what I said personally," said Megan. "I'm thinking out loud, trying to rearrange all the pieces of the puzzle so it creates a picture of what happened. There must be facts we don't know yet. We're only seeing part of the puzzle."

"In my opinion we're caught in an Agatha Christie novel," said Rosemary. "You know how difficult her puzzles are."

"But Agatha Christie had the option of creating her own clues," said Megan. "We have to take what we're given and make do with them."

"But we haven't discussed the clues we have," said Lorene in a hoarse voice.

"That's because we don't have any clues," said Randel. "Lisa is a bitch and then she dies. Not many clues there."

"Maybe we should look at the case from another angle," said Herb Jackson. "I'm a criminal defense lawyer as you all know, and a forensic psychiatrist affectionately known as Dr. Death because he always testifies for the prosecution in death penalty cases, says that all motives for murder fit within five categories. He refers to the categories as the five P's: passion, profit, psychosis, protection, and panic. In my opinion Lisa was killed for one of the five P's."

The reading circle was quiet, mulling over Herb's words. Megan thought that outside of Annabel, he had made the most valuable contribution of the evening.

"Your Dr. Death was probably right, but I don't know how we can decipher the correct motive," said Randel. "I certainly can't go to New York and investigate from that end. The problem with real crime is it's so poorly plotted, with loose ends unraveling all over the landscape and no way to tie them up. I like my crime tidy."

"Let's at least discuss the five P's," said Megan. "First is passion. Any ideas?"

"She wasn't trying to break up a marriage . . ." began Rosemary.

"That's because no one in the group is married," said Lorene.

"I was, but I'm divorced," said Herb. "And my divorce is years older than the month or so Lisa was in Amarillo."

"Okay," said Megan, holding up her hands for silence. "Anybody want to take the hate side of passion."

"She was a bitch, but I think hatred takes longer than a half an hour or so to grow to the point of murder," said Randel. "If anybody in this group is that loosely tied down, then the *P* for psychosis fits. But I don't think any of us are—although I wonder about you, Megan."

It took Megan several seconds to react, so shocked was she. "You made a joke, Randel!"

"I do have a bit of a sense of humor, I just seldom see anything funny. Try teaching Freshman English at a junior college for ten years. Your sense of humor is the first thing to go."

Candi patted his knee and gazed at him with an adoring expression. The surprise to Megan was that he returned it.

"Okay," said Megan, drawing everyone's attention from the phenomenon of Randel's having a sense of humor. "Let's talk psychosis. Does anyone believe Lisa was murdered by a psychotic? Is anyone under treatment for paranoid schizophrenia? Severe depression? Obsessive-compulsive disorder?"

"I don't believe anyone would admit it if he were," said Agnes. "I think we're all a little eccentric as opposed to crazy."

"I agree," said Rosemary. "Besides, almost anybody would recognize a true psychotic. That's not a minor disorder."

"What about profit?" asked Megan. "Who profits by Lisa's death?"

"Certainly Murder by the Yard does because we don't have to put up with her," said Lorene.

"I think profit means money," said Herb. "And the only way to answer that question would be to read her will if she has one. She probably doesn't. As a lawyer, I always advise my clients to make a will even if they own very little, and I'm always amazed at how many don't take my advice. If she had a will—and that's a big if—we can get a copy once it's filed for probate. That might take several weeks."

"I don't imagine she left her money to any of us, so I think the profit motive is moot," said Agnes.

"The next *P* stands for protection," said Megan. "What secret did Lisa know that would be so dangerous that someone would kill her to protect himself?"

"It's not sex," said Randel. "We're all single consenting adults."

"And even if one of us was gay, I don't think it would make much difference these days," said Rosemary.

"What about you, Dr. Stevens? Do you have any ideas?" asked Lorene.

"I'm a nonparticipant in this discussion," said Ryan. "And I don't think any of you ought to be discussing motives either. Did it ever occur to any of you that it might be dangerous to poke around in a murder case? Somebody murdered Lisa Heredia in a particularly grisly fashion and I don't want to disturb that person. I'm fond of my throat just the way it is."

"Ryan, we're not going to make a citizen's arrest," said Megan. "We're not stupid. We'll turn any information we develop over to Lieutenant Carr, and he can make the arrest."

He raised one eyebrow in disbelief, and Megan considered kicking his shin.

"What else would one kill to protect?" asked Candi.

"A child," suggested Agnes. "But the only children this group have are grown and gone. Unless you have young children, Herb?"

"They're teenagers, and I believe Lisa was smart

enough to leave them alone. I leave them alone. I'm sending them to military school next year."

"You have boys, then?" asked Lorene.

"No, they're girls."

There was silence.

Rosemary leaned forward. "What about reputation? Did she know some scandal about one of us?"

Megan shook her head. "These days I think cannibalism is the only behavior that would ruin one's standing in society."

"Jeffery Dahmer gave the practice a bad name," added Randel.

Megan frowned. Randel's sense of humor gave every indication of getting out of hand. "So no one is admitting to a soiled reputation. What about a criminal act? If someone were hiding a criminal act and Lisa found out, she might try blackmail. How about it, Randel—are you dipping into the till at Amarillo College?"

"If I were, I wouldn't be still driving a 1989 Plymouth."

"How about you, Herb? Are you defrauding your clients?"

Herb looked as gloomy as Randel. "My clients generally have to borrow a quarter from the arresting officer to call me."

"I know I haven't committed any criminal act," said Megan. "Unless you count forgetting to turn in overdue library books, and since I work at the library, I don't always pay my fines."

"You wouldn't kill someone over a library fine," said Agnes. "Now me, I'm a real criminal. I forgot to report my profit one year from a book fair at the Senior Citizens Center."

"That's not a crime. Scamming the IRS is the act of a patriotic American," said Randel.

"I filed an amended return," admitted Agnes.

"That does it, everybody. We're a boring, law-abiding

bunch," said Ryan. "We either give up this amateur sleuthing or find another set of suspects. There's not enough criminality between us to toilet paper a house on Halloween."

Sometimes Ryan overdid the humor, but he had a point, thought Megan. Nobody in Murder by the Yard was mean enough, scared enough, desperate enough, or passionate enough to commit murder.

"But somebody murdered Lisa Heredia," protested Megan.

"Honey, it wasn't any of us," said Ryan, then realized what he had said.

Megan and the other members of the reading circle watched a blush start at his neck and sweep up his face until it disappeared into his hairline.

Insensitive to the general interest in Ryan's indiscretion, Annabel took the floor. "What about clues? We haven't talked about clues. Got to be some."

Megan swallowed and tried to focus her attention on something besides Ryan's use of an endearment. "Did the lieutenant mention any leads?"

"The lieutenant is holding his cards close to his vest," said Randel. "You ought to know about clues, Megan. Didn't you examine the body? Isn't that what that young rookie told you, Candi?"

"Yes, but don't tell the lieutenant. I don't think Tommy was supposed to say anything."

"You're on a first-name basis, are you? When did that happen?" asked Randel. Judging by the sound of his voice, Megan thought he ought to be a delicate shade of green.

"I went to school with Tommy. We graduated from Amarillo High together. And he has a wife and a sweet little baby, Randel. He showed me pictures."

"The kid doesn't have any business hitting on you when he has a wife and family," said Randel.

"Randel, you're jealous!" cried Candi, her face so radiant that she just missed being pretty.

"Could you two postpone your lovebird act until after the meeting?" asked Ryan. "You're already close to a PG-13."

"Clues!" cried Megan. "Let's talk about clues. First, the throat was cut from left to right which indicates a right-handed killer. How many here are right-handed?" She waited until everyone held up their hands. "Okay, so everyone is right-handed. Scratch that clue. Next, the killer dragged the body about six feet and propped it up. That indicates—actually that doesn't indicate anything, because the victim was only slightly taller than me and very thin. I don't see anyone in this room who would be unable to drag the body six feet. The next clue is the best. The killer took the knife—I'm assuming it's a knife—with him or her. Does anyone carry a knife?"

The three men pulled out pocket knives, which Megan supposed could have slashed Lisa's throat in a pinch. Then Rosemary reached in her purse. "I have a cake knife. I always carry it when I furnish refreshments in case I need to do a quick repair on sliding icing."

Lorene waved a knife identical to Rosemary's. "Any cook responsible for catering even a small event carries a knife of some sort. Rosemary and I prefer cake knives."

Agnes waved her hand. "I generally carry a linoleum knife to cut open boxes and do whatever other chores around the store require a sharp-edged instrument."

Candi dug in her backpack. "I always carry a Swiss Army knife because it's got so many doodads. I can eat with it and open a bottle and slice kindling when I'm out camping."

"Got a letter opener in a brief case. It's sharp enough to cut a throat," said Annabel.

"Do you mean I'm the only person in the room who doesn't carry a sharp instrument?" said Megan.

"Looks like it," said Ryan. "Can we eat now?"

"We want to know about Annabel's book first," said Candi. "Annabel, tell us a little about the plot—but not too much. I don't want to know whodunit."

Annabel picked up several cookies and stuffed them in her skirt pocket, then came lumbering over to the circle. "It's called *The Five Pigeons*, and it's about a blackmailer who is slowly destroying five people—three men and two women—until the pigeons turn the tables on the blackmailer. It was a tough one to get through, but I like it."

"What a wonderful title," said Rosemary. "So old-fashioned. I'm looking forward to reading it, Annabel, and I'll expect a signed copy."

Annabel flushed and nearly smiled. "I'll save you one."

"Agnes, will you give Annabel an autograph party?" asked Candi.

"Yes, I always do," said Agnes with a frown.

"Now can we eat?" asked Ryan, already out of his chair and on his way to the refreshment table.

14

At one end of the inquiry there was a murder, and at the other end there was a spot of ink on a table-cloth that nobody could account for. In all my experience along the dirtiest ways of this dirty little world I have never met with such a thing as a trifle yet.

—SERGEANT CUFF in Wilkie Collins's
The Moonstone, 1868

"Ryan, did you hear everyone tonight? We all had the opportunity and the means to kill Lisa. The only reason that Jerry doesn't march us all down to Special Crimes, read us the Miranda, and give us the third degree is because none of us have a motive that stands up under scrutiny."

"Thank goodness for the American criminal justice system," I muttered, which earned me a sharp look from the redhead. Her sense of humor has been lacking since she stumbled over Lisa Heredia's foot.

"We're overlooking pieces of the puzzle. Unless Lisa's murder is a random killing, which I don't believe, then we ought to be able to see a pattern forming."

I raised my feet and placed my left boot heel in the indentation on the corner of the desk. There is nothing so relaxing and reassuring to a man than propping his feet on the top of a well-worn desk. I've spent hundreds of hours—maybe thousands—in just this position. I watched Megan pace my study, stepping over stacks of books automatically, gesturing with her hands, talking incessantly about what she referred to as "our case." I don't know where she got the idea that I felt any sense of ownership in the matter, because I didn't. I didn't want any part of solving Lisa Heredia's murder, and I was tired of the reading circle playing detective with Megan acting as chief.

"Megan, let's put the case to bed, shall we? In fact, why don't we retire it? You don't have the resources necessary to solve a case like this, the various technical reports on things like fingerprints and blood."

"Marsha Clarke and her entourage of prosecutors had all the technical support in the world on their side, and the human element beat them. It's just like Hercule Poirot says: 'It's the little gray cells that catch murderers.' I'm paraphrasing since I can't remember exactly how Christie said it, but what she meant was that in the end it was a thinking human being studying the human elements and finding patterns of inconsistencies that solved a murder."

"Megan! Agatha Christie wrote murder mysteries! Fiction, Megan, she wrote fiction, and fiction by definition means a lie. Look it up in Webster's if you don't believe me."

"I know that, Ryan. I have a Ph.D. and they don't hand those out to idiots. But what I'm saying is that fiction mirrors life. Murder—if it's not a random act for thrills, and this one isn't—is the culmination of human emotions prompted by one or more of Herb Jackson's *P*'s. To replay from the top, we're missing pieces, we're missing connections that would reveal a pattern."

"Megan, you've got patterns on the brain. Why don't you take up knitting like Miss Marpole."

"Marple! It's Miss Marple!"

"Whatever. The point is you're as bad as Jared and his witches when it comes to mixing fiction and reality."

Megan stopped her pacing with one foot on either side of a stack of reference books on the battle of the Little Big Horn, from which I was preparing lesson plans for a course I planned to teach in the fall semester. I expected it to be a big success.

"Jared is part of the pattern, Ryan. It's one of the human elements I keep leaving out of my equation."

"Jared is a kid with a George Lucas-size imagination," I replied, still looking at the stack of books. I thought they were overdue by a month or so. I must have misplaced the overdue notice from the library.

Megan gracefully lifted her other foot over the stack of books and glided over to my desk. Did I mention she took dance for fifteen years as a youngster? She did. Among other legacies from those fifteen years is the ability to glide across a room as though she were riding on a cushion of air barely an inch above the floor. She isn't, of course, and I don't know how she evokes that image, but she's beautiful to watch when she doesn't know she being watched. If she knows, she trips over her own feet.

She leaned over the front of my desk. "Jared is too a part of the pattern, Ryan. Otherwise, he wouldn't have been standing guard outside the bookstore." She grabbed a ballpoint and a spiral notebook.

"Megan, that notebook has my lecture notes for Custer and the Indians," I said, reaching for it.

She danced away, missing, so help me God, every stack of books on my floor. "Show your students *They Died With Their Boots On* with Errol Flynn, then talk about what the movie got wrong. Besides, I'm only going to use the last page and it's blank. . . . As I see it, we have a witch, Jared, Murder by the Yard Reading Circle, which includes Lisa Heredia, et al., and murder. If I write down these elements in a circle, what common denominator is in the center? What do all these elements have in common? Time and Again Bookstore! Don't you see, Ryan? All these factors intersect at the bookstore!"

"But Jared wasn't at the bookstore when Lisa was murdered," I said, interested in spite of myself.

"That's irrelevant, Ryan. If he hadn't caught chicken pox, he would have been, so logically the pattern holds. So, what else can we learn from our equation? That the one element related to all others is Time and Again Bookstore. That is where the reading circle meets and Lisa is a member of the circle. Lisa is murdered at the bookstore, and the bookstore is where Jared stands guard against a witch."

She glided around to my side and laid the notebook on the desk in front of me. In the middle of the circle of elements, she wrote "Time and Again Bookstore." Her theory was logical, even I had to admit that.

"Coincidence," I said. "Random chance, chaos theory, whatever. Just because these elements intersect at the bookstore doesn't prove that they are interrelated."

"Yes, they are, Ryan. What would be random chance or chaos theory *if* there were no relationship between Time and Again and the other elements. Once the facts or human elements are written down like this, so we can see their interconnectedness, it becomes obvious that Time and Again is the common denominator to actions that culminate in murder."

"You see that? I don't see that. I see a diagram that might—might, I said—be a lead that Jerry Carr *might* want to investigate."

Megan tore the page out of my notebook, folded it carefully, and tucked it into her back pocket. "The first step an archaeologist takes is to examine an artifact *in situ*. Our artifact is the bookstore. Let's take your truck. It's quieter than mine."

"What?" I shouted, lifting my feet off the desk and standing up. "It's one-thirty in the morning! I'm not driving down to Sixth Street and the bookstore and wak-

ing up Agnes to show her some damn fool diagram
which may, but more probably won't, have a damn thing
to do with the murder."

Megan shrugged. "Okay, I'll go by myself."

"Megan, it's one-thirty! Amarillo has a curfew for
kids seventeen and younger. The cops will pull you over
and card you. You know they will. You can't even get
in an R-rated movie without being carded. And what are
you going to tell the cops? That you were dropping by
the bookstore?"

"It's the truth, so why shouldn't they believe me?"

I closed my eyes momentarily. I do that when I need
to collect myself to deal with a difficult student. And I
had never had a student as difficult as Megan Clark. I
opened my eyes to an empty room.

"Damnation!" I exclaimed. She had left without me.
That could only mean trouble. Fortunately, I knew where
she was going, so it was only a matter of catching up
with her. Her black beast could outrace mine on the open
road and particularly, off-road, but I had the advantage
in town. I didn't have four gears to shift.

I took residential streets—Ong to West Fifteenth, left on
Fifteenth to Alabama, down Alabama to Sixth Street—
so I could speed without risking being stopped. I turned
in the alley that bordered the store's parking lot and
made another sharp turn into a little cul-de-sac in front
of the outside door to Agnes's apartment. I slammed on
my brakes just in time to avoid hitting Megan's black
behemoth and folding the front of my truck like an ac-
cordion. I saw Megan in my headlights, hammering on
Agnes's door.

I slid out of my truck and covered the ten feet or so
to Megan's side in a couple of running steps. "Damn it,
Megan, why did you leave without telling me?"

She turned to me and grabbed my shirt. "Ryan, Agnes
won't answer her door. I've rung the bell and I've ham-

mered on the door, and nothing! But her car's parked around front, so I know she hasn't gone anywhere."

"Don't panic," I said in spite of the fact that panicking sounded like a good idea.

"She's in there, Ryan, I know she is. I can *feel* it!"

We stood in front of the door, looking at each other in perfect accord. Whether you believe it or not, I could feel Agnes's presence, too. The wind set the leaves singing on the tall cottonwood tree at the end of the cul-de-sac. Despite what poets and romance writers may say, only the cottonwood truly sings, and the song tonight sounded like a dirge. Chills swept up my spine and I'll admit that I was scared.

Megan stood on tiptoe and whispered softly, as though she were afraid someone or something might hear. "Walk me around to the front door, Ryan. I still have a key."

"Where did you get a key?" I whispered back.

"Out of your pocket after you fainted last week. I had to get back in the bookstore to call the police and rouse Agnes."

She took my hand and we walked down the alley and across the parking lot, stopping short of the black shadows in front of the store. Megan turned on the tiny flashlight on her key ring and swept it across the shadows. It didn't provide much more light than your extra large firefly, but it was better than walking blindly into the dark.

Seeing no bloody corpse—if we had, I think both of us would have run screaming down Sixth Street—we stepped into the dark shadows. Megan is no more frightened of bodies, even fresh warm ones, than the average politician is of his constituents remembering what he promised last election, but I could feel her trembling. If you've never stood alone, late at night, with only the wind for company on the spot where a human being was slaughtered seven days before, then you don't understand how close we are to our primeval ancestors. The hairs on the back of my neck and on my arms prickled. I clenched my teeth until my jaws hurt.

"Give me the key and I'll go in first," I whispered in a voice that shook as if I had a chill.

"I'm not staying out here alone. You unlock the door and we'll go in together."

She handed me the key and clung to my hand as we approached the door. "Should we knock and tell her who's out here?" I asked softly.

"I don't want to warn anyone who might be inside," said Megan, her voice shaking so badly that it went up and down the scale, from bass to soprano.

I swallowed. "I'm thinking I want to give a warning, so if someone is in there, they can run out the back door while we walk in the front one."

"I like your idea," said Megan and let go of me to commence hammering on the door. "Agnes, are you in there? It's Megan and Ryan. I left my purse and it has my driver's license in it. Agnes, can you open the door? Okay, we're coming in. Ryan still has your key."

Every dog within hearing range of Sixth Street must have heard her, promptly responding with a chorus of growls, barks, howls, yaps, yips, and wails. Suddenly being inside the store rather than outside seemed like a good plan. I turned the key and slammed the door back against the wall to make sure that if an intruder was standing there ready to slip out, he would slip out seriously injured.

"Agnes," I hollered. "Agnes, it's Ryan. We came to get Megan's purse. Are you in your apartment?"

I closed the front door. Nobody fell on the floor. Agnes had left on three sets of track lights: down each side and in the middle aisle. As far as I was concerned, that wasn't enough. "Where's the light switch?" I whispered. "I want every light in the store turned on. I don't want a single shadow anywhere."

"Beside the door to Agnes's apartment."

"You want to stay here, or go with me?" I asked, hoping she'd come with me. The public area of the store felt empty, but I had an irrational fear of someone snatching Megan away from me, and I didn't think I could stand losing her.

"I'll come, but I want to get Agnes's baseball bat from the checkout counter. We need a weapon, Ryan, and I don't think your pocket knife is enough."

One lesson I gained that night was not to leave your weapon at one end of a building while you are at the other end. In addition to an empty cash box on the floor behind the counter, we also found Agnes.

15

Anyone's safety depends principally on the fact that nobody wishes to kill them. . . . We have come to depend upon what has been called the good will of civilization.

—MISS FULLERTON in Agatha Christie's
Murder Is Easy, 1939

"Tell me again, how you and the professor here happened to come knocking at Agnes's door at two o'clock, or thereabouts, in the morning," asked Jerry Carr, looking down at Megan where she sat beside Ryan on the bookstore's couch.

Megan yawned and rubbed her eyes. "Can't I tell you all over again tomorrow morning about eleven? I've already told my story twice, and you didn't believe me. Why would telling you a third time tonight make any difference? Maybe by tomorrow morning you'll see that my theory is logical, fits the facts as we know them, and is as a matter of fact the *only* story that takes into account all the human elements."

"Humor me, Megan. Tell me again. Maybe the third time's a charm, and I'll understand why you believe that this bookstore is the source of the conflict that has resulted in a murder and an assault."

"Quit harassing her, Lieutenant," said Ryan, slipping his arm around Megan's shoulders and pulling her close to his side. "She showed you the diagram she drew, and you have to admit that her theory makes a crazy kind of sense. Everyone involved in Lisa Heredia's murder is also involved in some way with Time and Again. This store is a common denominator for the action, and if we knew why, we'd be closer to knowing who killed Lisa."

Megan sat up and smoothed her hair back. She was exhausted from lack of sleep and stress. She needed twelve uninterrupted hours of sleep and she also needed to go to the hospital to check on Agnes. "Look at the diagram, study it, then we'll talk tomorrow morning, Jerry."

"I'm not finished yet, Megan. You still haven't persuaded me. Look, this is how I see it, how the evidence points. The front door was jimmied open, then locked again by the burglar. How do we know? Fresh scratches on the lock plate and the frame of the door where the burglar used a crowbar or other lever of some kind to force the door. It wasn't a dead bolt, although why Agnes didn't install one I'll never know. The burglar went straight to the checkout counter where he found the cash box. About this time Agnes thinks she hears something, puts on her robe and walks through the storage rooms to the public area. She probably makes some noise, hit something in one of the storage rooms on the way through. As a matter of fact, we found a couple of stacks of books knocked over back there. The burglar hears her, drops the cash box, and stands at the end of one of the aisles. Agnes walks in, spies the empty cash box, runs over to examine it, and boom, the burglar knocks her out with her own baseball bat, and takes off, running out the back door when he hears you two knocking at the front."

"Don't you think it's odd," demanded Megan, "that a murder was committed in front of this store seven days ago, and tonight a so-called burglar breaks in and just happens to hit Agnes so hard that the paramedics told me she may have to have surgery to relieve the pressure on her brain? Two violent crimes in a week's time at the same store? Doesn't that stretch credulity to the breaking point?"

The lieutenant shook his head, his eyes sympathetic. "Megan, I've seen the same store robbed once a month for a year by twelve different scumbags. I've seen the same con game worked in the same neighborhood by two different con artists. I've seen the same store manager take forged checks time after time. I've even arrested a rapist for raping the same woman twice. There's nothing unusual about violent crime happening in the same location twice. And there's nothing at this crime scene to indicate anything but a garden variety burglary."

"Jerry, it's not a burglary. That's too much coincidence for me," said Megan.

Jerry sat down on one of the easy chairs and leaned toward Megan. "I know that in those mystery books you folks read coincidence isn't allowed. It's not fair to the reader for the author to suddenly solve the puzzle by using coincidence. That's art and that's okay. But in real life, Megan, coincidence happens every day."

Megan shook her head. "If it is a burglary, then where is Agnes's receipt book for sales after the reading circle adjourned tonight?"

"Maybe she took it back to her apartment. Maybe it was full and she put it away for the tax man with the rest of her records. I don't know the answer, Megan, but I will find out. As soon as Agnes is conscious, I'll ask her," said Jerry.

"The receipt book is not in her apartment, and it's not with her other records. I looked," said Megan.

Jerry grimaced. "You were a busy woman after you called 911, Megan. Did it occur to you that you were contaminating a crime scene? Thanks to you, if we did find some evidence that this wasn't a simple burglary, we probably couldn't get it admitted into evidence. The defense would claim it was tainted!"

Megan bowed her head and swallowed several times in a vain attempt to get rid of the knot in her throat. How could Jerry Carr continue to be so blindly stupid?

"I was very careful when I searched, Jerry, and I know where Agnes keeps her records, so I didn't go tearing through her apartment like a bull in a china shop. You'll find my fingerprints on the doorknob on either side of the door, but otherwise I touched nothing. I used cooking tongs to lift her records to check for the receipt book, so I wouldn't leave fingerprints. Otherwise, you will probably find them in random spots where you would expect to since I'm a regular visitor. I did not 'taint' any evidence, and any halfway competent prosecutor could demolish any such defense argument that I did."

She stopped, trying to suppress the sobs she felt at the back of her throat. *I will not cry, I will not cry, she would not cry,* she repeated to herself. "I'm trying to be a good citizen and help the police, but you are determined to treat me like some kind of ditzy overgrown Nancy Drew. I am not Nancy Drew, and I am not ditzy. I'm not ignorant of the law either. I've answered your questions, I'm not a suspect or you would have read me my rights, so unless you are going to arrest me, I'm going to the hospital and Ryan is coming with me. Agnes is a spinster and she was an only child. There is no one to look after her but me and the other members of Murder by the Yard. So what are you going to do? Arrest me or let me go?"

Megan held her breath waiting for his answer. If Jerry Carr arrested her, she just might throw an hysterical fit. She had never thrown one in her life, but she knew the general principles and she would fake the rest.

"Go on, Megan. I'll see you and the professor at eleven o'clock tomorrow at Special Crimes. And please,

please don't stumble across any more crime scenes between now and tomorrow morning."

"The best way to assure that I don't is for you to listen to me," said Megan, feeling frustration turn to anger. "What difference does it make if I present my theory in diagram form on a page torn out of a spiral notebook instead of on a blackboard in the Special Crimes workroom? What difference does it make if my theory sounds like something out of Agatha Christie instead of a criminal justice textbook on evidence? The point is I'm right!"

Ryan grabbed her hand and tugged her toward the door. "Don't push your luck, Megan. Don't wave a mystery story under a real cop's nose."

Megan let herself be pulled along, but as she went through the door she couldn't resist one last remark. "I bet you'd take me seriously if I were six inches taller!"

"Hush up, Megan, or so help me God, I'm going to gag you," said Ryan with a grunt as he pulled her along at a slow run.

"You can let go of me now. We're out of Jerry's line of sight," said Megan.

Ryan stopped so suddenly that Megan bumped into him. "What are you playing at, Megan? Not three minutes ago your mouth was puckered up and your lower lip shaking, and you were seconds away from a crying jag."

"Keep walking," commanded Megan. "If I was about to cry, it was because I was so damn mad that Jerry was condescending to me like he would to a child! I'm okay now. I got the last word in. That's always very satisfying when someone is patronizing you, to get in the last word. I bet he's thinking right now of all the rejoinders he might've made."

Ryan was horrified. Megan could tell because he was looking up at the skies. She wished she knew what childhood trauma prompted his looking for answers in his ceiling or the skies. There might be a paper in it for one of the psychology periodicals.

"You staged that whole scene in there!" exclaimed Ryan, looking even more horrified. "And I thought you were on the verge of bursting into sobs."

"It wasn't a scene," protested Megan. "I meant every word of it. And yes, I was about to cry, but it was from sheer, unmitigated rage. If he thought otherwise, that's not my fault. He shouldn't stereotype women."

"I don't think I know you at all," said Ryan, looking at her as though she were a stranger who'd attached herself to him while he was walking through a crowd.

"Of course, you do, Ryan. You just persist in giving me the benefit of the doubt when you really shouldn't. Let's take your truck to the hospital. We can park it on a dime, and my truck needs the south runway at Amarillo International. We've got to get some answers from Agnes before the police do."

Ryan folded his arms across his chest and spread his legs out. "Megan, I've gone along with you in your Miss Mayberry impersonation . . ."

"Miss Marple!"

"Miss Marple impersonation, but I refuse to go along with your questioning a seriously injured woman. And what would you do with the information? You would immediately go make a citizen's arrest of a violent criminal, who, I might add, would probably shoot us both."

"Hand me your keys. I want to wait in your truck while you wrestle with your conscience. I'm getting cold."

"And I suppose if I refuse, you would climb in your own truck."

"Yes, and you might be sorry you refused to help me. You are parked directly behind me, and you know what kind of a driver I am."

"What kind?" asked Ryan, suddenly looking very worried.

"The kind who sometimes forgets to look before she backs up."

Ryan trotted over to his truck. "My conscience comes a poor second behind catering to a crazy woman who owns a GMC truck that growls when she turns on the ignition."

Megan slid into the small Ranger and huddled in the seat while Ryan turned on the ignition and punched the heater up to High. She felt guilty at blackmailing her best friend, but she would deal with her guilt later. For now she had to get to the hospital and hope that Agnes was conscious, because Megan had to ask her a question. The validity of Megan's theory rested upon Agnes's answer.

"To the hospital, Madam Blackmailer?" asked Ryan.

Megan winced. She knew she was an emotional blackmailer. If she were any other woman, Ryan would call her bluff. She was shamelessly manipulating him and she didn't much like herself for it, but she would like herself less if another one of the reading circle was the murderer's next victim.

"Yes, to the hospital, and Ryan, break the speed limit if you have to, but get us there before Jerry Carr."

Ryan hit the brakes, slowing the little truck down to the point that Megan thought she could run faster. "I mean what I said, Megan. I won't let you badger an injured woman. Let Jerry Carr beat us. Let him question Agnes on the identity of her assailant. Let him find and arrest the guy. He carries a gun and has the entire police department to back him up. Between us we have one pocket knife and no authority."

"Fine. Let him ask her who the assailant was. That should keep him occupied and give me time to solve the puzzle of motive without his interrupting me."

"What are you talking about?" asked Ryan, looking bewildered. Poor baby, Megan thought, he'd looked bewildered most of the time lately. She was beginning to think he had no natural aptitude for puzzle-solving.

"Ryan! I'm surprised that you really believed I'd make a citizen's arrest of the murderer based on Agnes's identification."

"Wouldn't you?" he asked, looking more bewildered than before, like a man watching the ground crumble under his feet and wondering how far he would fall.

"No! Agnes will have amnesia about events immediately prior to the intruder knocking her unconscious. It's called retrograde amnesia and it's usually not long-lasting, but if her head injury is more serious, then she could suffer posttraumatic amnesia, which is of uncertain duration. In other words, Jerry Carr will learn absolutely nothing from Agnes tonight, tomorrow, and possibly for several days to come."

Megan caught her breath before continuing. "Plus, I have better sense than to make a citizen's arrest. I think more of my own skin than to risk it on a stupid stunt like playing policeman."

"Then what in the devil are we going to ask Agnes that you don't want Jerry Carr to know? And more importantly, *why* don't you want Jerry Carr to know it, whatever it is?"

Ryan was still driving at the speed of an arthritic turtle, so Megan supposed she'd better tell him, or her hair would be long and gray before they got to the hospital. "I'm going to ask Agnes where she put her receipt book—if she put it anywhere. If she took it back to her apartment immediately after she locked up and balanced her cash drawer, then that should have been long enough before the assault that she should retain a memory of it. If, however, the receipt book was stolen, then I'll know I'm right. The receipt book is gone because it is in itself a clue. Each receipt has the customer's name and a list of the titles and authors of the books he or she bought on that particular day. If Jerry Carr finds out first that I was right, and the book was stolen, then he'll confiscate all the records for the past several months or years or whatever!"

"So what, Megan? He can examine the receipt books and figure out who killed Lisa and assaulted Agnes. I take it that you do think the two crimes are related?" asked Ryan.

"Please, Ryan! You're sounding like Jerry. Of course, the two crimes are related."

Ryan tapped the steering wheel for a moment, then glanced at Megan, a puzzled look on his face. "Uh, Megan, how will the receipt books lead to the killer?"

"The secret to the motive for Lisa's murder lay on the shelves and in the records of Time and Again. It's the books themselves, Ryan. There is something about the books themselves that trigger murder. Those receipt books would mean nothing to Jerry Carr if he studied them from now until forever. He's not a member of Murder by the Yard and he's not very familiar with the mystery genre. On the other hand, we—meaning the membership—are learned in the genre—so to speak. Jerry Carr would never recognize anything odd in those receipt books, whereas we would know immediately. But if he gets to Agnes first—and to her records first— then we will never have access to them and the killing will continue because we won't know how to protect ourselves, and we'll keep buying whatever it is that sends the killer over the edge. That mustn't happen."

Ryan turned into the parking lot of Northwest Texas Hospital. "Tell him about the receipt books, offer to consult with him. Tell him that Murder by the Yard volunteers to decipher those records."

"Ryan, Lieutenant Jerry Carr didn't take my theory seriously. He doesn't take *me* seriously. What do you think he'll say when I tell him that I and the Murder by the Yard membership can read the name of a murderer in those receipt books. He's more likely to believe me if I kill a chicken and examine its entrails."

•   •   •

Megan sat in the intensive care waiting room, listening to Ryan snore in the chair next to her, and thinking how slowly time passed, and how much more awful it must be for a family member than for a friend: ten minutes every two hours to see your loved one. If he unexpectedly died in between visiting periods, he died alone. Once a patient went Code Blue, and the crash cart and the emergency team failed to revive him, it was too late to call the family to hold his hand and say goodbye. He was beyond hearing voices.

Megan curled her legs under her and picked up a magazine dated the present calendar year. There was something to be said for old magazines: You read the headline stories of six months before, and realized that the dire predictions of the so-called pundits hardly ever came to pass. It was enough to give a person hope in the future. It was enough to give her hope that Agnes's coma was short-lived, that her head injury was less serious than it first appeared, that one day soon she would open her eyes and begin to pick up the pieces of her life. And that her memory would return, all but that few minutes before the assault. If God were merciful, she would never remember, for as surely as Megan knew she was a redhead, she was equally sure that Agnes almost certainly knew her assailant. She knew him as a customer, perhaps even as a friend; otherwise he would not know about the receipt books. How terrible it would be to suddenly remember seeing a friend come at you with a baseball bat. How terrible to remember such a betrayal.

"Megan." Rosemary tiptoed into the waiting room. "I've reached everyone in Murder by the Yard, and each of us will take a four-hour shift. Has there been any change since you called me?" She spoke in the quiet, unnatural, reverent tone that Megan noticed most visitors to the ICU adopted—an unconscious rehearsal for a funeral-home kind of voice.

Megan resisted the urge to scream, and spoke at a normal level. "She's out of surgery—they had to remove a hematoma and repair the damage—but she's still in a coma. The prognosis is good—Agnes is as hardheaded as I always thought—but she will have memory loss. If she's lucky, she might lose only a few days. Or she might lose weeks. The only certainty is that given her age, she will never remember the attack."

"I'm glad," said Rosemary, shuddering. "That would be too horrible to bear."

Megan uncurled her legs and got up, aching in every part of her body. She felt old, as old as Rosemary. Maybe that's how one felt when illusions died. "Tell the others what her condition is. I don't think I can go over it again without losing control of myself."

"I'll do it," Rosemary said, reaching out and giving Megan a fierce hug. "Go home, dear. I'll take charge now. Ryan, let me give you a hug, too. I haven't hugged a handsome man since my husband passed away, and I've missed it."

"I'll never turn down a hug from a good-looking woman, Rosemary," said Ryan as he wrapped his arms around her and lifted her off the floor. Over her head he caught Megan's eye. *Why did you lie?* he mouthed.

Megan looked down at the floor. She thought he was asleep while she talked to Rosemary, not that it mattered. She would have told him eventually; he was the only member of Murder by the Yard that she truly trusted.

16

*I can tamper with the law when, where, and how
I like. I have tampered with the law when, where,
and how I liked, and I will do it again.*

—HENRI BENCOLIN in John Dickson Carr's
The Four False Weapons, 1937

It was eight o'clock in the morning when we walked
out of the hospital, and we hadn't been to bed yet.
We were both lightheaded with exhaustion, but too tense
to sleep. By mutual consent I drove the few blocks to
Medi Park, a lovely expanse of grassy knolls and trees,
with various health care facilities scattered at discreet
distances from each other, as well as the garden center
and the Discovery Center, a baby-sized scientific museum and planetarium. I held Megan's hand and we
strolled around the small pond where swans and ducks
swam when not begging food from the featherless ones
who always seemed to want to share goodies such as
bread crusts and peanuts and candy bars. After being fed
nonstop from birth, they were too fat to fly, or else they
knew a cushy pad when they saw it. The sun was warm
and a light breeze was blowing just enough to make the
cattails in the pond bend gently. The day promised to
be beautiful after a night of violence. Megan and I
needed beauty.

"I think it's one of us, Ryan. That's why the receipt
book was stolen. It was a record of what each of us
bought last night."

Her voice was so soft I nearly didn't hear her. I wish I hadn't. I didn't want Lisa's killer and Agnes's assailant to be one of us. "How do you know it was stolen? Agnes is in a coma and can't be questioned. And while we're on the subject of Agnes, why did you intimate to Rosemary that Agnes might lose weeks of memory? The doctor didn't tell us that. He even said there was a possibility—small but there—of her eventually remembering almost everything right up to the actual attack. There's a chance she can remember who she saw before she was struck."

She turned her head to look at me. There was something different about her, a resoluteness that seemed too mature for one so young. "If the members of Murder by the Yard believe that Agnes has suffered permanent memory loss, she will be safe from another attack."

"You're serious, aren't you? You really believe it's one of us." The possibility sent chills marching up and down my spine.

She nodded her head. "It's the only theory that makes sense. We know that we didn't kill Lisa or attack Agnes, so that leaves six members: Randel, Candi, Annabel, Herb, Rosemary, and Lorene."

"Plus a stranger not known to us."

"No."

Her tone of voice was sharp and conveyed a certainty I disliked. I waited, but she didn't say anything else. "I don't want it to be one of us, Megan. Damn it all, I like all of us. I take that back. I don't like Randel all that much, but he's improving and eventually he might even be tolerable. Even Annabel is improving on closer acquaintance. You're tired and upset. Maybe your thinking is a little cloudy. Are you absolutely sure you're right?"

"Yes. It's the only theory that offers an explanation of the missing receipt book."

"If you truly believe that, then why in God's name

did you arrange for the Circle to take turns sitting with Agnes?"

"Who else does she have, Ryan? She's a spinster and an only child. Her parents are long dead and she has no cousins, no kin anywhere. Dangerous as one of us might be, we're all she's got. And my lie gives the killer a reason to spare Agnes, and I believe he will. If he wanted her dead, then he would have slashed her throat like he did Lisa. He could have even done it after he heard us banging on the back door. It only takes a split second to slit a throat."

I stepped around in front of her and grasped her arms. "Megan, this is Agnes's life you're gambling with. Tell Jerry Carr. Let him assign cops to stand guard outside her hospital room."

"Then the killer would know the police suspected an attempted murder rather than a burglary. He might panic and the rest of us would be at risk." I didn't like her monotone any more than I liked what she was saying. She was in shock, mentally if not physically.

I released her arms and took her hand again, and we resumed walking. "Because we don't know what books to avoid. Is that what you're saying, Megan?" I used a gentle voice that matched the day, talking to her as I would to a child facing tragedy for the first time.

"Yes. That's why I have to look at Agnes's records— so we'll know what buying habits are dangerous. I particularly want to know what Lisa bought that first time she visited the store. Somewhere in Agnes's receipts is a lead, and I'm going to find it. Fortunately I worked for Agnes when I was in high school, so I know her record system, and I doubt if she's changed it much."

We walked in silence while I mulled over Megan's reasoning. It was convoluted, imaginative as any crime novel, and totally improbable, but it made a terrible kind of sense. She might be in a kind of psychic shock, but she was still working on all cylinders.

"If Jerry would just believe that two violent episodes at a bookstore are not a coincidence!" Megan burst out. "How many people have to die before he believes that someone is knocking off customers who shop at Time and Again Bookstore? Three, four, eight, ten?"

When she used the word "customer," I remembered. "There may have already been two murders instead of one, Megan. Or maybe not. You would have counted the cleaning lady if you thought she was part of the pattern."

Megan stopped in the middle of the path, shooed a fat duck away who came begging, and turned to me, her forehead wrinkled up as it always is when she's thinking or worried. "What are you talking about, Ryan? What cleaning lady?"

"You ought to know. You inherited her beagle, according to what Agnes told me."

"Rembrandt? That's his name, although you've never asked. You must mean Violet Winston. But she was shot several blocks from the bookstore and that was months ago, long before Lisa Heredia moved to town. She would have had no connection with Lisa."

"According to your theory she didn't have to know Lisa, as long as she was connected to the store. She had been a customer of Agnes's for thirty years—and she had been in Time and Again the night she was murdered. Agnes said she had a large bag of books."

"Agnes never told me that Violet Winston had bought books that night. She just told me that Violet had been killed and would I take her beagle. Not that there was any reason then for me to care. That happened sometime in February." She wrinkled her brow in thought again.

"It still worried Agnes, because she told me about it after the first—or was it the second—meeting. She was angry that the police hadn't arrested anyone or even had a suspect."

"I can't believe Agnes didn't mention Violet after

Lisa's murder. She must not have thought there was a connection."

"How could she? She didn't know anything about your diagram. Remember, we were going to talk to her about it last night. My God, was it just last night?"

"If Violet's death is connected, then it reinforces my theory."

"Tell Jerry that you believe Violet is the first of the bookstore murders," I urged her. "That ought to make him more receptive to your ideas."

"I'll tell him, but I don't think he'll listen. And frankly, I'm more interested in getting hold of Violet's bag of books. Receipts are fine, but they aren't the books themselves. I want to know what's between the covers of certain books that is so dangerous to—someone."

"At least you didn't use the phrase, one of us. That's progress, I suppose. Besides, there wasn't a Murder by the Yard Reading Circle in February. Doesn't that mean that the killer might not be a member?"

Megan had that pensive expression on her face again that meant she was using her little gray cells, as Hercule Poirot calls them. Hercule Poirot? I was being tainted by association. Before long I'd know who Barbara Peters and Amelia Peabody were.

"What it means is that the killer was in the store at the same time Violet Winston was selecting her books. But we won't know who that was because one witness is dead and the other is in a coma."

"So when Agnes comes out of her coma, we ask her," I said.

"No, it's too dangerous."

Again she snapped the words out like a top sergeant chewing out a new recruit. The voice was totally unlike Megan's, which was usually sweet and mellow. This life as an amateur sleuth was having a detrimental effect on her personality. The sooner we figured out a likely suspect, the better. I wanted to turn this case over to Jerry

Carr before I needed to find an exorcist to drive the demons out of Megan.

"So tell your faithful Watson, Ms. Holmes. What is the next step in solving your first and last case?"

"We have to look through Agnes's receipt books. And we have to find out what books Violet Winston bought. Or traded rather, because from what I remember of Violet, she seldom bought, only traded. And to find that out we have to talk to Jerry Carr—which we have to do anyway. And let me do the talking, Ryan. I know exactly how to get the information out of him."

Those were literally the last words she spoke until we were ushered into Jerry Carr's office—which I found very unimpressive. The man in charge of a department like Special Crimes ought to at least have an office that would mildly overwhelm the public.

"Megan, Doc, sit down and let's go over what you told me last night." He was calling me Doc again. But what did he want me do? Burst out with some incriminating utterance? But I didn't know anything—except Megan's theories, which he didn't believe.

"I told you my story last night—twice—and I have nothing to correct or delete," said Megan.

"Doc, do you have anything you want to add?" asked Jerry, turning those laser-sharp gray eyes on me.

"Not a thing," I told him.

"You said that Megan was banging on the back door when you arrived at Time and Again, is that correct?"

"Yes, and getting very upset when Agnes didn't answer."

"How many minutes behind Megan do you suppose you were in arriving at the store?"

I stopped to think before I answered. I didn't like the direction in which that question seemed to be pointing. "I left immediately after Megan, so not more than two or three minutes, maybe not that much."

"And I suppose you agree?" he asked, switching his laser focus to Megan.

She was so pale that her few freckles stood out like specks of reddish paint. She saw where he was heading too. "I did not attack Agnes Caldwell," she said.

"I'm not accusing you," he replied, his face nearly as pale as Megan's and his expression more anguished. Even the most jealous man—myself—failed to enjoy the sight of the lieutenant in agony questioning the woman even I would credit him with loving. His suffering sprang from the unspoken word at the end of his simple declarative sentence: *Yet.*

"I think you're close to it."

"Megan, if you would throw me a lifeline here in the form of something logical and probable that I could believe instead of some scribblings on pieces of paper, I would let you go without any further questioning."

I almost felt sorry for Jerry Carr. He was a desperate man, a left-brained man being asked to take a leap of faith and believe two impossible things before breakfast. Left-brained individuals are not good at believing the impossible.

"Lisa Heredia's murder and Agnes's assault are related to each other and to Time and Again. Another murder, that of Violet Winston is related to Time and Again. Both women bought books from Agnes. If I could look at Agnes's receipt books, I could point out a logical suspect."

"I'm sorry, Megan, but you're reaching. The Winston woman died blocks from the store and more than three months ago. Last night's assault was a burglary gone bad. I can't reconstruct the crime scene any other way." He stopped, got up, and turned his back to us, massaging what had to be a stiff neck. He might also have been trying to get control of his facial expressions.

Finally he turned around. His eyes were bloodshot, and I remembered that he probably hadn't slept any more than Megan and I. "I also have to consider that you have discovered not one, but two violent crimes. The average citizen of your race and economic situation never discovers a murder victim in her entire life. Do you have a comment you wish to make?"

"Coincidence," Megan said smugly, throwing his own word back in his face.

"Damn it, Megan, this is not a word game!" he shouted. "Anyone else would already be a suspect. There is a correlation between the person who discovers a murder or an attempted murder and guilt of same, and it's a damn high correlation!"

"What about the correlation between location and three violent acts: two murders and an assault? Or is that just coincidence?"

"Megan, this is not helping either one of us. Don't force me into making a move I don't want to make."

"What kind of books did Violet Winston have in her bag? Agnes told Ryan that she had a bagful of books. What kind were they?"

"Violet Winston didn't have a bag of books when her body was discovered, and a cop was at the scene within five minutes."

"Who stole Violet's books? Who stole Agnes's receipt books? Answer those questions and you have a suspect," said Megan, not giving an inch.

"I don't know, but I intend to look for them as well as for the knife that was used to kill Lisa." He opened his desk drawer and took out a warrant to search Megan's home and her vehicle.

17

*A man always finds it hard to realize that he may
have finally lost a woman's love, however badly he
may have treated her.*

—SHERLOCK HOLMES to Watson
in Arthur Conan Doyle's
"The Adventure of the Musgrave Ritual,"
The Memoirs of Sherlock Holmes, 1894

Megan watched Jerry Carr and his menials from
Special Crimes take apart her home in search of
a knife and bloodstained clothes while Rembrandt provided the sound effects, his howling echoing through the
neighborhood like the baying of wolves in the old vam-
pire movies. Whenever she objected to the handling of
some belonging, Rembrandt darted at the miscreant so
unwise as to have aroused his beloved friend's ire, and
seized the object in question along with any fingers unfortunate enough to still be holding his beloved's pos-
session.

Finally Jerry Carr had enough. "Megan, control that
dog of yours or I'll call Animal Control."

Megan knelt down and put her arms around Rembrandt, who whined, wagged his tail, and covered her
face with doggy kisses. "If you do, I'll sue Potter
County, the city of Amarillo, and you personally. If you
think arresting me for obstruction would generate bad
publicity, just imagine the effect if you send my dog to
Death Row."

"Animal Control will not kill your dog, Megan, but he will be penned up so we can execute this search warrant without being bitten by that bad-tempered mutt!"

"He's not a mutt; he's a registered beagle, and you gave him to me. You didn't think he was a mutt then."

"I'm not getting into a war of what I said versus what you *think* I meant. Keep hold of that dog. I don't intend to have any more of my men bitten. Good God, Megan, don't you realize that I can legally have that dog destroyed?"

Megan tightened her hold on Rembrandt, who reveled in the embrace of his beloved. "You called me a liar, suspect me of murder, and now you want to shoot my dog!" She burst into tears, surprising both herself and Jerry Carr.

With a muttered curse that Megan couldn't hear over Rembrandt's growls and her own sobs, Jerry Carr turned away and stomped into Megan's bedroom where the officers had congregated. "Hurry it up in here!"

"Lieutenant, my finger's bleeding. That mutt raked my finger nearly to the bone," said one of the evidence techs, but not the one who had been so friendly to Megan at Lisa's crime scene.

"What the hell were you fighting the dog over: a piece of bologna?"

"I was searching her underwear drawer," said the tech.

"What did you do? Dangle a pair of panties in front of the dog's nose?"

"I was taking out each piece of lingerie and she yelled at me that no woman kept a knife in her underwear drawer, and I turned around with a pair of, um, underpants in my hand and the dog lunged, and I couldn't let go fast enough."

The evidence tech held up his right hand with a handkerchief wrapped around the middle finger. Megan tried to feel sympathy for the man, but failed. Her room was a mess with nearly all her possessions on the floor, the sheets pulled off the bed, and the mattress tipped off the frame. She wished Rembrandt had taken a piece out of the tech's posterior. Rembrandt seemed to read her thoughts because he growled at the man, who backed away, tripped over the tent poles he'd pulled out of her closet, and fell backward into her bookcase, which tipped over, pinning him to the floor. Rembrandt barked, and Megan thought she detected a snicker in his bark.

Jerry Carr ran his hands through his hair, studied the waving feet of his tech, who was calling for help, looked at Megan and Rembrandt, and shaking his head, walked over and grabbed the edge of the bookcase, heaving it up and against the wall. "Get your butt out to the van," he said as he pulled the tech out of the welter of scattered books and tent poles. He shrugged his shoulders as he left. "Damn rookies," Megan heard him say under his breath.

Megan wiped her eyes on her sleeve and tried to control her tears. She hated crying, because her nose always turned red and she looked like a woman on a drunken binge. Most of all she hated crying in front of Jerry Carr because she didn't want him to think her weak or frightened, although she was both. She couldn't remember her pride ever being hurt so badly since she was in the third grade and one of her snooty classmates told her that curly red hair made her look weird. She couldn't punch out Jerry Carr's lights like she did the snooty classmate.

Her knees aching from kneeling to hold Rembrandt, she changed positions and sat cross-legged by her bedroom door, leaning against the wall and hugging the fat beagle. Every now and then he growled at the strangers, then whined and licked the tears off Megan's cheeks. "I love you, Rembrandt," she whispered with a catch in her voice. His adoring look said the feeling was mutual.

Eventually she heard the front door open and the

sound of voices fade. She heard footsteps coming down the hall and leaned her head against Rembrandt's and closed her eyes.

"Megan," said Jerry, squatting down by her side. "We're done. I left a list of the items we took for lab testing on your kitchen counter by the phone."

"What did you take?" she asked, not opening her eyes. "I have to know if I need to buy a new outfit for the next murder."

"Don't kid about this, Megan. It's serious business."

"I know it's serious. I knew it when I first saw Lisa Heredia's throat gaping open like a second mouth."

"Megan, will you look at me, please?"

"I don't want to. Say what you have to say and leave. I need to pick up the house before my mother comes home. If you think Rembrandt was a pain, you better be glad my mother wasn't here. She cut her teeth protesting the Department of Energy's attempt to locate a high-level nuclear dump in the Texas Panhandle. If she could take on the Energy Department and win, she can chew up Special Crimes and spit you out."

"I'm a cop, Megan, and it's all I've wanted to be. I know that doesn't sound like much of an ambition to someone with three degrees, but keeping the peace is an honorable job. There are times, like now, when I wish I had never majored in criminal justice, never gone to the police academy, so I wouldn't find myself on the other side of an abyss from you. I don't want to think you killed anyone, and in my gut I don't, but being a cop means following a set of procedures, winnowing out those who are obviously innocent—like Dr. Stevens—and investigating those who keep appearing at a crime scene, and who have opportunity. We not only try to prove a suspect guilty, we also try to prove them innocent if we possibly can. We want the bad guys, not cute redheads who are in the wrong place at the wrong time."

"You have no idea how much better that makes me feel," she said, raising her head and looking past his shoulder. "Particularly since I don't have the means, i.e., the knife, and I don't have a motive. But I agree I'm probably dangerous, maybe even crazy. You're right not to listen to my ideas. Reading all those mysteries has warped my brain and induced hallucinations."

"Megan, please."

She raised her head and deliberately ignored the regret in his eyes. "Get out of here, Jerry. You executed your warrant and you're not welcome in my home. And what have you done with Ryan?"

Jerry looked away, the only indication that he had done something underhanded. "Dr. Stevens had trouble starting his truck. The cop in charge of upkeep on our cars looked at it as a favor to me."

"I just bet he did," said Megan.

"I just called, and the cop said he fixed the truck, but the professor took off running somewhere. I'm sure he'll be here soon."

"Why didn't you want him here? Jealousy?" Megan heard the nasty tone of her voice and felt embarrassed. This was an ugly scene and she wanted it over.

"Executing a search warrant can upset people, Megan. I didn't want to arrest the professor for obstructing a police investigation. I don't want to arrest you. I've never had to investigate anybody I lo—liked, and I don't ever want to do it again. If you have anything you want to tell me, do it now."

She looked at him and felt her eyes burning with exhaustion and suppressed tears. "I told you all I know, all my suppositions and theories. You disregarded everything!"

Jerry rose, his shoulders slumping. "I'm leaving now, Megan, but let me give you a last piece of advice. Get yourself a lawyer."

She rested her cheek against Rembrandt's head and

closed her eyes again. She must have dozed because Rembrandt's bark startled her.

"Hey, don't bark at me. I'm on her side."

Megan opened her eyes and looked up to find Ryan and Herb standing in front of her. "Ryan, the lieutenant said your truck was fixed."

"Yeah, right," said Ryan. "There was nothing wrong with it until I parked it at Special Crimes. When it wouldn't start and that mechanic was jacking around with the engine, I said to heck with it, and took off to find Herb. He gave me a ride over."

Megan tilted her head. "Are you here to fight the wicked lieutenant, Herb?"

Herb pulled her vanity bench over and sat on it. She guessed that three-piece suits didn't hold up well when worn sitting on the floor. "I looked over the search warrant that I found on the kitchen counter as well as the list of property collected by Lieutenant Carr and Special Crimes. The warrant is valid and the information provided by the lieutenant is true. And, since you are innocent, the lieutenant and Special Crimes were unable to find anything but a butcher knife in your mother's kitchen, and several implements from a green plastic tackle box."

"That's my digging kit, damn it! It took me months to collect all those tools." She sat up, energized by a sense of injustice. "What did that underhanded pond scum take?"

Herb raised one eyebrow, verifying what Megan had suspected all along: a Y chromosome was required for eyebrows to move individually. "According to the property list, Special Crimes took one hunting knife . . ."

"I used it in the Yucatan one spring when I was on a dig sponsored by the University of Houston," said Megan. "You can always use a good hunting knife in the jungle. I cut vines with that knife that were as thick as my middle finger. Thicker even. And I killed a lot of snakes with it. Yucatan means snakes, you know."

Herb sniffed and straightened his vest. "Very interesting, I'm sure. To continue, there was also a rock hammer, a sharp, pointed object resembling a spike . . ."

"I used that rock hammer in Israel one fall on a dig near Jerusalem. It's a rocky country. If Israel could figure out a way to export all their rocks, their economy would be running at a surplus. And the sharp object is a spike, one of the many I used as a tent peg on that same dig," said Megan, leaning back against the wall and thinking about the hot, clear light of Israel, and the scent of the olive trees.

"So these are innocent objects connected with your profession?" asked Herb. Megan nodded and Herb smiled. "Then I see no problem with those items. However, the list also includes a University of Texas T-shirt, a pair of cutoffs, and a pair of hiking boots with stains which might be human blood."

"It is human blood. It's Lisa's blood. I was wearing those clothes when I stumbled over her body. I also examined the corpse before the Justice of the Peace arrived, so there were lots of opportunities to transfer some of Lisa's blood onto my clothes. Then I changed clothes and dropped those in a plastic pail in the laundry room and forgot about them."

"This is bad, Megan. I don't like bloodstains on my clients' clothes. I particularly don't like the victim's blood on my clients' clothes. It complicates the defense. However, since you did examine the body . . ."

"For signs of life," interrupted Megan.

"For signs of life," agreed Herb. "Therefore we can argue that's when you inadvertently stained your clothes. In a humane cause."

"That is when I stained my clothes, Herb, but I did it before the police and JP got there."

Herb frowned. "That's unfortunate, but any fact can be interpreted in two different ways: one way by the prosecution and another by the defense. I wish Dr. Stevens hadn't been unconscious in the petunias—an eyewitness to your examination of the body would have been helpful—but I am reasonably confident that our interpretation will carry the day."

"I hope so," said Megan.

"And Megan, don't talk to the lieutenant or anyone else in law enforcement unless I am present. Even though Lieutenant Carr did not specifically say you were a suspect, we will treat any contact with him as if you were indeed under suspicion for murder. I find it's safer in conducting affairs for my client to anticipate the worst possible scenario. That way I'm never surprised. Surprise in defense work is deadly, although I admit that most of the surprises come from my clients. Criminals are addicted to lying—even to their lawyer. Maybe especially to their lawyer."

Herb stood up, straightened his vest, his tie, and his coat. "I think that's all we need talk about for the moment. I'll take Ryan back to Special Crimes to get his truck, and I'll go rattle the lieutenant's cage, make noises about unnecessary untidiness during the search, the suspicious malfunction of Ryan's pickup, et cetera. I'll have a whole litany of complaints by the time we arrive. I've found that numerous complaints delivered in a calm monotone generate many useful and inadvertent responses. Before I forget, is there anything I need to know more than what I already know about your unfortunate discoveries of Lisa and Agnes?"

Megan shook her head and lifted her hand so Herb could help her up. "I can't think of a thing, Herb, except that I'm incensed that an innocent person can be harassed by the police on no more evidence than an unfortunate matter of timing. It's un-American!" She noticed Ryan frowning at her and smiled at him, praying he would keep his honest mouth shut.

"Well, actually the lieutenant didn't step over the line,

but it's always disturbing the first time a person has any dealings with the police. They carry guns and that bothers certain people."

Megan took Herb's arm and walked out with him to his two-year-old Lincoln Continental, as waxed and shiny and immaculate as Herb himself. "If you don't mind, Herb, I'll go with you and Ryan, so Ryan can give me a lift back to Agnes's. I left my truck there."

"Actually, your truck was probably towed by order of Special Crimes, and is being searched for bloodstains as we speak. You may be without transportation for a day or two."

"That pond scum took my baby?" yelled Megan, incensed for real now.

"I'm afraid so, Megan. It was in the search warrant."

"I never read the search warrant. I knew that whatever they were looking for, I didn't have, and besides I was too busy trying to keep Rembrandt from biting the evidence techs, or biting them too hard, anyway."

"Megan, I advise you to always read a legal document of any kind before signing. You never know how much dishonesty there is in the world until you're a lawyer. Sometimes the worst offenders are members of my own profession."

Megan nodded and smiled, avoiding Ryan's questioning looks and hoping that Herb would continue with his dissertation-length discussion on the importance of reading documents, until they arrived at Special Crimes.

Herb didn't disappoint. He finished his lecture just as he turned off his ignition, and Megan shot out of the back seat. "Thanks, Herb, you are a wonderful man and I'll tell everyone I know that you are a terrific lawyer."

Herb smiled and straightened his vest.

Ryan started on her the minute he slid into his truck. "Why didn't you tell him your theory about the books being the motive for Lisa's murder and Agnes's assault?"

Megan snapped her seat belt and sighed. "Because I don't trust him. I told you that you're the only one I trust."

"Herb Jackson would never have killed Lisa while wearing his three-piece suit, Megan. I bet he wears a three-piece pajama suit to bed."

"I don't care, Ryan. Until I can figure out who is guilty on the basis of the books they bought, I trust no one! But he was sweet to come to my rescue. Is he a good lawyer, or did you get him because he's a member of Murder by the Yard?"

"Actually, he's supposed to be pretty good. Probably talks the prosecutors into making his client a good deal just to shut him up. And he does already know the circumstances of the case. Plus I was desperate. I needed to get a lawyer for you quickly."

"Thank you, Ryan. I really appreciate your taking care of me. I lost my composure and cried. I'm not used to being a murder suspect. It's humiliating to have your credibility questioned."

"I'm sorry I was late, Megan."

She patted his arm. "That's okay, Ryan. It's over now and I can go on with my investigation. Let's check Lisa's apartment first. Jerry will expect us to go back to Agnes's, so we won't do that today."

Ryan reacted as Megan expected. He slammed on the brakes, pulled over to the curb, and stopped. "Are you nuts? You came within an inch of being arrested. You're suspected of murder, and what do you want to do? You want to break into one of the victims' apartments!"

"I have to, Ryan. You saw how far sharing my ideas with the lieutenant got me. Do you really want to see me charged with murder? Because I'm beginning to think I might actually be facing that possibility. If I don't see to my own defense, if I don't solve the crime, then I may be sharing a cell with Guido the three-hundred-pound biker's girlfriend, Hilda."

18

Being a suspected murderer frees the mind from more mundane worries.

—MEGAN CLARK

"I've thought about the best way to get into Lisa's apartment, and I've decided that we should be up front with the manager: You're her brother and I'm her niece."

"That's up front?" I asked, appalled by the way Megan had taken to lying like a duck takes to water. "First you lie to Rosemary about Agnes's condition, then you lie to Herb."

"I didn't lie to Herb. I just didn't share all of my thoughts with him. Besides, look where truth got me: a search warrant and a scandal. Our neighbors were just recovering from my mother's daily press conferences on the front porch during her fight with the Department of Energy. Now they're wondering if I'm a serial killer. They're probably calling their real estate agents right now, so they can put their houses on the market and sell them before the police dig up bodies in the basement. The problem is that the truth sounds like a lie, and a lie sounds like the truth. If I told Jerry Carr I killed Lisa because she taunted me, he would believe me. But if I tell him that someone killed Lisa because of the books she read, he doesn't believe me. So I've decided to tell people what they want or expect to hear, then go right ahead doing what I planned to do in the first place. I don't intend to do nothing. I refuse to leave my fate in Jerry Carr's hands, or in Herb Jackson's, either."

No one but Megan could state her case in such a way that lying sounds like reasonable strategy. "Megan, you're a terrible liar. Your face turns red and your eyes look furtive."

"That's why I wanted you to be my backup: You're a good liar. Well, actually you're a bad liar because you always stutter, but no one expects you to lie, so you get away with it. I'll stand by your side and smile."

"Megan, this is not the right way to go about defending yourself."

She looked at me, her face somber and determined. "It may not be right, but it's the only way I have. Are you with me or against me?"

"Megan, it's not that simple," I said, even though I knew I stared defeat in the face.

She drew her brows together in a frown. "Yes, it is. It's black and white, yes and no, for me or against me. There are no gray areas today, no ambiguities to argue."

I was caught in a moral dilemma. What she was proposing probably broke, or at least seriously bent, several laws beginning with interference in a police investigation. Up to now, we hadn't really done more than dip our toes into the sea of illegality—when we beat the lieutenant to Jared Johnson—and Herb Jackson would argue that we were visiting the sick. Assuming a false identity and entering a murder victim's apartment without notifying the police or asking permission of the next of kin was jumping into that sea without a life preserver or even a leaky old rowboat. On the other hand—there was always the other hand with Megan Clark—to do nothing was to become a potential victim, and Megan Clark would never allow herself to be a victim of anybody's wrong thinking. She was born to challenge the status quo, to fight complacency, to defy the bureaucracy, to reject the self-righteousness of her parents' generation, and to accept responsibility for her own well-being. She was Generation X, and the bane of Madison Avenue admen who could not classify, categorize, or predict her behavior or buying habits in any consistent manner. The question: Was I ready to sign on with Generation X in the person of Megan Clark? Was I ready to stand tall and spit in the eye of authority if caught in Lisa Heredia's apartment. Why not? Guido the three-hundred-pound biker could have a sweet personality under his tattoos.

I swallowed, took a deep breath, and committed. "I'm with you. Let's go paw through your Aunt Lisa's belongings."

Lisa Heredia had lived in an apartment complex on Bell south of I-40 in the reputed better part of town. I remember that complex standing empty and unfinished for nearly five years during the savings and loan meltdown in Texas, while ownership—and debt—changed hands every quarter. Finally, a real estate management firm bought the complex at fire-sale prices, finished the units, applied a cosmetic exterior of faux weathered wood, put in landscaping, and rented each unit for twice what it was worth. Taxes are higher in the right part of town and so are rents.

The apartment manager took little persuading. In fact, I barely had time to perform my act as Lisa's brother before he was whipping out a key. He had a waiting list of tenants and one empty apartment to which the occupant would not be returning this side of eternity. Apartment managers are little known for their sentimentality, and this particular one was no exception to the rule.

"The cops never said nothing to me about making this apartment into some kind of museum, know what I mean? The Do Not Touch sign and the velvet rope? I got to answer to the company that owns this complex, and they aren't interested in a museum either. If it's empty, they want it rented , know what I mean?"

"We understand," I said. "I have a few rental units myself back in the Big Apple. Gotta keep those babies full. Insurance, taxes, they come due whether I got bodies in those units or not." Megan pinched my arm to let me know I was overacting my part.

She smiled at the manager, a thirty-something guy with a lot of miles on his face and a spreading waistline. "Did you ever talk with Aunt Lisa? I never got to say goodbye to her when she left New York, and I'd like to know, well, any little thing you can tell me."

She sounded like Scarlett O'Hara playing Manhattan, but the manager was too interested in the packaging to notice the sound. A stop for costuming saw me in a sport coat and slacks and Megan in a skimpy black dress from her undergraduate days. I say skimpy not because of cleavage, but leg. I felt an urge to tug on her hemline.

"To tell the truth, your aunt wasn't much for visiting," said the manager, demonstrating an unexpected mental dexterity in that he could ogle and talk at the same time. "She drove up in a rental car, wanted to lease a one-bedroom for three months max. We don't do that generally. We want a six-month lease at a minimum, but she offered to pay a little extra for the three months, so I said okay. The company's not losing anything. But beyond that, she didn't have much to say. And she didn't get any mail except what's addressed to 'Occupant.' We got a welcoming committee that always visits new tenants, hands out coupons from the local merchants, that kind of thing, but she didn't even let them in the apartment. She didn't want company, I guess."

"I see," said Megan.

"This here is her apartment," said the manager, tearing the yellow crime-scene tape to unlock a door and wave us into the apartment.

"Thank you," said Megan. "We'll stop by after we

pack Aunt Lisa's belongings to let you know we're finished."

"Yeah, well, I guess that's okay." The manager was reluctant to leave, but Megan eased him out the door with a smile that dazed him.

The apartment was the usual bland offering found in a thousand cities in fifty states and Puerto Rico: a cramped living room with cheap furniture, a tiny galley kitchen with a table and two chairs at one end, a bathroom with the usual toilet articles, and a bedroom. Besides a toothbrush, mouth wash, and makeup, the only other sign that someone had lived there was a few clothes hanging in the closet, underwear in the dresser drawers, and two suitcases. If Lisa Heredia had lived in this ugly apartment for nearly a month, then it should have been unnecessary to murder her. She should have been terminally depressed and ready to slit her wrists.

"Other than a sort of general pity I'd feel for any murder victim, I never felt sorry for Lisa Heredia until now," said Megan, standing in the middle of the bedroom. "This is terrible. How could anybody stand to live in a place like this for a month?"

I shook my head. depressed myself after only five minutes. "She must have wanted to represent Annabel awfully badly to go to this extreme."

"I can't stand this room. I'm at least going to pull the drape open to let in some sunshine."

"Should you do that? What if somebody sees us?" Entering an apartment under false pretenses made me paranoid.

"Ryan, the manager talked to us up close and personal. He can describe us down to our underwear—or at least mine. He spent most of the time trying to stare through my dress. If the cops ask him, we're dead meat, so I refuse to act furtive." She pulled open the cheap drape to reveal a sliding glass door onto a tiny patio big enough for one chair and a potted plant dying for lack of water.

"Ryan, come here." Her voice was high and urgent.

I immediately saw what riveted her attention: Lying on the patio by the uncomfortable-looking white plastic chair was a paperback book by Annabel Edgars Crow. A white receipt with the Time and Again logo at the top was tucked into the paperback as a bookmark.

Megan and I fought to unlock the glass door. Being younger and more dexterous, she won. She pounced on the book and jerked out the receipt. "Let me see, she bought ten books, two of Annabel's and eight out-of-print paperbacks for a total of $117.85. Agnes charges an arm and a leg for old paperbacks whether they're a valuable commodity on the rare-book market or not. She has nightmares about selling a first edition of some rare, out-of-print book and then the buyer turns around and sells it for fifty thousand dollars. Let me see what's on the receipt. I might actually have read one of these— you never know. *The Case of the Poisoned Tea Caddy, Five Easy Marks, Murder Betwixt and Between* . . . I don't recognize any of these titles and authors. They must be some of Agnes's obscure titles. But aren't they wonderful titles? They reek of the late thirties."

"They probably also reek of mold," I said, drawing a fierce look from Megan. I changed the subject in the interest of amiability. "Why would anybody pay more than ten bucks a title for old paperbacks nobody ever heard of?" I asked. I could justify spending nearly a hundred dollars for a first edition of a Max Brand paperback, and Louis L'Amour first editions were nearly priceless and worth every penny, but ten dollars for a moldy old book whose pages were falling out, by an author who couldn't write a postcard? Unbelievable.

"Buying old, out-of-print books is a bibliophile's equivalent of reckless behavior. For some buyers it's gambling that brings a bigger thrill than anything Las

Vegas can offer. It's treasure-hunting for grownups, because you never know when some book you find in a box in a junk store or garage sale will turn out to be worth a ton of money. And if nothing you buy is worth more than the pennies you spend, you still have a book to read, and life doesn't get much better than a good book and a cup of coffee."

I tried to think of a counter argument, but I couldn't. I even like the shape and feel of a book, and the smell of printer's ink that lingers in the pages of a new book fresh off the press is better than the smell of sixty-dollar-an-ounce perfume on the wrist of a pretty woman. Maybe not better than. Maybe equal to. I don't want to exaggerate.

"So let's scoop up these potentially priceless relics of a bygone age, and get the hell out of Dodge before the marshal shows up," I said, gently easing Megan back into the apartment. "I'm not in any condition to go another round with Jerry Carr."

From where we stood in front of the glass door, we could see the entire bedroom and bath. There were no books. Without exchanging a word, we each took half of the room and searched. Other than dust bunnies under the bed, I found nothing. I stood up, dusted my hands and the front of my slacks, and looked at Megan. She was leaning against the dresser with a frown that etched a fine line between her eyebrows. She visually examined the bedroom with the same intensity she would use on a mummy whose dry and wasted body lay helpless before her.

"I don't see a hiding place in here," she finally said. "And I checked the toilet tank for a plastic bag of books. Nothing. Did you check the pockets of her clothes in the closet?"

"I occasionally watch *Cops* on TV. I know how to conduct a search."

"So on to the living room and kitchen," she said,

marching ahead of me in that short black dress. I reso-
lutely focused on the back of her head to avoid any
distractions.

We looked in every cabinet and drawer in the
kitchen—bare—and the refrigerator—also bare, but for
a bottle of designer water, a shriveled apple, and a
wedge of cheese of unknown origin. In the living room
we removed the cushions from the couch—nothing—
and looked underneath it—more dust bunnies. Then we
traded places and searched all over again. Again nothing.
I had never met a person who failed to leave some im-
print on the place she lived until Lisa Heredia. A month
isn't a lifetime, but it's time enough to let your hair
down and expose bad habits like not hanging up your
clothes, or squeezing the toothpaste in the middle.

"Lisa Heredia did not exist," I announced after the
second search. I dropped onto the couch and put my feet
on the coffee table, my second favorite thinking stance
after staring at the ceiling. "A ghost lived here but not
a flesh-and-blood person. Nobody could leave so little a
trace as that woman. And the only book is the one you
found on the patio."

"The killer didn't go out on the patio," said Megan.
"He opened the door with the key he stole from her
purse, so there was no need to break in the patio door.
And he wouldn't have opened the drapes, because he
didn't want anyone to see him, and they would have
because it was dark."

"How do you know that?" I asked, fascinated by the
way her mind worked. The world lost a great detective
when she chose mummies instead.

"Logic. He would have come over here as soon as
possible to grab the books before the police got here,
probably unnecessarily, because there was no reason for
Jerry to make an immediate search. He didn't know Lisa
had been killed for the books. Now he knows it and
doesn't believe it. Anyway, the killer would have

searched immediately after the murder, say about ten-thirty."

"And we're certain that Lisa was killed for the books?"

"I give you exhibit A: a woman who buys ten books at a very hefty price, but there is now only one book, and that one remains because it was in a location the killer didn't search. My theory is holding up."

"So what's next, Ms. Holmes?"

"Let's get my truck out of jail, and ask about Lisa's rental car at the same time."

"I suppose we drive up to the impound lot, say we'll take the black beast over there, and by the way, do you mind if I search Lisa Heredia's rental car?"

I thought my remark was clever, but Megan didn't react all. "Something like that," was all she said.

The cop at the impound lot found Megan's little black dress as intriguing as the apartment complex manager. Megan's Scarlett O'Hara act didn't hurt, either. If anyone had asked me yesterday whether Megan Clark knew how to bat her eyelashes at a man, I would have said "not without laughing," and thought I was telling the truth. Today I believe eyelash-batting is directed by a particular gene in a woman's DNA. Of course, it helps that Megan's eyes are the color of the best Kentucky bourbon, with extra long lashes that match her hair. Whether it was the voice, the dress, the smile, or the whiskey eyes, the cop was out for the count five minutes after Megan looked up at him, an innocent child caught in the coils of a situation she neither understood nor could control. It was an Academy Award performance.

"I feel like I'm trapped in the Twilight Zone," she said to the cop. He believed her, but I didn't. She was too young to have watched Rod Serling, except maybe in reruns.

"I just don't know what to do," she cooed. I'd never heard a woman coo before. It was an interesting sound, resembling as it did that made by a fat pigeon on the trail of a particularly tasty bread crumb.

"I never thought just *knowing* a murder victim was enough to have the police pawing through my belongings. I was so *humiliated* when that young policeman searched my drawers where I keep my nighties and my undies." The way she said "undies" turned common underwear into something naughty. "Then they took my beautiful truck, and for what? They found it was as innocent as I am."

The cop kept nodding his head like one of those toy dogs you see in the back windows of some cars.

"And worst of all, Lisa Heredia—that's the victim's name—picked up my sack of books instead of hers after one of the meetings of our literary society, and had them in her car to return to me the night she was killed. And now I'll never get my books back, and one of them was autographed by *Annabel Edgars Crow*, who lives here in Amarillo, and I would hate to have her think I didn't care enough for her autograph to keep my book." Megan polished off this speech with a little catch in her voice as if she were about to cry.

"We didn't find any books in that rental car of hers," said the cop.

"You didn't?"

"No, ma'am, we sure didn't. Wasn't much of anything in that car, and I would of noticed a sack of books."

"Oh. Thank you, anyway. I must have left them somewhere else." With that remark Megan marched across the lot to her black beast, leaving the cop in a dazed condition, but not serious enough to require CPR.

19

It is stupidity rather than courage to refuse to recognize danger when it is close upon you.

—SHERLOCK HOLMES to Watson
in Arthur Conan Doyle's
"The Adventure of the Final Problem,"
The Memoirs of Sherlock Holmes, 1894

Megan parked her truck in the driveway, and dashed into her house to change into her Texas Crew T-shirt and cutoffs while assuring Rembrandt that she would be home again soon, and sat down to read the list of possessions taken from the black beast while waiting for Ryan to pick her up. He had really been obnoxious at the impound lot, skulking about in dark glasses and a Stetson pulled low over his forehead as if he were ashamed to admit he was with her. And he had worked his eyebrows overtime, raising one and then the other as commentary on her every word. If he objected to her flirting to elicit information, he would have to get over it. Maybe die-hard feminists felt flirting degraded the one who did it, but in Megan's opinion, flirting was half a woman's armament, and only a fool went into a battle of the sexes halfway to unilateral disarmament.

Megan was smiling to herself at her clever metaphor when a line on the inventory list caught her eye. She gasped and felt her heart slide down into her belly. She didn't own anything like that! She'd never owned anything like that. She felt sweat break out on her forehead and under her arms. Up until now she had been treating her suspect status as semi-serious, but not a real threat despite what she'd been telling Ryan. Not anymore. She was in real jeopardy.

Megan gave herself twenty-four hours at most until Jerry Carr arrested her for murder.

She climbed into Ryan's truck and glanced at her watch. "It's nearly time for shift change, so let's head to the bookstore—and park on the block behind the store. I don't want the cops to see your truck and get suspicious."

"They probably have my license number already, since they know I run with the big dog, namely you."

"They may," Megan said, ignoring his sarcasm. "Let's rub a little mud on your license plates before we leave."

"That's the best idea since the British decided to tax tea. Nothing will get you a second look faster than an illegible license plate, and I don't want to see Lieutenant Carr again today, thank you very much. A little bit of his company goes a long way."

"Then let's do what Poe recommended in *The Purloined Letter*."

"Hide in plain sight?"

"Yes. We'll throw an old drop cloth in the pickup bed, add a ladder or two, a few cans of paint, some brushes, and the cops will assume we're painters working on refurbishing some store or the other. They won't give us a second look. More important, they won't bother us while I go through the bookstore records." And most important, they wouldn't arrest her if they couldn't find her.

"I suppose you just happen to have a drop cloth and a few cans of paint?"

She nodded. "Left over from when my mother used to paint protest signs to use in demonstrations against the Department of Energy. My favorite was Fe, Fi, Fo,

Fum, Something Radioactive This Way Comes."

"If you change the wording to read Fe, Fi, Fo, Fum, Someone Stupid This Way Comes, it would describe us perfectly."

"Are you coming with me or not, Ryan? This is my life, and I'm not trusting Jerry Carr or Herb Jackson to see that I stay out of prison."

"They don't have a case against you, Megan. Herb was telling me that in his opinion the D.A. wouldn't even take the complaint, much less present it to the grand jury for indictment."

"Good for Herb, but that was before Special Crimes found my bloodstained clothes from the night Lisa was murdered. I had opportunity and I have Lisa's blood on my clothes. So, are you going to get the ladder and paint cans or not?"

Ryan loaded his truck and even drove it down a muddy alley to add verisimilitude to the image of a contract painter whose contracts had been a little sparse lately. Megan walked around the truck nodding her head. When pushed, Ryan was as good at masquerading, as anybody she knew. Herself, for instance. Her heart pounding and a cold spot in her stomach growing every minute, she climbed into the truck. Ryan might think this was a game she was playing to outwit the police and solve the case like her favorite amateur sleuths, and at first it was. Taunting—in a small way—the police, calling a meeting with passwords, but when the killer went after Agnes, Megan knew her cockeyed theory had validity. Now she had proof it did, but unfortunately the proof pointed at Megan Elizabeth Clark, librarian, forensic anthropologist, paleopathologist, and victim of a frame. Her life suddenly took on a surreal quality, as if reality had changed places with fiction. Maybe there was no real Megan Clark; maybe she was a creation of some mystery writer who then dropped her into a plot. Maybe all fictional characters believed they were real.

And maybe her elevator wasn't going all the way to the top floor these days.

She wrapped her arms around herself. She was shivering so hard, her teeth chattered.

"Megan, what's wrong? Are you cold, honey?"

There was that endearment again, and she didn't know how to respond now any better than she did the first time. Not only was she a murder suspect likely to be arrested on sight, but her bosom companion showed hints of wanting to change the rules of their relationship. Life was never simple, but Ryan just added an unexpected subplot.

"I'm scared," she said. And she was—of the police, of Ryan's feelings, and maybe a little bit of her own.

Ryan reached over and took her hand and held it all the way to Time and Again.

Ryan parked the truck a block away next to a corner, and Megan gestured toward the side street. "Let's go around the block and down the alley to Agnes's back door."

"What good will that do?" asked Ryan. "Our key's to the front door."

Megan pulled a key ring out of her pocket. "I took Agnes's keys while I was searching her apartment for the receipt books."

"I'm glad the criminal life is a hobby for you instead of a profession. You're too good at finding ways to get into places you have no business being in."

"I have business here," said Megan, trying several keys until she found the right one. "I'm trying to clear an innocent woman: me."

Agnes's apartment was filled with books. Where most women hung pictures, Agnes hung bookshelves. Her small living room had floor-to-ceiling shelves on two walls, with a comfortable couch and a chair with matching hassock on a third wall, along with lamps that could pass for spotlights. Agnes always told Megan that at her age a bright light was as good as a magnifying glass.

Down a short hall lined with narrow shelves just wide enough for paperbacks, Agnes's bedroom was a reader's paradise. A chaise longue sat in one corner with a low table to accommodate a coffee cup, a book, and a small reading lamp. Her queen-size bed had bookcases built into the headboard, and every inch of wall not occupied by a dresser and an antique highboy had shelves. Her guest bedroom was an office with large roll-top computer desk, a large filing cabinet, and a closet on one wall, and floor-to-ceiling bookshelves on the other three.

"I've died and gone to heaven," breathed Ryan, sitting down in Agnes's cushioned oak office chair. "What I wouldn't give for an office like this."

"You could add more bookshelves to your office, Ryan, but you would still have stacks of books on the floor. You're a piler, but it doesn't mean you're a bad person."

Megan pulled open the top drawer of the filing cabinet. "Agnes always keeps her current records in the top drawer, last year's in the second drawer, and so on for five drawers, five years. Then she stores the next five years in a filing cabinet in the closet. She says that if the IRS goes back more than ten years looking for back taxes, they will just have to send her to one of those country club federal prisons where you can play tennis and swim all day. She says that if the IRS can't catch her in ten years, then it's too bad, because she doesn't intend to smother in canceled checks."

Megan pulled out a stack of receipt books rubber-banded together. "Here we are, the rope with which we shall tie up a killer."

"Does Agnes write down title and author for every book she sells?" asked Ryan. "And make a note of the buyer's name and address?"

"No, just for the regulars. The odd customer or two

who stop in because they're on Sixth Street anyway just gets a cash-register-generated receipt, but regular customers want handwritten receipts on slips with the Time and Again logo. It's traditional and comfortable and makes them feel appreciated. It also gives them a record of their purchases written by Agnes herself. Readers like to keep track of what they buy, not only for tax purposes, but because they want a record of titles and authors. When I worked for Agnes, several customers kept a notebook listing of favorite authors and the titles they were missing. Agnes kept track on the computer of credit owed to those customers who only traded books. Violet would be one of those, but the members of our reading circle wouldn't, because we seldom bring back a book to trade. We just buy more."

"So there may not be a written receipt for Violet Winston?" asked Ryan.

"There has to be, Ryan, because obviously there was something special about the books she got the night she was murdered. I think Agnes would have given her a written receipt."

"Agnes told me that she gave Violet Winston some old, out-of-print paperbacks to show her appreciation for Violet's reading some of the new books Agnes ordered and making a recommendation on their target audience."

"Those old paperbacks again. What is it about them, Ryan? Are they suddenly very valuable and our killer knows it? But why wouldn't Agnes know, too? She keeps close tabs on the rare-book market."

"Maybe some of them are by famous authors writing mysteries under a pseudonym, or famous writers in another genre. A.B. Guthrie, the Pulitzer Prize winner for *Big Sky*, wrote four mysteries, *Murders at Moon Dance*, in 1943, and four others in the seventies and eighties, all set in Montana. They are supposed to be very fine books with extraordinary characterization, but nobody knows about them, or very few people, anyway. A first edition of one of those books would be valuable, wouldn't it, especially the first one?"

"I would think so," said Megan. "I didn't know Guthrie wrote anything but historical novels. Have you read them? Did you like them?"

Ryan flushed and coughed, and Megan wondered if she should slap him on the back. It was always so embarrassing to swallow the wrong way.

"I, uh, haven't gotten around to reading them," said Ryan, rubbing his eyes. "I've read his other novels, which are more in my field. I have so much reading to do that it's difficult to get to all of it." He coughed again and rubbed his eyes.

"Do you have something in your eye?" asked Megan.

"Allergy. Well, now, shall we get to these receipt books?" he asked, rubbing his hands together, then reaching for the stacks of yellow carbons.

"Let's divide them up and you look for the carbon of Violet's receipt—if there is one—and I'll look for the members of the reading circle," said Megan, picking up the receipt books and giving Ryan the earlier dates.

"Uh, just put my receipts aside," said Ryan. "I didn't get any out-of-print mysteries. No point in wasting your time reading the titles."

"Here's one of yours, but I'm not familiar with these titles and authors. *The Ox-Bow Incident* by Walter Van Tilburg Clark. I wonder if he's a relative."

Ryan made a grab for the receipt. "Give me that. I'll check it myself."

Megan straight-armed him with a move any running back would be proud of. "Just a minute, Ryan—some of the titles Agnes has marked 'OP,' which is the abbreviation for out-of-print. *Monte Walsh* by Jack Schaefer and *Sam Chance* by Benjamin Capps, *The Court-Martial of George Armstrong Custer* by Douglas C. Jones . . . Ryan, these are *Westerns!*"

"So? Do you have a problem with that?" he asked as

he reached over her shoulder and plucked the receipt out of her hands. "Presidents Eisenhower and Reagan read Westerns, famous scientists read Westerns, there's nothing wrong with reading Westerns."

"But we belong to a *mystery* discussion group!"

"You never asked me if I read mysteries, just told me that you had signed us up with the group."

"Don't get defensive about it, Ryan. I don't think any less of you."

"Just don't say anything about it, please. With all the revisionist historians hiding under every clump of sagebrush, I'd spend all my time writing essays to history journals defending my reading taste, and attacking them for trying to rewrite history when they never cite original sources in their papers. How do they know the private thoughts and beliefs of Lewis and Clark without reading the journals kept by the two men, and their subsequent letters and books? Most of them don't know that the term Native American was coined by a Washington bureaucrat in the 1970's for use on government forms. It's a meaningless label that further Balkanizes American society."

"You should talk to my mother. She's temporarily between causes. Seriously, though, I'll keep your secret. I devoured Zane Grey when I was younger. But tell me something, Ryan. Have you read a single selection for the discussion group?"

"Uh, no, but I was planning on reading this week's selection."

"*The Christie Caper?*"

"Yes, and I meant to ask you how Christie got away with using her name in the title of her book?"

Megan closed her eyes and wondered how an intelligent man could be without a clue in any field but his own. She opened her eyes and looked at Ryan's earnest face. "It's by Carolyn Hart, but never mind. Don't worry about keeping up with the group's reading list. It's probably better if you don't. Then you won't make a comment that results in a reenactment of the Custer massacre. This group takes no prisoners, Ryan. I think it would be best if you just came, snored through the discussion, and sampled the cookies afterward. It's what you've been doing all along and it's worked out well."

"I'm sorry, Megan."

"Don't apologize. After all I never asked if you wanted to join Murder by the Yard, I just signed you up."

"And I didn't mind, Megan. And I don't mind coming to the discussions even when I don't know what the devil or who the devil you're talking about. I like everyone, even that jackass, Randel Anderson. Best of all, I don't have to worry about what reckless pastime you'll take up next. You're safe with a discussion group."

"Ryan, I'm a murder suspect. There's a good chance I'll be in jail before dark."

His earnest look changed to a worried one that bordered on panic. "I won't let you go to prison, Megan. We'll buy false Social Security cards, change our names, dye your hair . . ."

"Have you ever for one second thought I might be guilty, Ryan?" asked Megan, blinking back tears.

"No! I'd sooner suspect Santa Claus of shooting Rudolph." He stood up and laced his fingers through her hair, and tipping her head back, kissed her on the lips. "I've never doubted you—even when we were illegally entering Lisa's apartment."

He sat down again and methodically began thumbing through the yellow carbons, while Megan licked her lips and wondered how she ought to interpret that kiss. As soon as she identified the murderer and turned the case over to Special Crimes, she and Ryan must discuss their relationship fully and honestly, holding nothing back. But first things first. She had to identify the killer or learn to like living in a cramped cell. She picked up one of the little books of yellow carbons.

The small apartment was quiet with only the sound of the furnace coming on or going off. Agnes didn't consider the temperature bearable under 85 degrees, so the office was uncomfortably warm to Megan. Or maybe the presence of Ryan, who suddenly looked bigger, stronger, more masculine, *more male*, than she had ever noticed him being before, had something to do with her feeling claustrophobic, as if she wanted to shed her skin and become someone else freer and more . . . what?

As she struggled with these unfamiliar thoughts, she nearly overlooked Rosemary's receipt. Dated the first meeting of Murder by the Yard, the receipt listed ten out-of-print books, but all of them familiar to Megan as written by contemporaries of Christie and Sayers. She could understand the twins needing to include these particular authors in their bibliography, but saw nothing about the titles that was the least unique or that would set the rare-book world to raving.

Immediately after Rosemary's receipt was Lorene's, which was similar in composition to Rosemary's—out-of-print books by contemporaries of Christie and Sayers. The only difference between the two receipts were the titles.

Quickly she found Randel's and Herb's receipts. Nothing unusual in either man's purchases. Randel was evidently completing a library of Edgar winners, because his list included *A Kiss Before Dying* by Ira Levin, *Beast in View* by Margaret Millar, and *Mortal Consequences* by Julian Symons, which won a Critical/Biographical Edgar. Herb's was more prosaic: a selection of Erle Stanley Gardner's Perry Mason novels including one of Megan's favorites, *The Case of the Sleepwalker's Niece,* and several courtroom dramas by less well-known but more accomplished writers. Candi's receipt listed only critical works on the mystery genre, including *1001 Mid-*

nights: The Aficionado's Guide to Mystery and Detective Fiction by Bill Pronzini and Marcia Muller, two among the scores of Megan's favorite writers.

"What about Candi?" asked Megan. "She always knows so many obscure facts about mysteries and mystery writers. Could she be the one?"

"The one what?"

"The murderer, Ryan."

"Candi? Nobody who blushes as much as she does can be a murderer."

"I don't think blushing and murder are mutually exclusive, Ryan. And she is the only member of the reading circle who might know as much about rare mysteries as Agnes."

"You might as well suspect Rosemary and Lorene."

"I've considered them," said Megan, wrinkling her brow. "But I just can't visualize Rosemary slitting Lisa's throat. It's such a messy way to commit murder and Rosemary is so, well, neat in her person. Now, if Lisa had turned up poisoned, I might seriously suspect her. Poison is more the weapon of choice for gentlewomen."

"My God, Megan! You're too young to be so cynical."

Megan shrugged. "I'm an anthropologist and archaeologist with a specialty in paleopathology. I've spent my whole academic life studying the behavior and artifacts of civilizations. There's not much new under the sun, Ryan. Murder has always been with us. I can make a persuasive argument in favor of every member of the reading circle being guilty."

"But why, Megan? What is the motive?"

"I don't know, but I don't believe it's something so commonplace as greed."

Eagerly she picked up Lisa Heredia's receipt, but it listed only paperback copies of all of Annabel's titles.

"Ryan, why would Lisa Heredia buy all of Annabel's titles when she must have already read all the books and probably owned copies. I mean, she came to Amarillo hoping to sign Annabel as her client, so surely she had already read her work."

Ryan shook his head. "I don't know unless she wanted them for props, you know, toss them around on end tables and kitchen counters, tuck one in the old handbag for show."

"I don't think she'd invite Annabel to that horrible apartment. I wouldn't if I were trying to impress a writer."

"Maybe Annabel wouldn't notice if her taste in furnishings is as bad as her taste in clothes." He handed Megan a receipt. "Here's Violet Winston's last purchase, or at least it's the only receipt I could find and it's dated February. Isn't that when she was killed?"

"Yes, and this receipt is dated the day before Jerry brought me Rembrandt, so this must be the one we're looking for." Megan scanned the list, then looked up at Ryan. "One of the out-of-print books is the same as one Lisa bought: *The Case of the Poisoned Tea Caddy.* I don't think it's a coincidence that both women bought that particular title, and both women are murder victims. I wish I knew something about that book, but I don't. And it's an old paperback, so none of the book editors at that time would have reviewed it. Damn it, Ryan, what's the secret of that book?"

Without waiting for an answer, Megan put aside Violet's receipt and flipped quickly through the yellow carbons and pulled out two. Again she scanned the lists of books, then whistled. "Let's go, Ryan. I found something!"

Ryan laid down his carbons and rose, fishing his keys out of his pocket. "What is it, another copy of *The Poisoned Tea Caddy?*"

Megan tucked the carbons into her hip pocket. "That, too, but something better and something weird at the same time. You remember how Rosemary and Lorene misplaced their books?"

"Yes," said Ryan, looking bewildered, a recurring expression, Megan noticed.

"Rosemary and Lorene each bought twenty-five old out-of-print paperbacks. How do you misplace or forget twenty-five paperbacks?'

"I don't know. I've forgotten one book before or misplaced one, but twenty-five? That would take a conscious effort."

"Exactly!" exclaimed Megan. "But I don't think it was the twins who made the conscious effort."

20

If you knew anything about detective work, you'd know that the most seemingly impossible conditions are often the easiest to explain.

—FLEMING STONE in Carolyn Wells's
Vicky Van, 1918

Megan called Rosemary and Lorene before we left Agnes's apartment, so we wouldn't make a wasted trip. "I don't know what Jerry Carr is planning," she said, "so I don't want to go home. I would be up the creek without a paddle if he arrested me before I know the answer and can prove it."

I was still wondering what she thought of my kiss, whether she put it down to friendly excitement of the moment, or whether she read something more into it, so I didn't react to what she said for a few seconds. When I did, I turned off the ignition and removed the key. "What's this about proving it? You mean you'll write a report detailing all the evidence and how one piece relates to another and how it all supports a conclusion? That's what you mean, isn't it?"

"Certainly I'll have to provide a written report, Ryan. You don't think left-brained Lieutenant Carr will accept anything he can't see in black and white, do you?"

"I was apprehensive for a minute. Remember you're the woman who wanted to bungee jump from the rim of Palo Duro Canyon except the park ranger threatened to have you arrested."

"I don't see the connection. That was a new sport that looked like it might be fun. This is serious."

She wore that frown again that gave her mother fits, but I decided it was cute—a word I would never use in her hearing. It made her look like a worried twelve-year-old. I would never say that aloud either.

"The connection is you're a daredevil, always risking a broken neck on some foolish stunt. It wouldn't surprise me if you planned on confronting the murderer and ordering him to turn himself into the police."

"I thought about it, but I don't think that would work at all, at least not at present," she said, rocking in her seat in her impatience. Like a lot of mildly obsessive personalities, once Megan made up her mind, come hell or high water, she would bull ahead toward whatever goal she had set. Sometimes she didn't need a goal; sometimes an impulse would do.

"Let's go, Rosemary's waiting. It's her bridge night and she doesn't want to miss it. She saw the hostess buying the prize for high score at Hasting's Books, Music and Video, and it was a copy of Patricia Cornwell's new book. Rosemary plans to win it."

I was relieved that even Megan used her common sense sometimes. "Now, what is it we're going to ask Rosemary? I'm a little unclear on that point," I said as I eased out into the five o'clock traffic on Sixth Street. A patrol car was coming toward us in the opposite lane of traffic, and Megan slid down in the seat as much as her safety belt allowed.

"I'm going to ask her some questions about her forgetfulness," said Megan to her belly button as she leaned over until her head was below the level of the dashboard.

"I don't think I'd do that, Megan. I remember my grandmother was very sensitive about her forgetfulness until the day she forgot her own name. My mother made her a nametag to wear around her neck with her address and phone number on it, so whoever found her could bring her back home. Grandmother always said that she met more nice people after she forgot her name than she ever did before when she remembered it."

"I'm sure your grandmother was a terrific lady, but I don't think Rosemary is quite ready for a nametag."

"Actually my grandmother was an old witch who thumped us kids over the head with her thimble any time we messed around with her 'stuff' as she called it," I said, pulling into the driveway of a three-story Depression era mansion on Tyler Street, the kind with a gazebo in the back yard and the maid's apartment above the garage.

Rosemary answered the door herself, smiling and waving us in. I was secretly disappointed. I always wanted to be invited in by a real butler who said, "This way to the withdrawing room, sir," whatever a withdrawing room is.

Rosemary led us to what I guess you would call the conservatory, a pleasant room with plants hanging from the ceiling, growing in pots along the tall windows that made up the south wall, and blooming in planters on either side of a rattan swing big enough to sit in. On the west wall was a cabinet of lacquered cane next to a bamboo plant that reached the ceiling. The floor I'm sure was real marble. Megan was right when she said Rosemary had money.

Our hostess invited us to sit down on a rattan couch upholstered in lime-green with white willow branches all over it, and offered us tea or lemonade. I expected Madeira in fine crystal. It was that kind of house.

"We don't have time, Rosemary. You'd miss your bridge game, and the police may be looking for me. Lieutenant Carr thinks I murdered Lisa."

Rosemary sank down on an ottoman as if her legs had suddenly given way. She plucked a handkerchief from somewhere about her person and patted her cheeks and forehead.

"Rosemary, are you all right? Can I get you some water?"

Rosemary pressed her hand against her chest and shook her head. "Water, hell! Get me some Southern Comfort out of that cabinet against the wall, and Megan, pour it in a big glass." She blotted the back of her neck with her handkerchief, exhaled, and looked at me. "Did I hear her correctly, Dr. Stevens—Ryan? Did she really say that handsome lieutenant suspected her of murdering Lisa?"

"I think she's exaggerating myself, but he did search her house and her truck and took the clothes she wore the night that Lisa was killed."

Megan handed Rosemary her Southern Comfort. "Don't try to downplay the situation, Ryan. Yes, I believe Jerry suspects me. He doesn't want to, but the only evidence available points to me, so he doesn't have an option."

"The bloodstained clothing?" asked Rosemary.

Megan nodded, her face so pale it was almost blue-white.

Rosemary clasped Megan's hand. "Oh, that's serious. I was reading a mystery last night in which the heroine was found bending over the body with blood on her hands. Naturally the police immediately suspected her, but . . ."

"Stop it, both of you!" I shouted. Two shocked faces turned toward me, and I lowered my voice. "This is not a murder mystery by Agatha Christie."

"No, I wasn't reading one of Agatha's stories, Dr. Stevens—it was a new author who showed promise. I can't recall her name right now, but I'll remember it in a moment. I've told you how my memory is slipping lately." She took a huge swallow from her glass that would have had me shuddering from the fire racing down my esophagus, but it didn't seem to bother her.

"I want to talk to you about your memory, Rosemary," said Megan, taking a tiny sip from a glass smaller than Rosemary's but not by much. Everybody was knocking back strong liquor but me. Maybe I was the designated driver and Megan had forgotten to tell me.

"I think that you and Lorene might be the murderer's second and third victims, Violet Winston being the first and Lisa the fourth," continued Megan after another, larger swallow.

"Violet Winston was my cleaning lady," said Rosemary with a delicate belch. "Such a wonderful woman. But why do you say she was the murderer's first victim, Megan?"

"Because she and Lisa both had the same out-of-print paperback when they were killed. *The Case of the Poisoned Tea Caddy* was its title. I think that's a little too much coincidence, don't you?"

"Absolutely!" agreed Rosemary. "Particularly since I bought the same paperback. If only I hadn't lost my book bag."

"You didn't lose it, Rosemary," said Megan. "It was stolen—stolen right off your hall table. And I don't think you forgot to lock your doors either. I think someone jimmied your lock to gain entrance and steal those paperbacks."

This was the first time I had heard that particular explanation for the missing books, but it made more sense than believing Rosemary was ga-ga. Any slippage in her mental gears was due to ingestion of Southern Comfort, not a rusty cog.

Rosemary rose from the ottoman, tottered a moment before finding her balance, and led us to her kitchen door. "I found this door unlocked the same morning I missed my books."

Megan and I knelt down to check the lock. There weren't any scratches around the lock on either side of the door that I could see. I stood up and turned around to face Rosemary. "I don't see any evidence of someone forcing the door, Rosemary. Could someone have stolen your key?"

"Nobody has keys to my house except my children, who both live in Houston. I didn't give out keys to anyone else . . ." Her voice trailed off to a whisper. "Except to Violet Winston so she could clean the mornings I volunteered at the hospital."

"Another connection," said Megan.

"Another clue," said Rosemary.

"Another coincidence," I said, and both ladies stared daggers at me. A cliché is a cliché for a reason, and the reason is that no other phrase so perfectly describes the displeased kind of look one may be a target of after making what others—in this case, Rosemary and Megan—believe is an idiotic statement totally at odds with the truth.

"Let me explain before you both question my intelligence and imagination," I said, gesturing with my hands held palm-out like a traffic cop. "Agnes sells out-of-print books, so what is so unusual about three copies of an out-of-print book? I'm sure I could find multiple copies of the same book in Time and Again. It just indicates that one, the print run of that particular book was larger than the average, or two, that title was distributed more widely in this area."

"Can you explain why two of the people who bought that particular title were murder victims, and the third person the target of a burglar who only stole out-of-print books of which that title was one?" asked Megan. "I bought out-of-print books and no one killed me. Many of the Edgar winners that Randel bought were out of print and he's still alive," said Megan while Rosemary nodded agreement.

"Can you explain why the murderer may—and I emphasize *may*—have stolen Rosemary's key after murdering Violet in February, but never used it until now? This is the first week of May. Was he waiting for Rosemary to purchase *The Case of the Poisoned Tea Caddy* before he broke into her house? Think about it, Megan."

"I have thought about it, and your guess is right. He didn't break in until he had a reason."

"*The Case of the Poisoned Tea Caddy?*"

"Yes. There was no reason to break in before that."

"And what about Lorene? Do you think she has a copy of that particular title?" I asked with a heavy hand on the sarcasm.

"No," replied Rosemary. "We never bought duplicate titles, just traded them back and forth if either of us thought a title belonged in our article. That way we could read twice as many books." She shivered and rubbed her hands up and down her arms. "I'm calling the locksmith today to change the locks, and that security company that keeps calling me about installing some kind of fancy security system. The very idea that some-one was creeping around my house while I was asleep terrifies me. It remains me of the Manson Gang. They used to do that, break in houses at night while the own-ers were there, and crawl around on the floor without waking up anyone just to prove they could do it. Vincent Bugliosi wrote about it in *Helter Skelter*."

I didn't blame Rosemary. I would install a nine-foot fence with razor wire at the top and buy two of the biggest Dobermans in Amarillo.

Megan patted Rosemary's shoulder, then pulled the yellow copies of the receipts from her back pocket. "Lorene bought a copy of *Murder Betwixt and Between*, and so did Lisa. Lorene was robbed and Lisa was killed."

"Why were Lisa and Violet the ones who were killed? Why not Rosemary and Lorene?" I asked, pointing out what I considered the fatal flaw in Megan's reading of the murderer's game plan.

"It's really very simple," said Megan, "if you weren't so determined not to see. Violet had to be killed because of Rembrandt, her beagle which is now my beagle. No way can a burglar set foot within a hundred yards of my house without Rembrandt barking loud enough to wake the dead. So the murderer kills Violet while she's sitting in front of the antique store because he can't break into her house and steal her books. If Violet hadn't owned Rembrandt, I wonder if she would have been killed at all."

"That makes some sense," I grudgingly admitted. "But what about Lisa? She didn't own a dog."

"She also lived in an apartment house with people coming and going all day and all night. The murderer couldn't take the chance of standing in that hall with doors to three other apartments opening on to that same hall. He might be lucky and he might not, so he killed Lisa in front of the bookstore and took her key. Then he could get into her apartment easily and quickly at will."

Megan was buildidng her case with the obsessive's attention to detail. "What about Lorene?" I asked.

"The killer broke into her house and stole her books without her knowing it," Megan said. "Otherwise she would be dead."

All three of us shivered.

"Lorene lives on Jackson, north of I-40 and close to downtown," said Megan.

"Not a great neighborhood," I said. "Or rather, it's a mixed neighborhood that's not sure if it's moving up or down the economic scale. Some of the houses are huge and luxurious, while others are 1920's bungalows. Some are well maintained and others are rooming houses or have yards decorated with wrecked cars. I can see why Lorene might be apprehensive about forgetting to lock her door."

I parked in front of a white bungalow shaded by two giant elm trees, with colorful flower beds, pansies I thought, and a pale green ground cover the name of which I couldn't even guess at. Beyond roses, daisies, iris, and pansies—maybe—I was a botanically challenged individual. My wife always took care of the horticultural end of our marriage, which I greatly appreciated since any plant that pollinates—which is nearly all of them—makes me sneeze. I've hired a lawn service since my wife's death, or occasionally Megan tends the flower beds. I guess she was fated to be an archaeologist because she loves digging in the dirt.

Lorene answered the door. "Come in, Megan, Dr. Stevens. I've just taken a pan of peanut butter cookies out of the oven. Can I offer you some with coffee?"

I was quick to accept before Megan got to state her case. If I was her volunteer chauffeur, then I was staying long enough to eat a cookie. "Sounds good to me, Lorene," I said, controlling my saliva flow enough to avoid slobbering on my collar. "And my name's Ryan. Calling me Dr. Stevens makes me feel like I ought to give you a grade."

She laughed and ushered us into an honest-to-God American Arts and Crafts-style living room, with dark paneling, stained glass panes on the upper half of the windows, a little cubbyhole next to the fireplace with cushioned window seats, and an authentic Morris chair. I don't know which I coveted more: her living room complete with Morris chair, or a dozen of her peanut butter cookies.

When we were seated—I in the Morris chair—with coffee and a tray of cookies, Lorene nervously clasped her hands and looked expectantly at Megan. "You said you had some questions to ask about the books I misplaced? I can't tell you much. I selected them on the basis of the copyright date, so I could be sure each was written after Christie and Sayers established their reputations. I didn't pay much attention to the cover copy. With those early paperbacks—and recent ones for that matter—cover copy was exaggeration and adjectives. I don't know how many times I've read that an author has written a masterpiece, when he's really just written a mediocre story. The more hype on the cover, the less likely the book is to tell an interesting story. I wish some writers would understand that a dedicated reader wants a good story first, and a masterpiece second."

"You did buy a copy of *Murder Betwixt and Between*?" asked Megan. "Can you remember anything about the plot line?"

"Yes, I bought that one. I thought it had a wonderful title, and maybe the writer had an imagination to match. But the cover copy didn't say much, just that the stingy stepmother was murdered in a most unusual way. That can cover a lot of ground. I can think of lots of ways to commit murder besides using a blunt instrument, can't you?"

I wasn't sure to whom Lorene addressed the question, since she was looking from one of us to the other, but I was quick to answer in the negative. Having anyone think I might spend my leisure time planning unique ways to kill my fellow man made me nervous. "I don't think much about murder, so beyond shooting or stabbing, and the blunt instrument, I'm at a loss as how to best do away with a victim."

"You don't have to come up with an original idea, Ryan," said Lorene. "Just think of all the wonderful ways our favorite authors commit murder."

In the Western, the favorite weapons are the Colt .45, the Navy Colt, or a Winchester rifle. There is also hanging, but that's a legal means of execution—unless we're talking of vigilantes, or a rancher who catches a cattle or horse thief in the act and applies a little rough justice by means of a rope over the nearest tree branch. In comparison to mystery writers, Western writers prefer their deaths short, sweet, and straightforward. Bang, bang, thank you, ma'am.

"I haven't given a lot of thought to the means of murder, as much as I have to what Megan calls 'the human elements,' so I'd make an unimaginative murderer." I saw Megan smile and was glad she found something to amuse her. I wasn't amused. I felt like a fraud on the eve of his discovery.

"That just proves that you're a kind and gentle man," said Lorene.

Kind and gentle? That's nearly as bad as being called a sensitive man. I've never seen the so-called sensitive man get the girl.

"Not to be unfaithful to my favorite, Dorothy Sayers, but I have to admit that Christie's using thallium to poison the victims in *The Pale Horse* is brilliant," said Lorene. "I think it's my favorite poisoning mystery. What's your favorite means of murder, Megan?"

"*The Speckled Band*, the Sherlock Holmes short story, is one of them. I thought Conan Doyle's use of the snake was clever, and it would work today. Who's going to question a poisonous snake bite?"

"You said one of them. What else do you like?" asked Lorene.

"*The Winds of Evil* by Arthur Upfield in which the murderer suffered from what Upfield called somnambulism brought on by the winds blowing from the outback. I like it so much because it reminds me of our own winds in the Panhandle, and how newcomers are nearly driven mad, but if we grow up here, the wind is just background."

We sat quietly for a few minutes, and I thought about this Upfield that Megan mentioned. He understood about wind. I might have to read that book.

Megan set her coffee cup down and patted her mouth with a napkin. "Lorene, which door did you forget to lock the night you misplaced your bag of books?"

"The kitchen door," said Lorene, looking puzzled. "What difference does it make?"

"I noticed that your front door is a solid piece of wood, very heavy, with a dead bolt."

"Yes, I had a dead bolt installed several years ago when the neighborhood started attracting transient renters. What's this about, Megan?"

Megan wiped her hands, laid the napkin on the tray by her coffee cup, and stood up. "May I see your kitchen door before I answer?"

Looking more and more puzzled, Lorene led the way to her kitchen, another dream room of dark woods and cabinets that would bring a fortune on the antique market. She pointed to the door, a flimsy-looking affair with veneer covering its surface and a glass pane in the top half.

"This isn't original to the house, is it?" I said, kneeling down to check out the lock.

"No, that door was splintered and ruined when my husband and I bought the house, and we couldn't afford to buy a solid wood door like the front one, so we bought a hollow-core door and replaced it whenever we needed to."

Megan locked the door, then did something I didn't observe and the door swung open. She held up an American Express card. "Simple. Slip a credit card or any other piece of stiff plastic between the door and the frame and flip the lock back. Lorene, I'd get a solid core door with a dead bolt, or else install another kind of lock."

Lorene turned pale and leaned back against one of the kitchen cabinets. "I've read about that trick a hundred times in mysteries and never thought to apply it to my own doors."

She turned even paler as Megan explained her theory of a nocturnal intruder who stole Lorene's books. "Now I know what a rape victim feels like," Lorene said. "I've been violated and humiliated by some *bastard* who came in my house and touched my things, stared at me while I was sleeping. I want to take a bath, but I'm afraid to. It's like *Psycho* by Robert Bloch except nobody stabbed me. It's terrible not to feel safe even in your bathroom."

I wedged a chair under the door knob, and we left Lorene on the phone with a local contractor, offering to pay him a bonus if he installed a solid core door with a dead bolt before the sun went down.

"I want to apologize for doubting you, Megan," I said as we pulled away from Lorene's house. "Your theory, wild and convoluted as it is, may be on target."

Megan had that intent look on her face again. "I still have one more supposition to verify as fact; then I'll have the solution."

"What fact is that?" I asked.

"Drive me to Jared Johnson's house. I think Jared holds the final piece to the puzzle."

"Are you going to tell me what that piece is?"

"I'll let Jared tell us both."

"Then we can turn the case over to Jerry Carr, signed, sealed, and ready for delivery," I said.

"Not exactly."

21

Murder is always a mistake; one should never do anything that one cannot talk about after dinner.

—LORD HENRY WOTTON to Dorian Gray
in Oscar Wilde's
The Picture of Dorian Gray, 1891

Megan sat in Ryan's truck, reluctant to step inside Jared's home again. If Jerry Carr had used his influence to get the Johnsons help, then well and good—if the family would accept welfare. She knew many who would not, their pride driving them to struggle along as best they could. Generally they pulled themselves out of poverty, and kudos to them, but Leon Johnson was fighting an unequal battle. A one-armed, one-eyed man had two strikes against him before the battle even started, but with help to feed and clothe his family, maybe he could explore using his mind instead of his body. He seemed intelligent enough to talk to and with a few courses at Amarillo College, then perhaps West Texas A&M University after that, Leon Johnson could find his way to a better life.

"Are you getting out?" asked Ryan, holding her door open.

Megan slid out of the truck. "It hurts to walk in that house, Ryan."

"I know it does, but look at it from another perspective. They only lack 'stuff,' Megan. They're rich in what's important. With a little help—if they'll take it—the Johnson family will be fine, but don't push them. You're a fixer, but some people want to fix themselves."

Megan nodded. Everything Ryan said was true, even pointing out her character flaw. She was a fixer or a pushy woman, whichever way one might classify her. Like it or not—and she really tried to curb her impulses to "fix" things—Megan Clark was her mother's daughter, and there was no bigger fixer in the Panhandle. It was like being born into a family of alcoholics: The urge was always there.

Ryan knocked on the door, and Megan let him take the lead while she tamped down her obsession with correcting whatever was wrong in the world.

Mrs. Johnson answered the door, looking little different from their first visit. "Miz Clark, are you here to see Jared? He's feeling better than he was and is like to drive me to drink. I'd appreciate a visitor for him. The Social Security folks stopped by the other day with some papers Leon needs me to help him fill out."

Megan smiled. "Dr. Stevens and I will entertain Jared long enough for you to help your husband. Is he applying for disability?" She felt Ryan pinch her arm, and knew he was telling her to mind her own business.

"He didn't much want to, but I talked him into it. I call it a breather until we can catch up on the bills."

"Maybe he could take a few courses at Amarillo College," said Megan, and felt Ryan pinch her again. She didn't care. If nothing else good came out of this case, at least Leon Johnson got a chance.

Mrs. Johnson tilted her head to study Megan. "I thought that policeman sent the Social Security folks out here, but it was you, wasn't it?"

Megan hesitated, picking her words carefully. "I told the policeman to call them and a few other people. I hope you're not mad."

"I'm not, but Leon's got his pride hurt, so maybe you

better not say anything about it. You know how men are."

Megan wasn't sure that she did, but she nodded anyway. Growing up without a father left her handicapped when it came to reading men. She didn't even understand exactly why Ryan kissed her.

"We'll go on back to Jared's room if that's all right, Mrs. Johnson," said Ryan, taking a firm grip on Megan's arm.

"You know your way, I guess," said Mrs. Johnson.

"We do," said Ryan, nearly pushing Megan along.

Jared was sitting up in bed playing with the plastic truck he'd bought with the tooth fairy money, his face, arms, hands, and even scalp covered with red, scaly scabs. He grinned, exposing the gap where his front tooth had been before he gave it to Megan.

"Hey, it's the tooth fairy lady. You been talking to any more fairies?"

"No, but I've been thinking a lot about witches since I visited you last, and I need your help."

Jared scratched the top of his head. "I can't stand guard for another couple of days, Miz Clark. I'm a whole lot better, but I promised my ma that I wouldn't go out until she says I can. I don't know if she'd let me or not."

Megan clasped his hand, scaly spots notwithstanding. "No, I don't want you to stand guard, Jared. I want you to tell me about the first time you saw the witch."

Jared fidgeted, looking around his room as if he'd never seen it before. "I'm scared," he said in a voice that trembled on the verge of breaking out in sobs.

Megan sat on the bed and hauled the little boy onto her lap and held him tightly. "Dr. Stevens and I will not let the witch get you, cross my heart and hope to die."

Jared laid his head on Megan's shoulder and looked at Ryan. "Do you promise, too?"

"Absolutely," said Ryan. "And remember, I'm packing a water gun."

Jared didn't say anything for so long that Megan felt the urge to fidget, too. Finally, he spoke in a soft voice that both Megan and Ryan leaned closer to hear. "You got to promise not to tell the cops, 'cause she's a real smart witch. She'd know if you told, and she'd come hurt me."

Megan held up her hand. "I promise never to tell the police what you told me, Jared, but someday you'll have to tell Lieutenant Carr yourself. You'll know when the right time comes."

Ryan bent to whisper in her ear. "Megan, you can't tell him that. He has to tell Jerry Carr what he saw."

"And he will—when the right time comes. My first obligation is to keep Jared safe, and if that means we wait until we have more evidence, then so be it. I won't risk Jared by gambling that Jerry Carr will buy a bird in a bush when he thinks he has me in his hand. And I won't let you risk Jared either, so give me your word that you'll wait."

She could see Ryan becoming more and more frustrated. "Megan," he said. "You're no amateur sleuth in one of your mystery novels."

"I'm not Nancy Drew, Ryan. There's nothing amateurish in my methods." She looked down at Jared. "Go on, Jared."

"He ain't promised," said Jared, pointing at Ryan.

"Promise him, Ryan, or go sit in the truck while Jared tells me. And if you call Jerry, I'll refuse to say a word and so will Jared. And Jared won't break either. I know what kind of kid he is because I was just like him."

It wasn't often that she saw Ryan caught on the horns of a dilemma, but he was seconds away from being impaled. She wished she wasn't responsible, but she didn't wish it enough to take back her words.

He capitulated. "I'd never go behind your back, Megan. I promise—not a word until you tell me differently."

He was more honorable than she, Megan reflected, since she'd go behind his back without thinking twice if the stakes were high enough—like a little boy's life. "Go on, Jared, tell us about the witch."

Jared wiped his nose on his sleeve, then began, his voice as soft as before. "It was winter time and real cold. It was February—I know because I can read a calendar—and I was down on Sixth Street playing spy."

"How do you play spy, Jared?" asked Ryan, kneeling down so he and Jared were eye to eye. He sounded interested, as if he were talking to another adult, and Megan thought again that he was better with kids than she.

"I creep along from planter to planter, and sneak down alleys. I'm real careful about peeking around corners, and I ain't ever been caught. And besides, if kids are careful, and don't knock anything over or make much noise, grownups don't see them."

"Is that what you were doing in February when you saw the witch?" asked Megan.

"Sort of. I was practicing tailing—you know, following somebody so they don't see you. Anyway, I was following the lady with the book bag who just came out of the bookstore, and I was being real careful so nobody saw me. 'Course there wasn't nobody anyway. It was real cold and nobody was on the street except me and the lady. That's how come I seen the witch, but she didn't see me. I was crouching real still in the alley next to where the lady was sitting down, and I peeked around the corner just in time to see the window break. I ducked back and my stomach was hurting like I was about to throw up, I was so scared. The alarm bells went off in the store, and I took another quick peek. The lady was turned round like she was going to look in the window, and there was a bright red spot on her back. I could see it in the streetlight in front of the store. I was so scared

I couldn't move or say anything, and that's when I saw the witch drive up on the sidewalk going the wrong way. She leaned out of the car, and grabbed the lady's books and purse. I got a real good look at her because the light came on inside the car when she opened the door. Anyhow, she slammed her car door and took off and so did I."

"He's an eyewitness," said Ryan in a low voice.

"I should have caught on sooner," said Megan. "He kept telling me the 'witch hurt a lady,' but I never made the connection. Not until I guessed Violet was killed for her books, then remembered that Mrs. Johnson said there was a period in February that Jared stayed home. Then I knew his witch was real."

"Jared, could you tell us what the witch looked like?" asked Ryan. "You've seen her and I haven't."

"You have, too. She goes in the bookstore every time you do."

"I must be too old to know a witch when I see one, Jared," said Ryan. "Only kids recognize witches no matter how they disguise themselves. That's why we're asking you."

Jared snuggled down against Megan, and she was shocked by how natural it felt to be holding him. It must be something genetic that kicked in without any conscious thought on her part. She couldn't help contrasting the peaceful domestic picture she and Jared made with the words he spoke that revealed a murderer.

Ryan sat down on the floor as if his knees suddenly gave way. "My God, Megan, do you know who he's describing?"

"I suspected it when I realized that three different women bought the same old paperback, and two of them are dead, but I wanted to talk to Jared just to be sure."

"We've got to tell Jerry Carr."

"We promised Jared. Besides, we don't have any proof. I'm still the only one in the circle who had the opportunity and against whom there is any physical evidence at all."

"So tell Jerry and let him find the proof. That's his job, Megan! It's what he does for a living!"

Megan heard Ryan, but his voice seemed to come from someplace far away, or else she had cotton in her ears. She wondered if her mother experienced a similar sensation when one of her supporters urged her to compromise with the government, like she heard the sound of people's voices, but the words were in a foreign language.

"So we break our promise and tell Jerry that a six-year-old boy saw a witch kill Violet Winston three months before Lisa's murder, and Jerry barrels out here to interview Jared. What do you think happens then? Does the D.A. go to court on the word of a kid and nothing else? In your dreams, Ryan. I'd be the one sitting in the dock."

"Jerry can get a search warrant for the clothes. Surely they'll have Lisa's blood on them. And the books, he'll find the books," said Ryan.

Megan shook her head. "Sure he will, Ryan—like the police found the bloody knife and clothes in the O. J. Simpson case. He'll find zip, zero, nothing, not even ashes from burned books."

"You can't be sure of that, Megan."

"I'm sure enough not to bet forty years without parole."

"So what are you going to do with this information? Sit on it? For how long? Or are you planning to let a murderer go free?" demanded Ryan, standing over her and Jared like a recording angel taking Megan's statement on Judgment Day.

"I have a plan."

22

Real crime detection lies not in the microscope and test-tube, but in asking innumerable questions and weeding out the answers.

—INSPECTOR HARRY CHARITON in
Clifford Witting's
Measure for Murder, 1941

I argued with Megan all the way home, but she's the most obstinate woman God ever put on this earth, so I achieved nothing but a hoarse voice. Actually, I did accomplish something else. Megan insisted in crouching on the floor of my truck, so any number of drivers stared at the spectacle of a man yelling at an empty front seat. I hoped nobody I knew saw me.

I turned into my driveway and stopped. "We're home, Megan, you can sit up now."

She looked up at me from her seat on the passenger side floorboard. Her hair was a mass of wild curls, and violet circles underlined each eye. She not only looked exhausted, she looked apprehensive, and for the first time since Jerry Carr pushed that search warrant across his desk at Megan, I was scared.

"Megan, are you telling me everything?" I asked, my heart and stomach icy cold, while sweat beaded along my hairline.

"Drive into your garage, Ryan. I don't want anyone watching the house to see me get out of the truck."

"Damn it all, Megan!"

She closed her eyes and looked drained, as if she lacked the energy to hold them open. "Please, Ryan, drive in the garage."

I gave in to her plea. I didn't know what was wrong, but something was—something worse than a few blood-stained clothes for which Megan had a believable explanation. I drove into the garage, turned off the ignition, and stretched for the benefit of whoever was watching—if indeed anyone was.

"Tell me," I demanded, and do it fast because I can't sit here very long without somebody getting suspicious."

"Get out of the truck and unload it, but slowly so you can listen," said Megan's disembodied voice from the floorboard.

I slid out of the truck and left the door open like people occasionally do, so I could hear Megan's whisper. I lifted two cans of paint out of the pickup bed and glanced around the garage as if I couldn't decide where to put them. "Talk," I ordered out of the side of my mouth.

"Special Crimes found a hunting knife in my pickup," Megan said, her voice shaking like she was freezing to death. "It's not mine, Ryan. Mine was in my digging kit in my bedroom. I've never owned two hunting knives."

I froze, a paint can in each hand. "How long have you known?"

"Since before you picked me up. There was a note on the inventory list I had to sign. I never noticed until I got home and read the list carefully. I didn't tell you because I didn't want you demanding to see the lieutenant and making a scene in general. Once the police lab checks that knife, they'll find Lisa Heredia's blood on it, and then not only did I have opportunity, but I had a weapon—*the* weapon."

"You don't know that," I managed to utter in a hoarse voice.

"Ryan, you are such an optimist. Of course, they'll find Lisa's blood. Why else plant a hunting knife in my pickup?"

I couldn't think of a reason, mainly because I agreed with her. The hunting knife was the murder weapon. "How did it get in your truck?"

"I think she was in the store, hiding among the shelves probably, when we opened the front door. We were distracted by finding Agnes, and she slipped out the back way and . . ."

"Dropped the knife in your pickup," I finished for her.

"Worse than that," said Megan. "She hid it under the seat on the passenger side. She wanted it found, but not by me."

"But why?" I cried. "What does she have against you? She could have left well enough alone, the lieutenant would have eventually given up suspecting you, and the case would have gone unsolved. But to deliberately plant that knife in your pickup shows a maliciousness that I never gave her credit for."

Megan rested her head on her knees for a moment, and I wanted to lift her out and carry her into the house, tuck her into bed, and watch over her while she slept. There is a certain aura about Megan that brings out a man's protective nature, an aura she is unaware of and would deny if I mentioned it. To a woman of Generation X, self-reliance is a religion.

Megan lifted her head. "She isn't malicious, Ryan. She doesn't act from a desire to hurt me so she can watch me suffer, because that motive would at least recognize me as a separate entity with emotions. She doesn't care one way or the other about me any more than she would a cockroach. If I'm arrested and go to prison, fine. If I escape without any charges, that's fine, too. She's acting in pragmatic self-defense, throwing suspicion on me to deflect it from herself. There's no passion to it, just as there was no passion when she killed Violet. It was something that had to be done to protect herself. If she could have stolen Violet's books like she did Rosemary's and Lorene's, she would have done that instead of murdering her, because there was less risk involved. It was all the same to her."

"My God," I said in lieu of remaining silent.

"Finish unloading the truck, close the garage door, and go on into the house. When it's completely dark, I'll climb out the window in the back of the garage and crawl to your back door. Special Crimes doesn't have infrared glasses, so they won't see me if I'm careful. Before Jerry thought I was a mad killer, we used to go out sometimes. He told me all about Special Crimes because I was interested. He's probably regretting it now, but thank God I asked all those questions. At least I know what strategies he might use, so I'm not completely ignorant of my opponent."

"I suppose I'd be wasting my breath if I told you to talk to Jerry, lay out your case for him, trust him not to be a damn fool," I said.

"You're right, you would be wasting your breath."

Her voice was firm and conveyed a determination that raised the hairs on the back of my neck. Whatever she was fermenting in her fertile brain I was certain I wouldn't like it. "What are you planning to do, Megan? I'll give you sanctuary until hell freezes over, but I think Jerry would tear my house apart until he found you. All you're doing is buying time."

"That's all I need, Ryan, a little time and Murder by the Yard. Call them, tell them to meet here at nine o'clock, but use the front door this time. The Poe strategy again. A secret meeting in the open, but tell them to use passwords again. We don't want to let in somebody from Special Crimes by mistake. I'll have one chance to prove I'm innocent, and I don't want to blow it because Jerry Carr came to visit."

"How are you going to prove you're innocent, Megan?" I asked, ignoring a premonition that I wouldn't like the answer.

"By proving Annabel Edgars Crow guilty."

I couldn't get another word out of her no matter what argument I used, so I closed the garage door, walked across the yard to my house, and picked up the phone. "Rosemary," I said when she answered. "Megan wants to know if you could get a substitute for bridge tonight. She needs a little help to catch a killer."

Beyond greeting the members of Murder by the Yard, Megan stood quietly in front of my fireplace while I poured coffee and tea or handed out bottles of soft drinks. Occasionally someone—usually Randel—called out a question, but Megan never answered, and gradually conversations died, and everyone sat in a semicircle around her. No stranger would ever have chosen Megan Clark—cute, petite, and looking years younger than her age—to be a leader. But no strangers sat in my living room that early May evening. In an amateur sleuth situation, which is what we all found ourselves in whether we liked it or not—and I didn't—the leader of the pack is the one who solves the crime and names the killer. Not by guesswork, or spectral intervention, or by accident, but by a logical discussion of clues that lead in progressive steps to a solution. As amateur sleuths go, the Circle believed Megan Clark outdid their favorite fictional heroines. Not having a background in mysteries, I couldn't say if I agreed with that opinion or not, but even I was impressed by her deductions.

When everyone was seated and quiet, Megan began to talk, and I think it was her intensity, her determination to carry through her plan alone if nobody would help her that forever secured her place as the sleuth of the reading circle.

"Thank you all for coming. If at any time you feel uncomfortable listening to what I have to say, please leave quietly. I won't ask anyone to help me who feels he or she will be violating their sense of right or wrong."

"Get on with it, Megan," said Randel Anderson. "We don't need the disclaimer. All of us knew before we came that we might be pushing the envelope if we helped you with whatever it is you have in mind. Personally, I decided to help you anyway. I've been a schoolteacher at one level or another all of my life, and I've reached the point that I even bore myself. So I'm kicking over the traces, to use a deadly cliché, and grabbing for the brass ring."

"Randel, you're not boring," protested Candi.

He stroked his goatee, which was beginning to look almost elegant—almost being in all probability the best Randel could expect. "Most of the time I am, kiddy, but thanks anyway for seeing me in a better light."

I was surprised—no, make that shocked—by Randel Anderson's confession, and it was all Megan's influence. Well, maybe not all Megan's influence. Candi probably boosted Randel's testosterone levels to the point where he thought he was a real man.

"Thank you, Randel. I appreciate your confidence in me. Rosemary, Lorene, if you leave, I won't be angry. Herb, you're my attorney, so I guess whatever I tell you is covered under the attorney-client privilege, although if you feel obligated to resign, I'll understand."

Casually dressed in a suit and tie sans vest, Herb stood up to answer. I guess he felt better on his feet in front of an audience.

"Megan, I consider this an attorney-client conference which, of course, is entirely confidential, so if you'll step into the dining room for the sake of privacy, you may begin."

My estimation of Herb Jackson III as a lawyer took a quantum leap. That was the slickest bit of slicing the law paper-thin that I ever saw. By holding their conference in my dining room, which was separated from the

rest of Murder by the Yard by an open archway, Herb
was technically within the law. Of course, we could hear
every word Megan said, which was the intention. Really
clever on Herb's part. I didn't make such a bad judgment
call in retaining him for Megan. He might even manage
to keep her out of jail.

"As you know—Herb," Megan began, with a glance
at the rest of us, "from the diagram I showed you at the
last meeting, I believed that Time and Again was the
source of the conflict that has killed two women—Violet
Winston, a cleaning lady who was murdered in February, and Lisa Heredia—and led to the burglary of Rosemary's and Lorene's homes, during which nothing was
stolen but out-of-print paperbacks, and three dozen
cookies. I was partly right. It was not the bookstore itself
but what was on the bookstore shelves. In other words,
certain books were the motive for murder."

"*Murder Betwixt and Between* for one," said Lorene.
"If my back door had been stronger, I might be dead
today." Everyone looked puzzled as they tried to figure
that one out.

Megan smiled at Lorene, if you could call her effort
a smile. Those violet circles under her eyes looked
darker, and the skin on her face was stretched too taut,
as though it had shrunk against her bones. "That was
one of the titles, but there were others. I was certain that
the killer was a member of Murder by the Yard because
any other explanation violated all common sense."

There was a stir among the members on hearing that
Megan had suspected them all of murder, but Rosemary
shushed everyone. "This is more exciting than Hercule
Poirot explaining how his little gray cells solved the
crime. Everybody be quiet. I don't want to miss a word."

Megan smiled again, another automatic stretching of
the lips, and went on to discuss our finding Agnes, Jerry
Carr's suspicions and his search warrant, our search of
Lisa Heredia's apartment, which made Herb Jackson

wring his hands, and finally, our examination of Agnes's receipt books.

"I studied the receipts for Rosemary's and Lorene's purchases the week before the murder. When I saw that they had bought twenty-five books each, I knew that was too many to misplace. I believe that Rosemary and Lorene were the murderer's first two victims—after Violet Winston, of course. The murderer didn't kill them—obviously—just stole their books to persuade them that they were losing their memories. But that wouldn't work with Lisa. Lisa had to die."

You could have heard the proverbial pin drop on my hardwood floor, so quiet was everyone. I took another sip of my cola and waited for the important part—the part I didn't know: how Megan planned to prove Annabel guilty. Judging by Herb's face, nothing she had said so far was proof of anything but breaking and entering.

"The most frequent name to appear on Agnes's receipts is Annabel Edgars Crow, who earns her living writing mysteries, the same Annabel Edgars Crow who also bought *The Case of the Poisoned Tea Caddy*, *Murder Betwixt and Between*, and *The Five Easy Marks*."

I sat up a little straighter. I didn't know that. Megan hadn't mentioned a word about the books Annabel bought.

"Why did Lisa have to die? To answer that we need to review what we know about Lisa Heredia. She was a New York agent who allegedly came to Amarillo to sign up Annabel as a client, charging her a twenty percent commission, which is outrageous. Annabel would have been wiser not to mention Lisa's commission, because then I wondered why in the world Lisa thought Annabel would pay that. According to Annabel, she turned Lisa down. But Lisa pestered her. Why did Lisa continue to pester her when Annabel had already told her no? Perhaps because she would rather not play her trump card."

"What trump card are you talking about, Megan?" asked Randel. "Come on, cut to the chase."

Megan ignored him. She was taking her time, building suspense as if she were writing a mystery herself. "Who mentioned that Annabel's books all seemed so different?"

"Lisa Heredia!" shouted Candi, then blushed. That girl blushed so much, I wondered if leeches were not called for.

"Exactly! And who stands to lose financially if her books are revealed as plagiarized from old, out-of-print paperbacks by obscure authors?"

"Annabel Edgars Crow!" cried the twins in unison.

"My goodness!" exclaimed Rosemary. "Why didn't we catch on sooner? *The Case of the Poisoned Tea Caddy* must have been plagiarized as *The Orange Pekoe and Pekoe Mystery.*"

"And *Five Easy Marks* must be that newest one Annabel was describing—what was it called?—*The Five Pigeons,*" said Lorene. "This is so easy once you know how. I bet if we compared Annabel's books to Agnes's collection of old paperbacks, we'd find that she stole all her work from someone else."

Megan waited until the conversation quieted again. "And who was going to write an article on old paperback mystery writers until they decided they were too infirm mentally?"

"Rosemary and Lorene," said Randel in a somber tone of voice. "You ladies are lucky to be alive."

"You're good at this guessing game," said Megan, complimenting the Circle. "It's all very logical, isn't it, once you ask the right questions. But I had one last test. A young boy I helped at the library kept watch over me at the meeting, to keep me safe from a witch that he said 'hurted a lady once' in February, when Violet Winston was killed. I asked the boy to describe the witch, and he described Annabel. I will not identify the boy in case my plan fails and Annabel doesn't confess. I don't want him to be a target of Annabel's rage."

"My dear Megan," said Herb in his most lawyerly voice. "We need to contact Lieutenant Carr immediately with this information, so he may build a case against Annabel."

"That may be difficult, Herb, since Lieutenant Carr found a hunting knife in my truck which I suspect is the murder weapon. Now, with my bloodstained clothes and a hunting knife, is Jerry Carr going to pay any attention to some wild story I tell him about Amarillo's own Annabel Edgars Crow, the same Annabel who always mentions at least a dozen cops on her acknowledgment page?"

There was that dead silence again, and Megan smiled, the saddest, most resigned smile I had ever seen on her face. "See, even you, mystery readers ready to believe the improbable, know it's unlikely that my story will be taken seriously."

"What will you do, Megan?" asked Randel.

"I have a plan."

23

*Life is the process of finding out, too late, everything
that should have been obvious to you at the time.*

—In John D. MacDonald's
The Only Girl in the Game, 1960

"Tell me again why I agreed to do this," said Ryan,
standing at the bottom of the bookshelf directly
in front of the door at Time and Again, and looking up
at the top shelf. "It's a good ten feet to the top of this
thing."

"You didn't agree to do it, Ryan, you demanded to
do it, and Randel and Herb nearly had to gag you because you were yelling like a banshee. People three
blocks away could hear you. I don't want you whining
about my plan now. Just climb up the bookshelf and lie
down on top of it, and I'll hand you the video camera.
If a video sent Rodney King's abusers to prison, then a
video will send Annabel to prison. Just please don't forget to take off the lens cover."

"I'm insane," repeated Ryan over and over again as
he climbed the three-step ladder that Agnes provided for
her customers, then gingerly put his foot on a shelf and
hoisted himself to the top of the bookcase. He lay down
on his stomach and promptly sneezed.

"Don't do that," snapped Megan. "Put your finger under your nose. That will prevent a sneeze.

"I couldn't help it. It's dusty up here. Doesn't Agnes ever dust the shelves?"

"I wouldn't if I were her age," said Megan. "She's too old to climb up high enough to do it. Besides, why bother? She doesn't have any customers ten feet tall."

"It's the principle of the thing."

"Quit complaining, Ryan. I'm nervous enough without listening to you," she said, climbing up the ladder and handing him a small video camera.

"I suppose this isn't the time to tell you that I'm allergic to dust."

Megan grabbed a handful of Kleenex from the box Agnes kept on her counter for the customers. "Wipe the shelf off, and Ryan, your shoulders are sticking out on this side."

"I can't help it if my shoulders are broader than the bookcase, Megan. I can't cut off a couple of inches on both sides."

"Then I'm going to turn off the lights except the ones on either end of the bookstore."

"I won't have enough light to film," Ryan said, turning on his side so his shoulders didn't hang off on either side of the bookcase.

Megan chewed on a fingernail. This idea had sounded fine in the abstract, but in the real world some holes were showing. "Okay, how's this? I'll leave on the lights in the last row on either side, and those three track lights over the checkout counter. I'll stay behind the counter, and Annabel will stay in front of it."

"How do you know?" asked Ryan, holding the camera up to his eye and grimacing as he focused. At least Megan hoped he was focusing and not about to sneeze again.

"Don't talk in shorthand. How do I know what?"

"How do you know Annabel will stay in front of the desk?"

Megan felt a chill dancing up and down her spine.

She didn't know, but she didn't want to tell Ryan. He had hair-trigger reactions tonight, and he might just pick her up, throw her over his shoulder, and walk out of the bookstore. He'd threatened to do exactly that earlier, at his house, when she told him her plan.

"It's logical, Ryan, that we should each stay on our side of the counter."

"This woman is not logical, Megan. She's a murderer, and as far as I can judge, she's a pretty damn good one."

"She should be. She's a mystery writer even if she borrows her plots, characters, and probably her descriptive narrative. Even borrowing, Annabel must have learned something about how to commit a murder without getting caught."

"You certainly know how to comfort a fellow," said Ryan, lathering on the sarcasm.

"When that phone rings I may jump out of my skin," said Megan, ignoring his comment.

"Where are Rosemary and Lorene?" asked Ryan.

"They're hiding behind the pillars of the church across the street, so they can see in both directions. Rosemary will call on her cell phone when she sees Annabel approaching. That's when you take off the lens cover and focus on the door."

"I'm glad we've got a backup system. It's always good to have a backup system—I've said that a hundred times. Is the wire comfortable?"

"Terrific, Ryan. I always wear two microphones taped to my chest under my Texas Crew T-shirt. The tape itches and I hope I don't get struck by lightning, but as long as Annabel doesn't suspect I'm wired for sound, I can stand a little discomfort."

"Can Randel and Candi hear you, do you think?" asked Ryan, taking the lens cover off the video camera.

"I think so. We tested it from a block away and they could pick up the audio. As long as they record it, I imagine someone in Special Crimes can augment the sound, make it louder or whatever."

He didn't reply and Megan took a deep breath and tried to calm her nerves. Time and Again smelled faintly of vanilla bean and cinnamon and old paper. With Agnes in the hospital there was no one to put out fresh potpourri or straighten the books, and the store already looked a little neglected and shabby. Like a small child, a business needed constant care, and Time and Again's caretaker was gone.

"I wish Rosemary would call," said Megan, forcing her thoughts away from the state of the bookstore.

"Where exactly is our lawyer waiting?" asked Ryan. "I want him close enough to save our necks from Lieutenant Carr after Special Crimes arrives."

"Didn't you listen when I went over the plan?" asked Megan, consciously relaxing her jaw. If she gritted her teeth much more, she'd have to have caps.

"I was too busy expressing my opinion of your using yourself as bait to lure Annabel to the store so you could con her into confessing her sins while I filmed her on video like I was Steven "Indiana Jones" Spielberg. The only reason I agreed to go along with this cockamamie plan is because I didn't trust anybody else. Rosemary and Lorene are too old to lie around on the top of bookcases, and Candi is too flighty and might break out in a fit of giggles—if giggles come in fits—and I wouldn't trust Randel with anything more mechanical than a hammer."

Megan drew a breath. "Listen to me while I go over it one more time. Herb is waiting at a telephone booth six blocks away. Randel will call him the minute he hears Annabel incriminate herself, and Herb will place an anonymous call to Lieutenant Carr from the telephone booth. It'll have to be anonymous because as an officer of the court, he would be in serious trouble with the bar association if he's caught participating in my plan. I think he's precious for helping me in spite of the risk."

Ryan peered down at her, and she flinched at the sight of his frown. "Let me get this straight. Randel and Candi are recording the audio from your chest phones. When Randel hears Annabel incriminate herself, he calls a phone booth where Herb will be waiting. When Herb hears from Randel, then Herb will place an anonymous call to Lieutenant Carr, who comes speeding down Sixth to the bookstore and arrests Annabel. Do I have the sequences right?"

"Yes," said Megan in as crisp a voice as possible given the fact that the plan didn't sound nearly as good when Ryan described it as it did when she was thinking it up.

"I hope the old saying my grandmother always repeated is true," said Ryan after a long pause.

"What did your grandmother always say?"

"God protects fools and children, and He has one of each in this store tonight."

The phone rang and Megan started. She picked it up, hoping she could hear Rosemary over the pounding of her heart in her ears. "Hello, this is Time and Again."

"She's coming, Megan. Lorene saw her car pass the church." There was a pause; then Rosemary whispered in a voice that shook. "Good heavens, she's nearly at the door! I didn't see her until now. I don't know how she slipped by me. Be careful, Megan!"

Megan hung up the phone and tried to swallow, but her mouth was dry as cotton. Her hands shook until she clasped them together under the counter so Annabel wouldn't see. She felt sweat trickle down between her breasts and hoped it wouldn't short out one of the microphones, or if it did, that the microphone wouldn't set fire to her T-shirt.

"Get ready," she said in a quiet voice. "She's coming."

"Oh, my God," said Ryan just as quietly, and turned on the camera.

He shifted his position and knocked the lens cover off the bookcase. It hit the tile floor and bounced. "Damn it! I'm sorry, Megan."

"Will you be quiet, please," said Megan through gritted teeth.

"See if you can find the lens cover," said Ryan, peering over the edge of the bookcase.

"I don't have time to look," whispered Megan. "She's coming."

Megan took several deep breaths to flood her brain with oxygen, supposedly an aid to relaxation and concentration. If there had been sufficient oxygen to her brain earlier, she wouldn't be here now. She would have thought of a better plan, a safer plan, like fleeing to a country that didn't have an extradition treaty with the United States.

She saw the knob on the front door slowly turn, and she waited, her stomach twisting into knots, and the cold spot in her chest expanding as she shivered. Under the bright light illuminating the counter, she felt like a target in a shooting gallery. A target! Why hadn't she thought of that? What if Annabel pulled the door open, stepped in, and shot her like she did Violet Winston?

The door began to open one inch at a time, stretching Megan's nerves to the screaming point. The best defense is a good offense, she thought to herself, and plunged into the scene that would either remove her as a murder suspect, or remove her, period. "Annabel, come in. Don't be shy. I've been waiting for you."

Annabel flung open the door the rest of the way and stalked in, a thick figure dressed in black slacks and a black T-shirt, a linebacker in drag. She looked around the bookstore, then walked ponderously toward the counter. Megan hadn't noticed until then what small eyes Annabel had, like little black currants stuck in a doughy face.

"What do you want?" asked Annabel, her voice as hoarse as ever. It was also a monotone, a flat emotionless sound that set Megan's heart racing even faster.

"I compared a copy of *The Case of the Poisoned Tea Caddy* to a copy of your *Orange Pekoe and Pekoe Mystery*, and guess what I found? The two books are nearly identical, too much so for coincidence."

"You don't have a copy of *Poisoned Tea Caddy*. Agnes only had four. I got one and I burned the other three."

"After you murdered Violet and Lisa."

"You don't have a copy," repeated Annabel, revealing no reaction to Megan's accusation.

"You're sure of that, are you, Annabel? Remember I worked for Agnes while I was in high school, and she gave me a lot of books. With school and working I only had time to read a few and I put the rest in my bookcase. Guess what one of those books was?" There was no response. "You don't care to guess?"

"You're lying."

"You know what your mistake was, Annabel? You plagiarized a book that had a bigger print run and wider distribution than say, *Murder Betwixt and Between*, published under your name as *Breathless.*"

"What do you care?"

Megan couldn't believe what Annabel had said. "What do I care? I care because you shot a woman who had nothing but an old dog and a love of reading. I care because you bludgeoned Agnes, who was always supportive of you, and didn't deserve what you did to her. And I care because you frightened Rosemary and Lorene, two elderly woman with few years left to them, who are terrified of losing their memories. That was cruel of you, Annabel, nearly as cruel as if you had killed them."

"They'll get over it," said Annabel.

Megan sucked in a breath and exhaled, started to chide Annabel, but decided that wasn't the best idea. "I even care about Lisa, although she was a terrible person."

Annabel lumbered closer to the counter, then began moving around it. "You ought to mind your own business."

"Murder is my business, Annabel—it's everyone's business. You can't run around Amarillo killing people who might discover you're a fake. It's against the law." Megan began backing up toward the shelving area as Annabel moved closer. "And so is plagiarism. You're a copycat, Annabel. You want to be a writer, but you can't write, so you steal other writers' ideas."

Megan kept backing up to keep her distance from Annabel, and wondered when the woman would confess. Everything she said implied her guilt, but Megan wanted a confession in simple words that any jury could understand, words that would send Annabel to prison.

"So you want money to keep quiet? Then you're no better than that agent. A twenty percent commission! She was a thief!"

Megan wanted to laugh at the irony of Annabel's calling Lisa a thief, but that was about as safe as stepping on a bad-tempered, poisonous snake. "How did she find out about your hobby of taking credit for someone else's work?"

"That's none of your business," said Annabel, awkwardly rounding the counter until she stood on the same side as Megan.

Megan immediately slid around to the front, so the counter was still between her and Annabel. "I think she must have run across a copy of a title published under your name with no changes except cosmetic ones. Being a literary agent, she immediately recognized a case of plagiarism when she saw one, and thought the chance for making big bucks off you was worth the cost of a plane ticket to Amarillo. Once here, it was a matter of making the rounds of used bookstores asking if you were a regular customer. In the process she bought three more books you had plagiarized. I'm certain she thought she was about to become a very wealthy woman, and to cover her blackmail, she wanted to claim you as a client. She could brag that she was the agent of best-selling author Annabel Edgars Crow. Isn't that the way it went, Annabel?" Megan asked her.

Annabel stood across the counter from Megan, clenching and unclenching her fists. "You think you've got everything figured out, don't you? You don't know anything about it. She was a bloodsucker! I offered her twenty percent, but she wasn't satisfied. She wanted it all."

"I don't understand what you're saying," said Megan, watching Annabel's eyes. Conventional wisdom held that the eyes telegraphed action. If Annabel intended to grab for her, Megan should be able to read it in her eyes.

"Publishers send royalties to the agent, who deducts her commission and sends the rest to the author. If Lisa Heredia was my agent, she would control my money and dole out pennies to me, and if I objected, then she'd call *Publishers' Weekly* and give an interview. She was going to bleed me dry, but I bled her dry first. That's what you do to bloodsuckers."

Megan nearly sagged to her knees with relief. Finally Annabel confessed. Now Murder by the Yard would spring into action: Randel would call Herb who would call Jerry Carr. All told, maybe ten minutes until Jerry and Special Crimes rushed in. Just ten minutes to hold Annabel at bay.

"I understand better now why you killed Lisa. Greed is a dangerous habit that Lisa should have avoided, but I guess she thought there wasn't any reason to be afraid."

"She found out better, didn't she?" said Annabel in

that hoarse monotone that Megan found more frightening than hysteria.

"Tell me about Violet Winston. How did you know Agnes gave her two old paperbacks?" asked Megan, glancing quickly at her watch. Five more minutes until liftoff.

"You're making things too complicated. I was in the store when Agnes gave her those two books, so I shot her after she left."

"Because of her dog," said Megan. "You didn't want the dog barking and waking up her neighbors, so you shot her before she got home. I deduced that much. I knew if Violet hadn't owned a dog, you wouldn't have killed her."

"You been reading too many mysteries. Dog didn't make no difference," said Annabel. "I just didn't want to drive all the way over to her apartment. Killing her really put me out, though, because I had to find a new cleaning lady. Hard to find anybody you can trust."

"My God, you're a cold woman!" exclaimed Megan, then flinched. *Good going,* she thought. *Insult the mass murderer.* "I didn't mean cold as in cruel. I meant cold as being in control of your emotions."

"I don't put up with people messing with me," said Annabel. "Those that do are sorry for it."

"Lisa and Violet certainly are," said Megan, tilting her head to listen for Special Crimes. If they didn't hurry, she would be out of topics for conversation, and she would much rather converse than do whatever else Annabel might have in mind. Annabel was too fond of sharp instruments and metal objects that went bang for Megan's taste.

"May I ask you something else, Annabel? I'm checking my deductions against your answers, and I've got a passing grade so far. I thought the dog had more to do with your decision to shoot Violet outside her home, but other than that, I'm good."

"What do you want to know?" asked Annabel.

"Why didn't you kill Rosemary and Lorene? It would have been so much easier to do than creeping around their homes and risking being caught."

"Didn't need to. It's easy to get old people all stirred up and worried. Besides, if I'd killed them, who would bring cookies to the reading circle?"

"They'll be glad to know that their cookies saved their lives," said Megan. Perhaps Rosemary and Lorene might bake a special batch as a going-away present, say sugar cookies sprinkled with arsenic.

"Too bad you don't bake cookies—but it's a little late now to revise. I'll go with my outline the way it is," said Annabel, circling around the desk to the front, the butcher knife in her hand reflecting the light from the fixtures above the desk.

Megan ran, keeping the desk between Annabel and her. "Don't do anything you might be sorry for later, Annabel."

"I won't be sorry, now or later," said Annabel, rounding the corner of the desk on Megan's heels.

"Everyone in Murder by the Yard knows I'm here and that I'm meeting with you," said Megan desperately. Too bad Annabel had a linebacker's speed as well as his build.

"Don't think so. You don't like egg on your face if I didn't show up."

"Please, Annabel," pleaded Megan. "Don't do it." Suddenly there was a loud crack, and she caught a glimpse over her shoulder of Annabel stopping and picking up a black, plastic cap. In horror, Megan recognized the lens cover.

Annabel held the cap in her hand and slowly perused the bookstore from her position a few feet from Megan. "Where's the camera?"

"What are you talking about, Annabel? I don't have a camera."

Annabel suddenly took two running steps and forced Megan back against the reference shelves. She grabbed a handful of Megan's hair and held the knife to Megan's throat. "Better tell me where you hid that camera."

Megan held her breath even though she knew it wouldn't help if Annabel cut her throat. Not much would help, but it was the principle involved. Never trade active for passive. She swallowed and tried to deny one more time that there was any camera. As it turned out, she didn't need to.

Ryan, lying on top a bookcase full of dusty old books, and terrified that Annabel would actually murder Megan in front of his eyes, was caught unawares by the loudest, longest, deepest sneeze that cracked like a rifle shot through the quiet store.

Startled, Annabel let Megan go and swung around searching for the source of the sneeze, a tactical error on her part as Megan seized the first weapon she saw and bludgeoned Annabel Edgars Crow over the head with a copy of *Webster's Second International Unabridged Dictionary*.

Used, of course.

24

Nothing is simpler than to kill a man; the difficulties arise in attempting to avoid the consequences.

—NERO WOLFE in Rex Stout's
Too Many Crooks, 1938

A gnes came home to Time and Again one crisp morning at the end of May when the yucca bloomed on the prairie outside of town. Her hair was a silvery stubble, which she claimed to like. "It's a new millennium, so why shouldn't I have a new hair style. And this is so easy to take care of. Just wash and blot."

We all pretended to laugh, wanting to make her homecoming a happy one, but she wasn't fooled. Agnes is owner of Time and Again and one of our aging ladies, and not much fools her.

Agnes clapped her hands, which she does whenever she wants our attention. "This is the most sober-sided bunch of people I've seen since several of us patients got together over lunch and discussed our surgeries. I'm fine! My neurosurgeon was excellent and swore that in another six months I could shave my head if I wanted to and there would be no scars visible to the naked eye. I don't plan on being quite that radical, of course. I might scare my customers. And speaking of customers, who is going to give me the real lowdown on Annabel? All I know is what I read in the papers, as Will Rogers used to say. Come, come, tell me. Murder by the Yard owes me a good tale. While I was laid up in the hospital where the health care providers insist on asking personal questions about one's bowel movements, you people were having an adventure. You solved a murder!"

Randel Anderson, who is unfortunately never at a loss for words, began the story with a synopsis of Megan's plan. "It was a bit dependent on absolutely everything working out exactly on time and as planned, but it was clever. Agatha Christie couldn't have written a better ending. My hat, if I wore one, is off to Megan."

Megan smiled and inclined her head in appreciation, like Queen Victoria at a royal reception. A month ago she would have jumped up and bowed, but a month ago she hadn't faced Annabel Edgars Crow who held a knife to her throat. That kind of experience will wring out the youthful wildness in almost anyone.

"It was dangerous, too," said Rosemary. "Luring a murderer to an empty bookstore at night? My heavens, what were we thinking, letting our sweet little Megan take such a risk. But it worked and it was exhilarating! Except for the arthritis aggravated by kneeling behind the church pillar for so long, I feel so much better than I have in years."

"And we did our job," said Lorene. "The part of the plan involving Rosemary and me worked perfectly and came off right on time."

"Randel and I were one block away recording the audio from the microphones taped to Megan's chest," said Candi, "and according to Lieutenant Carr, we also did a super job. Special Crimes was able to do a little electronic enhancement on our tape, and it's so clear that you can hear Megan's heart beating."

I didn't offer any comments on the plan, even though Megan claims I saved her life by sneezing. It's enough that I'm a hero. Not many of us heros left in the world

"Were you scared, Megan?" asked Agnes.

"No, not scared, I was terrified. And I'll never do anything so risky again. I'm cured of my foolhardiness. From now on you'll see a sensible, level-headed female. If it hadn't been for Ryan, I would probably be dead, and I'm not wasting my second chance."

"Well said, Megan," said Randel, leading a round of applause.

Agnes looked as if she didn't believe Megan's pledge, and I didn't either. In the years I've kept chaste company with Megan, I've heard her swear to put away her recklessness on an average of once a month and twice on holidays.

"What was your job, Herb?" asked Agnes.

There was a long—very long—silence during which everyone looked everywhere but at Herb. I felt sorry for him, because it was something that could have happened to me. The incident was not a statement on Herb's manhood, it was just one of those things that happen to us on occasion.

Finally he spoke, and I'll give him this, he never offered an excuse of any kind. I like that in a man. "I was at a phone booth six blocks away waiting for Randel to call. Once he did, I was supposed to call Lieutenant Carr anonymously to report an assault on Megan at the bookstore."

Herb stopped talking, although his mouth kept opening and closing in search of the perfect sentence to explain what he did. I could tell him that in my experience there is no such thing as the perfect sentence.

"Spit it out, " said Randel. "At this rate we'll have long gray beards before you finish."

"I received Randel's call and started to drop my money into the phone to make the call, but my hands were sweating from all the tension, so I dropped my only quarter, which rolled out of the phone booth, and down the storm drain. I had to run six blocks back to Randel and borrow a quarter. By the time I called the lieutenant,

Megan and Ryan had already pulled Annabel's fangs—
so to speak."

Herb finished and stood up as if he expected us to
fling him against the wall and execute him. If Megan
had been hurt, I might have done just that, but all's well
that ends well as Bill Shakespeare said. I was feeling
mellow toward my fellow man.

We adjourned to the refreshment table, where Rosemary and Lorene had outdone themselves. I resolved to
eat nothing but salads for the rest of the week and filled
a napkin with cookies and my cup with coffee. At peace
with the world I went back to the Circle and sat on one
end of the couch, and nibbled on my goodies. By the
time I finished, Megan and Randel were going at it over
some obscure point in a book called *Murder at Moot
Point* by somebody named Charlie Green.

"Millhiser obviously wants us to believe in the supernatural," said Randel.

"No, she doesn't! She uses the supernatural to distract
the reader, so he misses important clues. That's an ac-
ceptable use of ghosts."

I folded my hands over my belt, rested my chin on
my chest, and prepared to doze away another meeting
of Murder by the Yard. Before I fell asleep I wondered
who this Millhiser person was, and why the group was
reading a ghost story. I thought we only read mysteries.